DISCARD

By Madeleine Roux

FOR ADULTS

Allison Hewitt Is Trapped

Sadie Walker Is Stranded

World of Warcraft: Shadows Rising

Salvaged

Reclaimed

The Proposition

FOR YOUNG ADULTS

The Asylum series

The House of Furies series

The Book of Living Secrets

The Proposition

The Proposition

A Novel

MADELEINE ROUX

DELL

NEW YORK

A Dell Trade Paperback Original

Published in the United States by Dell, an imprint of Random House, a division of Penguin Random House LLC, New York.

DELL is a registered trademark and the D colophon is a trademark of Penguin Random House LLC.

LIBRARY OF CONGRESS CATALOGING-IN-PUBLICATION DATA
Names: Roux, Madeleine, author.
Title: The proposition: a novel / Madeleine Roux.
Description: New York: Dell Books, 2022. |
"A Dell Trade Paperback Original"—Title page verso.
Identifiers: LCCN 2022002997 (print) | LCCN 2022002998 (ebook) |
ISBN 9780593499375 (trade paperback) |
ISBN 9780593499382 (ebook)
Subjects: LCGFT: Novels.
Classification: LCC PS3618.O87235 P76 2022 (print) |
LCC PS3618.O87235 (ebook) | DDC 813/.6—dc23
LC record available at https://lccn.loc.gov/2022002997
LC ebook record available at https://lccn.loc.gov/2022002998

Printed in the United States of America on acid-free paper

randomhousebooks.com

2 4 6 8 9 7 5 3 1

Book design by Dana Leigh Blanchette

For my mother

To participate in matrimony is to abdicate one's duty to the dignified state of solitude. Upon completion of the contract, a woman becomes property owned by man, surrendering all autonomy and power, diminishing herself in every conceivable way.

—Bethany Taylor, *On Marriage*

The Proposition

1

Sussex, 1819

The small and saintly quiet town of Round Orchard was never known for anything. Absolutely, it held the expected Sussex charm and the expected hedges and gardens, the expected paved town square decorated with the expected bunting and wreaths, but it was otherwise unremarkable in every way. That is, but for its one hidden claim to fame, which was known only to a few residents, and most of those would categorize this "claim" to be something less than attractive. In fact, it was now a closely guarded secret, like a bit of shameful tat kept in the lowest drawer under the heaviest blankets, a pet nobody loved buried in the backyard in an unmarked and shallow grave.

Like a brief and embarrassing infidelity.

All but one inhabitant of Round Orchard wished to hastily sweep this secret under the rug. Only young Clemency Fry remained the keeper of this tiny, hidden flame—the flame in question was a Miss Bethany Taylor, a woman of middling family and middlinger prospects. Some described her as "severe" and "a scold" while other more charitable Round Orchardians allowed that she had an intense sort of beauty that only specific and brave men coveted. This Miss Bethany Taylor produced and published a treatise against marriage, aimed at convincing other members of her sex that the institution was both humiliating and cruel. *To participate in matrimony,* wrote the severe scold of intense beauty Miss Taylor, *is to abdicate one's duty to the dignified state of solitude. Upon completion of the contract, a woman becomes property owned by man, surrendering all autonomy and power, diminishing herself in every conceivable way. Solitude is subsequently diminished also, as the state of contented aloneness cannot be improved upon—even a love match requires some degree of compromise. Thus, with society thrusting women into a state of compromise, only a single lady happy in her charms, her accomplishments, and the quality of her morals achieves a truly enviable state of being.*

Marriage was, in Miss Taylor's controversial and embarrassing opinion, a swindle: To marry was to give one's self up; this could not be argued with. Nobody agreed with her except of course the keeper of her flame and one devoted reader, Clemency Fry. Clemency did not style herself a historian, but she did obsess over Miss Taylor's work and felt nothing but conviction when it came to preserving the heart of the late Miss Taylor's writings.

In the year 1801, the men of Round Orchard and surrounding towns were outraged and began an effort to quash all access to Miss Taylor's work. Many fires were lit and many pages burned. The vicar at the time offered his restrained critique of the treatise, calling it, "A disgrace, an abomination before God, and an affront to the understood and natural order of things." Some overheard him saying it made a case for "bringing back the stake," though these remained unconfirmed rumors. A local man, urgently asked for comment, reportedly told a room full of good society that, "Miss Taylor, like all unmarriageable women, turns her pen against men rather than confront her own deficiencies." The tirade continued for some time. "A real shrew," the man concluded.

Scant copies of *On Marriage,* by Miss Bethany Taylor, remained after the predictable outcry and response. Word of its existence scarcely reached beyond the county. But as mentioned, one young lady, brought up in the small and saintly quiet town of Round Orchard, found a moldering copy of *On Marriage* in the woodshed one day. She was then eleven, and the papers had been stuffed into a suspected vermin nest. Despite the papers' poor condition, Clemency Fry took them, dried them, smoothed them, and like a diligent restorer of ancient artifacts (but only just like one, for after all she was only eleven), painstakingly scraped away the mouse droppings and dirt until a somewhat legible and faintly stinking copy of *On Marriage* existed.

It was, as one might imagine, a formative experience for small Clemency Fry. Those redolent, faded pages were perhaps the last copy of *On Marriage* in the whole world, and they belonged to her, and she protected them, the solemn guardian of this most hated work.

So too did the reading of this treatise prove momentous for young Clemency.

Was it not so that marriage was unfair to women? Were the laws of property, of patrilineality, not by definition unjust? *What,* young Miss Fry longed to cry to the heavens, *about women?* Eventually it came to her mother's attention that little Clemency was in possession of what was meant to be mere kindling, words that had become a very different sort of kindling. A young mind once ignited is difficult to snuff out, but Mrs. Fry gave it her best attempt. Mr. Fry, a generally frail and distracted person, failed to intervene, giving many the perception that the Fry children were left somewhat to run roughshod, with only the supervision of an overtaxed governess. A fearful and exasperated Mrs. Fry repeatedly threatened to confiscate what was "essentially poison" but she, seeing how dearly her daughter loved the dropping-stained relic, never had the heart to follow through on her threats. Still, she hoisted that same cudgel whenever Clemency acted out (which was frequently) and won a few battles, but by the time her daughter had become a young lady, Mrs. Fry had utterly lost the war. Reading Bethany Taylor led Clemency to an appreciation and study of Olympe de Gouges, and Mary Wollstonecraft, and so on, until Round Orchard secretly harbored another harbinger of rights for the fairer sex. *Quelle horreur.*

Mrs. Fry begged her daughter not to take after women who were "shrill and intolerable, scary, and probably up to a not insignificant amount of witchcraft." After such strong language, a more obedient child might have been warned off the material and frightened, but then, Clemency had never been an obedient girl, nor a cowardly one.

She grew up to be an even less obedient woman.

Clemency Fry stared at the man who may be her husband while her flesh, her heart, her very soul turned as cold as the chilled salmon gelée jiggling on her plate. Whenever she glanced at him, at Turner Boyle, a flash of love passed before her eyes like a strike of lightning. His face, handsome in a fragile and cherubic way, elicited a momentary blast of warmth before the chill inevitably came on.

For in recent memory she *had* loved him, and, she felt reasonably certain, he had loved her. She had loved him somewhat against her will, her suspicion of marriage ever bolstered by the philosophy and feelings of Miss Bethany Taylor, her idol. Those words had formed a sort of protective armoring over Clemency's heart, a padded gambeson of sense and control only lately pierced by the arrow of Lord Boyle's affection. But now that affection was gone, and the arrow wound felt less like a wound of love and more like an infection that had begun to fester. None of that affection remained, not even a smear like the one on Lord Boyle's plate, where his salmon had been.

Yet he smiled.

"Excellent as always," Boyle crowed. He had a raucous pile of gingery hair that seemed always to style itself roguishly and fell in different attractive configurations whenever he ran his hand through it. It was a nervous tic of his, a tell, and he did it just then, as he no doubt felt Clemency's eyes boring into the side of his cheek.

If Miss Bethany Taylor were there to see her in that moment, she would have withered and died all over again of embarrassment.

I am so sorry I did not listen, Miss Taylor. You were right all along.

After exchanging a dozen or so words at a party and six secretive letters, Lord Boyle pronounced them friends, adding that, "Friendship is a serious affliction; the most sublime of all afflictions, because it is founded on principle, and cemented by time." She had been so impressed by his attempt to echo Mary Wollstonecraft that she had initially neglected to notice the error in the quotation. (Affection, not *affliction.* Obviously.) This failure she realized by and by was rather an epidemic of wishful thinking on her part vis-à-vis Lord Boyle. At any time, Miss Taylor's ghost would stir from the loose earth of a Round Orchard graveyard and come to haunt her, and Clemency was convinced she would deserve it.

"Of course, you must serve the salmon at your wedding breakfast," Mrs. Fry, her mother, crowed from the other end of the long, long table. A dozen dishes lay between them, her mother seemingly separated by an entire country's worth of jellies, spreads, roasts, vegetables, and half-empty wineglasses. This out loud planning was all a bit hasty, thought Clemency, particularly when considering nothing official had been signed or announced. The snail's pace of the whole affair being due to her father's chronically poor health and spates of quasi-reclusion.

"I shall leave all of that to Clemency," Boyle replied. He glanced in Clemency's direction, but managed to land his eyes only on her gloved left hand. He had striking blue eyes and fair skin, but he looked even paler then, faced with the daunting possibility of eye contact. "She has all the taste and sense, and it is every young woman's wish to dot every i and cross every t on the nuptial plans."

She had forgotten she was holding a silver fork, and in that moment, hearing him lie so plainly to her own mother, she felt strong enough to bend it with the sheer power of her despair. At once, she was reminded of Jane Austen. *Men of sense, whatever you may choose to say, do not want silly wives,* wrote Austen. Well. Did women of sense want silly husbands? After all he was a baron, but now in her mind he no longer seemed like a serious person. Clemency's fingers pinched the fork harder.

"Surely you cannot mean my daughter!" Mrs. Fry gave a polite titter. Clemency's mother was an exact mirror image of her daughter, plus five and twenty years. They had the same oval face and full mouth, the same freckled skin and strawberry-blond hair, naturally wavy and styled into ringlets, and matching pale gray eyes.

Gray eyes that Lord Boyle had once called "arresting" but now could not be bothered to even meet. Her certitude in the folly of marriage had stood like a moat around her for her entire life, and Boyle had managed to build a bridge across it by simply disagreeing with her, relentlessly, in an amiable and starry-eyed way.

Marriage is foolish for others, Boyle had told her at a quiet gathering after she rebuffed him yet again. *I am different. You are different. Together we can make a different sort of union.*

"Clemency is dear and sometimes obedient, but it is miraculous that anyone at all could persuade her to marry," Mrs. Fry continued.

Lord Boyle knew this, of course. Probably he had forgotten. Sometimes, when her rage was at its peak, Clemency fancied that he could not even remember her face, so little did he regard it now. But he knew that Clemency had always avoided matrimony. The ton had whispered that no man would ever conquer her, that her willfulness and disinterest in marriage would lead her to be a lifelong, and content, single woman. Clemency had never feared spinsterhood, and now she all but longed for it.

Lord Boyle had built a bridge across her moat, and now she had to wonder if that was all the fun there was to be had—in the building of the bridge, and the crossing it, in the winning of an unwinnable hand. Men did so enjoy games and gambling, pursuits of challenge and daring, and often in such things, gambling in particular, one must develop a flair for bluffing.

And he had bluffed her into the one thing she wanted least in life—marriage. Boyle of course knew this, as did the others seated at the table in Claridge House, the Fry family estate. To Clemency's right, her elder brother, William, sat with his beloved wife, Tansy. They were too engaged in new-lywed whispers to notice that Boyle had taken complete leave of his senses. Mr. Saines, a clergyman and family friend, was seated beside Tansy, his attention fixed on the sherry. On the other side of the table sat Clemency's sister, a widow, Honora, quiet but listening. Their aunt and uncle, Mr. and Mrs. Drew, had come and were sandwiched between Honora and Turner Boyle.

Naturally, Clemency's parents presided over the meal at the head and foot of the table. Mr. Fry sat to Clemency's left, while Lord Boyle had been placed immediately across from her.

"Y-Yes," Boyle was now stammering out, fluffing his hair nervously. The tell. "Indeed."

"Clemency dear," her father was saying in a whisper, "have mercy on your fork."

"If I must," she bit out, placing it with a tremble back on the cloth. Mr. Fry was having one of his rare good nights, and Clemency was glad for his presence. She often found herself missing him, though for some years he had been like a ghost haunting their home, pale and only occasionally glimpsed.

"How silly! Truly ridiculous." Mrs. Fry was not going to drop Lord Boyle's forgetfulness. She had seized on it, the one interesting development in the whole of dinner. "Our Clemency! Can you imagine it, Mr. Fry?" she all but screamed down the table. "Can you imagine it? Our Clemency! Eager to marry! No, no, it took a stalwart, persistent knight to storm that castle, and thank God for that, and thank God for you, Lord Boyle!"

Moat. Bridge. Clemency wrinkled her nose.

Mrs. Fry dissolved into rapturous laughter, and a few at the table indulged her, just as ready for some distraction from the screech of forks and knives across the dinnerware. Poor Mr. Fry did not so much as chuckle, his frequent bouts of gout and grippe leaving him tragically humorless. Boyle, however, threw back his gingery head and laughed with all his might, though to Clemency it sounded rather more like choking.

Without realizing it, she had picked up the fork again, this time in her fist.

"Dear . . ." Her father touched her left forearm lightly. He was a frail man in his sixties, snowy-haired and with a lined yet pleasant face. He possessed the soft, white luster of a cut turnip. "You must relinquish the fork, sweet girl, before anyone realizes your murderous intent."

Clemency snorted, grateful for her father's intervention. They shared a brief glance, and then she was laughing in earnest. She couldn't stop. It was all too funny, too, too funny. And horrid. One full-bodied guffaw led to another, for the noise and feeling was neighbor to sobbing, and that she very much wanted to do. Eventually, everyone at the table noticed that she was laughing at something else entirely, utterly in her own world; her face and neck reddened as the sound threatened to resolve into crying.

"Clemency?" her mother shouted down the table. Out of the corner of her eye, she noticed Boyle wince. "Are you quite all right?"

"Oh! Yes!" Clemency at last found her voice, out of breath. She stood, shaking. "I am all right. In fact, I am splendid. Just . . ." She clapped her eyes on Lord Boyle, and the swiftness of it caught him off guard. At last they met eyes, and she watched him blanch, and freeze, and swallow a deeply sour mouthful of something. She hoped it lodged in his throat. "Just magnificent," she said, stepping unsteadily away from the table, rattling the cups and plates. "If you will excuse me, I suddenly very much need to be sick."

Clemency fled the table, her vision blurry as she found her way to the sitting room, then to the grand front hall, and then to the stairs leading up and away. The bannister caught her before she could fall. She stayed there for a moment, finding her feet, then dragged herself up the steps. General chatter of alarm had erupted in her wake, but she didn't listen, gaining her equilibrium and racing for her bedchamber, breaking through the door just as the first shuddering sob left her mouth.

Backing into the door and shutting it, she let the pain come. She had been holding it in for weeks, months, feeling it fill her up like smoke in a burning house. Just to be in Boyle's presence was an insult. And yet she must try to marry him. When he first mentioned the possibility of an engagement, it had been the happiest moment of her life, his love, his assurances, making her feel as if anything was possible. She had always been labeled unmarriageable for her opinions and her stubbornness, and deep down she had always wondered that maybe she wasn't unmarriageable but *unlovable*.

Then, Turner Boyle had starkly declared his love for her, and like a fool, just for a short while, she believed.

He had come to her just after Christmas, taking Clemency's hand beside the hearth in the east sitting room while the snow fell beautifully and silently outside. The whole house had seemed so quiet, as if it too held its breath while Turner Boyle smiled tearfully down into Clemency's face and said the words.

The words. The night after the proposal, Clemency had written them down in her diary, wanting never to forget them. She knew them by heart of course, and now they struck her not as a declaration of love, but as a curse, a curse binding her to him.

Will you love me forever, darling Clemency, and make me the happiest man in the whole of England?

What a magnificent bluff! In hindsight, she should have seen the traps hidden in the field of those words. Pretty they were, and perhaps truly meant in that moment, but like everything to do with their relationship, it was all about *him*.

Clemency hurled herself onto the bed and beat her fists against the pillows. Her hair and face would be ruined for the dance, but that hardly mattered. She needed to let all of this escape before it flamed hotter and consumed her from the inside out.

If she could cut off the understanding, in an instant she would, but Turner Boyle was a baron, an heir, his fortune dwarfing her family's. William had married well, but Tansy Bagshot's once-promising inheritance was now dwindling, her father's lucrative shipping business struck with tragedy after tragedy, merchant vessels lost to storms and pirates. Unless a miracle turned the Bagshots' circumstances around, William's lovely wife might soon be penniless.

Their father's ailments had kept him from meeting formally with Boyle to discuss the financial ins and outs of the arrangement, though she was assured by both men that it would all be seen to shortly. Yet over and over again, one or both of them stalled, leaving Clemency's future hanging on the flimsy hook of mere words. In her heart, she wondered if her father kept postponing and dawdling because he simply disliked Boyle, money or no money.

Her sister Honora's fate seemed similarly bleak, her husband dying unexpectedly, struck by a carriage in London. Their marriage had been so short that his family balked at her taking the majority of his inheritance. Honora had loved Edwyn Hinton mightily, and so he had loved her in return, but the Hinton family did not share his infatuation.

And of course, what a devil would Clemency be to let her sister be pressured quickly into another match? No, it fell to Clemency to secure their futures, and she had done it, against her own prejudices and hesitations, truly against her sense and beliefs, landing a baron. Lord Boyle.

Her fists beat harder against the pillow, so hard she almost didn't hear the door opening and closing. A rustle of skirts and pitter-patter of slippers later, and her sister was there, stroking the hair back from Clemency's forehead and sighing.

"Mother is concerned," Honora murmured. Even before Edwyn passed, Honora had always spoken softly, now her voice barely rose above a whisper.

"Oh, hang Mother! *I'm* concerned!" Clemency flipped onto her back, staring up into her sister's face. Her brows met in consternation. "He does not love me, Honora. He did! Oh, he did. But now . . . now . . ."

"Dearest," Honora said, pulling Clemency up until she could hug her properly. "I thought something might have transpired between you. He does not gaze at you as he once did. What happened?"

"I do not know! I can only guess and conjecture. He will not even speak to me, Nora, and he will not drop me out of pity. How I wish he would just end it! I would rather be humiliated and scorned, and have the whole world laugh at me for daring to change my mind and fall in love. Miss Taylor wouldn't even laugh at me now; she would feel only pity. Oh, but I should have taken her lessons more truly to heart."

"Perhaps it was foolish to rail so against marriage, dearest, one does tend to succumb to it, in the end." Honora squeezed her tighter. "But the humiliation should be his, unless you did something to make him go so cold."

"Nora!" Clemency pulled her head back, aghast.

"I am not accusing you! Sweet sister, I would never." Honora shook her head, her darker ringlets bouncing against her cheeks. "I only . . . I know you can be willful, and opinionated, and . . . Well, and stubborn. Occasionally impropriety gets the better of you. And men are strong in their guises and fragile in their hearts, perhaps you unknowingly gave some offense."

It came out like a question, but Clemency was too upset to answer. Yet she did search her mind. Had she said something? *Done* something?

"Nora . . ." She let out a giant gust of breath and sank against her sister. "All I did was love him with all my heart. I loved him better every day and feared I should use it all up long before we were dead or bored with each other, but while my affection grew his simply faded away. Now he will not so much as look at me, and I will be married to a heart of stone."

But the family would go on, and there would be a roof over their heads, and food on the table, and nobody would be turned out in disgrace. That it all came down to money made Clemency more disgusted with herself. They were quiet for a moment, and Mariah, their maid, entered to light the room with candles and pull the curtains shut and then, she was gone again. Honora rubbed Clemency's back, and gradually the urge to cry dissipated.

"I can be courted again, dearest. There is no need for you to continue in this way if you think he is lost," Honora said.

"No! Absolutely not. No. I forbid it!"

"You cannot forbid me—I am your elder sister."

"I can and I do. No, Nora, this is my error," Clemency insisted, turning until she sat with her legs dangling over the side of the bed. She took both of her sister's hands in hers and checked Honora's face. Her sister was willowy and had a more elegant face, wiser yet still unmistakably feminine. If Clemency was a rose, then Honora was a lily of the valley, delicate and sweet, shy and ever drawing inward.

"This is my error," Clemency repeated. "And I will . . . I will simply learn to live with it. I have soldiered on for weeks now; I can do so for longer. For us. For the family." She forced a thin smile. "But mostly for you."

"Perhaps the Bagshots will have a better season," Honora suggested hopefully. Her eyes sparkled with optimism, but it was a dull shine. They all had that look lately, a family of bright eyes gone dim in the face of so much adversity and horrible surprise. "If their profits rise again, then you can be free of him, dearest. Maybe your freedom is near at hand."

"Maybe," Clemency said. *But probably not.*

Honora, taller, leaned her head down and rested it on her sister's shoulder. "Say you will come to the Pickfords'. I cannot survive it alone. There are always so many pitiable glances at these dances; I hate it. I hate to be pitied and fussed over and made to feel the loss all over again."

"Then let us both stay here and feign illness."

"Mother will be cross, and it will disappoint Tansy so—you know how she loves to dance and be seen, and she needs something to lift her spirits now," Honora pointed out. "She has talked of nothing else all week! Miss Brock will be there, and she has all the best fashions, and Mr. Greer's cousin is returning from abroad, and Mrs. Sable will have the latest gossip from London. So says Tansy, of course. Repeatedly."

"You must stop being so sensible," Clemency said with a long sigh. "And persuasive."

Honora wrinkled her nose and sat up, climbing up from the bed and smoothing out the folds in her dark green gown. "A distraction will do us all a world of good," she insisted. "And I will fill your dance card, and find you a better prospect, and free you from this cold entanglement."

At that, Clemency had to laugh, for who else would ever seek to court her, Clemency Fry, the woman who had sworn off marriage and called herself unconquerable? The headstrong girl who had surrendered to one man only to find herself locked away in the frigid and unforgiving prison of his total indifference.

Miss Taylor was right—it was all, quite frankly, a swindle.

2

Mr. Audric Ferrand supposed that under a different moon, he might find the village of Round Orchard tolerable, even charming. But his poisoned mood did not allow for such generosity. He had tracked the scoundrel to Round Orchard, and that was all that mattered. His purpose. His mission.

Audric had tracked many such rakes to many such secluded villages, but this time it was altogether different.

His cousin Mr. Frank Greer acquired an invitation to the dance for him easily enough. Like any genteel English family, the Pickfords were eager to make more rich acquaintances, and Audric was certainly that. Rich.

Rich and determined. A dangerous combination in any man of wit and means, in a man like Audric, with acuity to spare and a lightning-fast sword hand, it was lethal. He was a seeker under a hunter's moon, come to do what he did best: bring unruly dogs to heel.

The last freezing gusts of winter blew his greatcoat hard to the left as he made his way to the door. The Pickford residence, a comely if rustic estate called Harrop Hall on the outskirts of Round Orchard, south of Heathfield, glowed with a welcoming light, every window filled with a cheery candle, each of them a promise to banish the chill. He had come late but not impolitely so, hoping to blend into an already drunk and rowdy crowd. If he was lucky, the music and laughter would be so loud that nobody would notice him being announced.

The wind brought with it a breath of nostalgia that he drank down greedily. It reminded him of the woods and fields of his boyhood, the idle hours spent educating himself in his father's library, collecting insect specimens and chasing frogs along the banks of the Vesle River. It was there, along that river, that he had learned to hunt and gained a talent and a taste for it. That he only ever enjoyed the thrill of the chase and not the act of killing troubled him and embarrassed his father. Yet it was undeniably so—to spy a hare in the brush was galvanizing, to spill its blood a minor devastation. Always the scent of woodsmoke and cool gravel transported him to the Vesle, to the crunching leaves, the hares, his father standing like a marble column at his back. . . . He banished such sentimental thoughts from his mind, remembering that somewhere inside the Pickford estate the focus of all his rage and ire waited, unwitting, ignorant of what was soon to befall him.

That thought he relished. He let it nourish him, let it propel each step toward the front door. It was painted dark green and swung open as he approached, a ready manservant on the lookout for late guests. His coat and hat were taken, and Audric stood adjusting his sleeves in the expansive foyer, his keen eye taking stock of every detail in the place. The front hall was choked with people, their combined heat creating a swelter, but he was glad of it—he might just go unnoticed. The Pickfords had decorated Harrop Hall in a strong hunting motif—furs, antlers, and stuffed rodents

pouring from every available corner and shelf. He had to admire their commitment, for the tapestries and heavy rugs
were out of fashion but did somewhat lend a timeless air to
the house, as if a medieval knight could stroll around the
corner at any moment and not look out of place.

A large, wide staircase framed the hall leading toward the
ballroom. To his left and right, corridors led to salons over-
flowing with guests. A sea of ladies in white silk and muslin
was dotted with the occasional blue or red or black gentleman's coat.

"Sir." The manservant had returned, a young man with
white-blond hair and a spotty complexion. "If you will
please follow me—"

"Not necessary." Audric waved him off. Not necessary at
all. The bumbling young man would draw only more attention. Here, he wanted to be as vapor. As smoke. There and
gone again, and never remembered. "I will make my own
way. Billiards room?"

The young man's eyes blew wide with surprise, but he
composed himself, bowed, and gestured to the right. "Follow
through to the gallery, then you will find it the second door
on your left."

Audric set off, wading into the crush of rustling skirts and
wine-red faces, expensive perfume wafted by swishing fans.
A quartet in the main ballroom played a sprightly tune, while
more quietly in this sitting room a girl hammered artlessly
away at an étude. Her friends and suitor were delighted. Audric cut a path through it all, and most let him pass. He was
hard to miss, tall and broad-shouldered, dressed in sober
black, cut to perfection. If ladies eyed him as he passed, he

did not care to notice, and his doggedness instantly dissuaded them. Only three people in Harrop Hall were of any interest to him that night—his cousin, his quarry, and the quarry's woman.

Everyone else in the estate might have been just set dressing for the drama to unfold, papier-mâché dolls, as far as he was concerned.

His cousin would be in the billiards room, and so that was his first destination. He kept a wary eye on the moving heads before him, aware that he might stumble upon his target at any moment. Not that it would necessarily change anything. The blaggard had no idea what he looked like, or that he was coming, or the myriad ways Audric would make him suffer.

Still. Audric was a man who could appreciate the poetry of things. The symbolism. He wanted it all to unfold just so, for this to be like any satisfying revenge story, a quiet simmer to start, a roaring boil later. His other hunts were to satisfy a client, but this was just for him. It would somewhat spoil things if he were to blunder into the man now, instead of making a precise and calculated introduction at the time and place of his choosing.

He did not yet know if he would savor the kill, but oh how the pursuit would sustain him.

The music from the ballroom grew louder as he sidled by two open doors in the gallery that gave a glimpse of the rows of dancers merrily skipping toward one another and taking hands. Audric could not remember the last time he had danced at such an event; he expected it never to happen again. His was no longer a soul for dancing; it required a degree of buoyancy that he simply did not possess. The quartet no doubt played well, but to him it all sounded hopelessly out of tune.

Thankfully, the billiards room was less full. All the men were wanted on the dance floor, apparently. He spotted his cousin at once, a man of four and thirty, with thick black hair curling down to his shoulders and full, ruddy cheeks. He had the signature Ferrand ink-black hair and shockingly bright green eyes, inherited from Audric's aunt, Cecile. She was long dead, but the family resemblance endured, strong enough to mark Frank Greer as his blood even though they had not seen each other in many years.

"By God! You really have come!" Frank caught sight of him while watching a game, sipping from a small crystal glass. He strode across the deep red carpet, reaching to clasp Audric by the hand. "Cousin. You look well! Or tall. Tall and well. How long has it been? God. Too long! Sixteen years at least."

"At least," Audric agreed, stiffly accepting his cousin's hand and shaking it.

"And how do you find Sussex?" Frank asked, stepping back to look Audric over from top to bottom. His eyes sparkled. "Is Delphine with you?"

Audric frowned. "No. She is at the inn with my man."

"Heathfield?"

"Obviously." Audric glanced around the room, making certain his target was not there.

"Are you looking for someone, Cousin? Whom else could you possibly know here?" Frank laughed and steered him toward the liquor cabinet near the two billiards tables, both occupied with players that gave Audric a quick once-over, brows raised in curiosity. "Ah! But that is on me, yes? I must make introductions. You are not yet a married man, and there are so many young ladies here that would cherish your company, no?"

"No." Audric allowed him to press a glass of wine into his hand. In truth, he had no interest in courtship or flirtation, only a single-minded need to find one woman in particular. "There is only one lady I should like very much to meet."

Frank huffed, eyes widening as he clapped Audric playfully on the back. He seemed to notice how much Audric disliked it and immediately withdrew his hand as if burned. "Do tell, Cousin. I am at your disposal. I must say, it is damn wonderful to see you again. Have you given up Fox Ridge for good? Have you been in Calais all this time? Your accent is not as strong as I expected."

He had forgotten that Cousin Frank was a little light on brains. Already his attention wavered. Audric sniffed the wine, deciding it was decent enough to drink. "Fox Ridge has not interested me in some years. Alas, I am never in one place for very long, though I hope to change that."

"Yes! The estate!" Frank hurried to finish his sherry and went to pour another. The clack and thump of billiards continued around them. Men came and went, retiring to rest from the dance, refresh a drink, then loom in the doorway and watch the ladies drifting by like swans on a lazy river. "I think Beswick might suit you and Delphine; it has a perfect view of the river. Or Ashford, since you so adore the hunt; the birds are better, and I'm told the grounds are in excellent condition. . . ."

"Delphine would quite enjoy a river," Audric told him coolly. "Beswick will suit us well, I am sure. As you might imagine, arrangements must be made tonight."

"T-Tonight?" Frank's eyes bugged. "But . . ."

"I am not leaving Delphine in town one more night."

"Right. Of course. Tonight then. I do wish you had brought her," Frank said with a sigh. "Was she not well enough to attend?"

"Her frailties keep her much indoors," he replied.

"Pity that, she might have made some lovely new acquaintances." Frank seemed to finally circle back to Audric's previous concern, his mouth dropping open as he guffawed. "Too much sherry, I suppose, forgot entirely that you wanted to meet someone here. Who might you be interested in?"

Audric didn't appreciate his tone. But of course his cousin would speculate. He was a single man of fortune about to take another great country house; Frank would be stupid not to wonder. And actually, Frank was closer to the truth than he might know.

But Audric chose his words carefully. The plot had begun in earnest now. The curtain was rising. All that remained was for Audric to find the players and put them on the stage. "I am told Clemency Fry is passably fair. Do the society gossips in London have it true?"

"They do, they do," Frank snorted into his sherry, eyeing Audric all the while with reddening cheeks. "Fair as a June morning, with the most brilliant gray eyes . . . She and any other lady here would be glad to make your acquaintance, with you as rich as Croesus."

Audric granted him a thin smile. "I have done some modest business in Marseille, certainly."

"Modest? Good Lord, man, you will own the entire south of France by year's end from what I hear; that is hardly what I would consider modest." Frank shook his head, tumbling his dark curls this way and that. "Wealthy *and* humble. Is it true you've taken up a different kind of sport?"

Audric stared at him, knowing perfectly well what he implied.

His eyes widened as if afraid. "You're now a kind of man hunter?"

"Clemency Fry," Audric prompted him, weary. He didn't suppose a man of Frank's country narrowness had the imagination to understand how Audric spent the majority of his time.

Frank turned and set down his sherry on a folding table near the liquor cabinet, flustered and maybe disappointed, then led Audric back through the room of cherrywood bookcases and embroidered sofas to the open double doors, where they joined the handful of gentlemen surveying the field.

"I can arrange an introduction, Cousin, of course, but we shall have to find some other maiden to tempt you," Frank explained. His jacket was crooked; his cravat sprayed with a fine mist of sherry.

"And why is that?" Audric knew, but this was a play, and he would respect the script.

"Well, because you see she is quite attached, and expected to marry soon."

"Marry whom?"

He braced to hear the name, knowing it would send a delicious shiver of deadly anticipation down his back. And it delivered.

"Lord Boyle," Frank said, playing his part beautifully.

"You wait here, Cousin, I will bring her to you. Perhaps instead you might be interested in her sister, Honora. She too is very pretty, prettier some say, and recently widowed."

"Perhaps." Audric would consider no such thing.

"I will return shortly," Frank promised with a flash of a smile before disappearing into the crush of people veering away from the gallery and back into the ballroom.

Audric did not wait idly; he kept his vigil, studying every face that went by. Hunting. It was tedious to stare at so many strangers in turn, but his diligence paid off. Before Frank could return, he spotted a familiar face. Well, familiar in that he had seen a small portrait of the man, a likeness kept in a large silver locket. But the resemblance could not be clearer. The thin nose, ivory skin, and garish red hair. It had to be him.

The woman accompanying him bolstered Audric's suspicions; she fit the description of a fair-haired, freckled, rather short young woman. Her face was now glossy and pink from exertion. Audric took one step outside the billiards room, ready to follow them at a discreet distance. As he eased into the crowd, the young woman turned toward him, glancing over her shoulder, and somehow, of all the dozens of folk she might have laid eyes on, it was him she saw.

Audric almost gasped. Her eyes were startling, gray and icy, and within those arresting eyes he saw a hint of confusion and something else, something he knew intimately, something that had been his bosom companion for the last five years: rage.

3

Clemency hugged herself, following Turner out into the vicious cold. The contrast stole her breath away, for the dance had grown hot enough to make her dizzy, but one step outside the door and she was covered in gooseflesh. Her dancing slippers crunched across frost, teeth chattering as Turner strode to the ornate bannister at the edge of the south-facing veranda. He appeared immune to the cold, and immune to her pleading, his back to her as he gripped the railing and sighed.

But she was not deterred, not by his icy reception or the icy weather. This was the first attention he had paid her all evening, and she was determined to take advantage of it.

Clemency marched up to him, arms still wrapped around herself for warmth.

"Why will you not dance with me?" she asked. No, demanded. "Turner. Look at me. Please, will you look at me?" He would not.

"I have no interest in dancing this evening," he muttered. His shoulders had bunched up around his ears.

"And yet you happily led Tansy out!"

Turner let go of the bannister to rub his temples. "She is your sister by marriage, of course I led her out."

"I thought I was to be your wife."

That drew only another disgruntled sound from him. More and more infuriating. Clemency threw her hands up in the air, pacing back and forth behind him. Other couples emerged from the large doors at the back of the house, bringing with them snatches of the merriment inside, but Clemency ignored them. Let them see how desperate his behavior had made her, it didn't matter to her anymore. He had already humiliated her by refusing to dance, repeatedly, rudely snubbing her.

"Truly, Turner, I have resorted to begging just for a scrap, a morsel of your regard, when only months ago I could do no wrong in your eyes. You pursued me relentlessly, followed me like a trained puppy, and I, a woman who thought never to be induced to marry, accepted you. What has changed so?" Clemency stopped, eyes fixed on the back of his head. "Please, I beg of you, just tell me what have I done to give such offense? Do you even wish still to marry me?"

At last she heard him draw in a ragged breath, and his words began slowly at first, then came faster and faster, building in volume and intensity. A dam had broken, and she was standing right in the path of it.

"The Clemency I fell in love with could not give two figs about marriage, or romance, or sentiment, or any of it! You were a sphinx, but now you are a kitten!" He whirled to face her, raking both hands through his hair, his cheeks prickling with red heat. "One whiff of an engagement and you are a completely different woman. Perhaps your so-called aversion to matrimony was simply a ruse all along, a snare meant to entrap me!"

Clemency glared up into his face. "Ah. So now *I* am the

liar?" He scoffed and turned away again, retreating to the railing. "Forgive me. Forgive that my affection for you was too ardently and genuinely given once I knew that you shared my regard. Forgive the intensity of my feelings—"

"For God's sake, Clemency!" Someone on the other side of the veranda gasped, and then she heard them run inside. Turner advanced on Clemency, daring her to move, but she stood her ground. She had never seen him so angry, so hysterical. "You were smothering! You *are* smothering! *No* man could tolerate the intensity of your feelings."

"Or consider," she bit out, "that you are simply not man enough to withstand them."

Turner reeled back as if struck. "I will not be spoken to this way; it is insupportable. I have tried, I have truly tried, but y-your behavior is insupportable. Collect yourself, madam, and endeavor to be better, or this entanglement will end, I promise you that."

An image of Honora, sweet and shy, refusing every man at the ball because she was still not ready to dance again or give up Edwyn's memory blazed across her vision. She could not bear to let her sister down. An invisible clamp squeezed her heart until she wanted to collapse, but Clemency pushed her shaking fists to her sides and gave a single nod.

"Very well, Turner," she said softly. "If my passion offends you so, I will strive to be a . . ." *Colder. Deader. Sadder* . . . "Steadier sort of woman."

"Good." Turner jerked on the bottom of his jacket, then plucked at his sleeves. He ran his right hand through his hair again, the red splotches on his cheeks beginning to fade. "See that you do, the simpering and fawning must end. I wouldn't wish it upon my worst enemy."

He was ready to go back inside, but Clemency blocked his path for a moment. She hoped he wouldn't touch her, for she knew even a feather landing on her shoulder would shatter her like frost-brittled glass. But he had fussed so much with his hair during his infuriating speeches. It forced her to wonder if he was lying. But what about? Did he still love her, or was there something else?

"And if I make this promise to you," she murmured. "To be a quiet woman, a . . . coy one, will you at least dance with me this evening?"

Turner narrowed his blue eyes, perhaps sensing that she was seeking a concession from him. For all his changeable moods, he was not stupid.

"That is agreeable."

He pulled on his left sleeve again and arced around her, purposefully avoiding even the very edge of her skirts.

The doors closed, but the sound was muted by the storm of thoughts in her head. Still fragile, teetering between consuming fury and despair, she forced herself to walk carefully back inside, head high. There was no sign of him in the considerable crowd gathered near the door for a breath of fresh air, and so Clemency threaded her way through the guests, knowing Harrop Hall well enough to navigate to a solitary place. The library at the far end of the corridor, through the portrait gallery, that was where she might find a moment's peace. Her hands still rigid at her sides, she hurried away from the laughter and music. All along the journey, she felt someone watching her, but Clemency simply ran faster, breezing by the sober faces of five generations of Pickfords, each portrait seemingly more judgmental of her unladylike speed as she careened across the wooden parquet and through the doors, taking a harsh right past two fern-filled vases and into the blessedly silent east library.

It was a cozy nook of a room, not dusty but stuffed with the old mustiness of books. And it was occupied. Two wayward lovers had found their way there, nipping away for a quick grope near the map section. The chestnut-haired boy had his paramour up against a bookcase, both of them drunk enough to make their kissing sound like two pigs snorting around in a trough.

"Out!" Clemency bellowed. The lovers broke apart, red-lipped and shrieking. "Get out at once!"

They were too shocked to argue and scuttled by her, both wiping guiltily at their mouths as they went, the woman's green satin ball gown trailing behind her, the last thing Clemency saw as they streamed out the door.

The hearth, opposite the doors, was lit, and Clemency ran toward it, outside's chill settling in her bones. No matter how close she stood to the fire, she couldn't get warm. The frost spreading inside her had everything to do with Turner.

How could she have been so careless? What had she done? What sort of person had she attached herself to? All of her high-minded ideals were abandoned to accept Turner's love—and for what? Now it was only for the money, that much was clear, and it felt horribly like selling herself. Worse, she must play a part, the meek and quietly doting woman, and a greater insult she could not imagine.

What about your family ravaged by destitution? Can you imagine that?

Clemency's hands slowly lifted, her strength fleeing her as

the weight of her predicament descended. She placed her palms on the heated mantel above the hearth, letting her head fall forward, and letting the tears spill. Her chest burned from the pain in her heart. Was she really all that Turner said? Was her love unbearable?

Was she, in the end, as she had worried and suspected, unlovable?

She had written him poems, yes, and hid them in funny places for him to find. Once, she had sweets from his favorite bakery in Heathfield sent to London to surprise him. And yes, at balls, she wanted to dance every dance with him. Was that wrong and *smothering*?

A sphinx, he had called her. And that was so. She had been immovable during their courtship, for she had a brother marrying well, with William and Tansy announcing their intention to unite just before Boyle came into her life. Clemency had stood in the position to marry for love if she so desired, but even that was not entirely clear to her. In her girlhood, she had read so many fantasies of love, romances that seemed impossible in their perfection. She ached for just such a thing, but the sensible corner of her heart knew it was all just fiction, and Miss Taylor's writing had convinced her that the indignity of marriage, the prison of it, was not worth the potential fantasy.

And like a fool, she had not listened to that part of her heart or her idol. The sphinx, as Turner put it, had become the kitten. Kittens could be adored and cooed over, but they inevitably grew up into a plain cat, no longer so fluffy or so sweet, just a nuisance, something to fling out into the barn and forget about. Clemency had learned her lesson. She would never be a kitten again, and she would never open her heart to another man. The fantasy, the romance, must be locked up tight, and she must become stone.

I will protect my family, do what I must, but I refuse to pretend it is agreeable.

The tears flowed faster, and Clemency did not stop them. She cried harder, mourning the happy, cherished person she had been for those heavenly months when all seemed right, and Turner Boyle doted on her just as she doted on him.

A floorboard creaked behind her. Clemency gasped and raised her head. For a single, stupid instant she thought it might be Turner. That he had come to find her, apologize, mend the bridges he had torched with his unkindness. Pure fantasy, of course. He had not come.

"Do not dance with him."

Clemency turned, quickly pressing the backs of her hands to her cheeks, but there was no hiding that she had been crying. A man stood watching her from the open doorway, his face half in shadow.

"I wish to be alone," she said, walking across the thick carpet toward him. Then she stopped, brows knitting. "Do not dance with whom?"

"Turner Boyle. Do not dance with him tonight, or ever."

His voice made her shudder. Clemency forced herself to remember the promise she had just made to herself, that she would be stone. No man, however handsome or intriguing, would infiltrate her defenses again. She continued advancing toward him, her anger rising with each step.

"You were spying on me."

The man inclined his head slightly. He took up almost the entire doorframe, tall and commanding as an oak. A careless mane of black curls fell over one equally dark brow. Some might have considered his face too severe, sculpted by a hand that had no patience for excess, but that sparseness only enhanced his best feature, his vivid green eyes.

Lock. Sphinx. Stone.

Just green, Clemency assured herself. *Not verdant or leaping or paralyzing, just green.*

"Forgive me for doing so." The man bowed slightly once more. When he looked at her again, he smirked. "You two were making rather a noticeable commotion."

Clemency sighed and glanced down at her feet. "We were, weren't we? My passion moved me to impropriety, sir. If you have come all this way to scold me, then fear not, I am now contrite."

His smile deepened, dimples carving themselves around his lips. "You mistake me, I have not come to scold. I have come to lift your spirits."

Clemency almost snorted. Instead, she rolled her eyes and wiped at her tearstained face again. "Then you have come in vain. My spirits are quite unliftable, sir."

"Oh, I doubt that." There was something curious about his voice, an accent of sorts, almost too subtle to detect. He moved deeper into the room, the shadows lifting from his face. Clemency admitted to herself, in an academic sort of way, that this stranger was cuttingly handsome, not soft and boyishly attractive like Boyle, but with a hollow-cheeked, hungry look about him. Dangerous.

"I have a proposition for you, Miss Fry."

Clemency glanced at the hearth behind her. She wasn't sure she could dash around him quickly enough to make an escape, and the only other route was back, and straight into a fire. "We have not been introduced, sir."

"Now we have," he insisted, opening his right hand and then sweeping it toward his chest. "My name is Audric Ferrand, and I have traveled from Marseille to Round Orchard with one aim and one aim only. . . ."

"And what is that?" Clemency saw a muscle twitch along his jaw, and felt the fire roar hotter behind her, as if stirred to higher flames by the sheer intensity she saw, then, in his gaze.

"To ruin the reputation, name, and livelihood of Turner Boyle. To that end, Miss Fry, I think you will find collaboration would benefit us both."

4

To her credit, Clemency Fry waited at least a moment before balking at his suggestion.

"You are a stranger to me, sir," she reminded him. In trying to avoid him, she had gotten so close to the fire that he was afraid she might singe her skirts. "And an impertinent one at that. I am meant to marry Lord Boyle, why on earth should I wish to damage his reputation? Any disgrace he suffered would be mine to suffer too."

Audric had expected resistance; in fact, had she agreed to help him without inquiry, then he would have immediately questioned her sanity. But he had not expected to be granted such a shocking boon; having overheard their argument on the terrace, he came equipped with plenty of sharp edges to chip away at her defenses.

"Not if you were to cut off any understanding."

"Oh?" She raised one pretty little brow. "And why would I do that? Simply because you, a stranger, asked?"

"No, of course not, though I should think the way he spoke to you just now outside should be justification enough." Audric made a wide circle around her, planting himself near the hearth. This allowed her to escape, if she so chose, and he wanted her to have that option. None of his plans would work if she felt forced into the arrangement. She had to decide for herself.

She had to *want* to see the cur destroyed.

In an ideal world, Clemency Fry would desire it as much as he did, might even be one of his clients, but that was probably impossible. She retreated to the middle of the library, drawing half away from him, as if shielding herself from an oncoming blast.

"So you *were* spying."

Audric shrugged and swiveled toward the fire, holding out his hands to warm them idly. "Gathering information, more like."

"Right. Spying." Clemency rolled her bright gray eyes.

He could confess to himself that her beauty was something of a relief. If—when—she agreed to his plan, they might eventually marry, or at least mimic a courtship, and a sudden infatuation with a lovely young girl was easy enough to explain away. To the inevitable nosy gossips, it would not look at all suspicious. And her forthright manner, generally an unattractive quality in a woman, also made her uniquely suited to this challenge. The role she had been cast in required tenacity and wit, and a softer, duller girl would not do.

No, Clemency Fry had been perfectly cast. She simply did not know it yet.

"I do hope he was a degree or two more civil during your courtship," Audric said. She was already shuffling toward the door, evidently intrigued by his bizarre proposal, but also smart enough to be wary of it. As stated, perfectly cast. Audric couldn't help but pat himself on the back—it was all going to align just so. "If a man spoke to my sister the way Boyle spoke to you, I should hide him raw."

Clemency blushed and froze, and he could swear the smallest smile flickered across her lips before she reined it back in. Indeed, he did not doubt the image he had just conjured for her was all that displeasing. "The nature of our courtship is none of your business, Mr. Ferrand, and before I leave you, I will politely suggest that you take less interest in the affairs of strangers."

She began to go, the elegant train of her sapphire-blue dress whispering across the library rugs.

Audric calculated carefully, waiting until she was almost to the door, pitching his voice low, but still loud enough for her to catch as she left. "And what a sordid affair it is."

It was almost too easy, pulling her strings. He somewhat hoped the other portions of his plan would be more satisfying to execute. She stopped midstride, then gradually spun to look at him, sending a withering glance in his direction. Continuing to warm his hands, he feigned surprise at her return. Streaking across the floor like a blue comet, she marched right up to him. At that range, her eyes were even more striking, and they were shining with violence.

"Pray, say that again."

"I said nothing that should surprise you," Audric told her evenly. "The man you have attached yourself to is not who you think he is."

Clemency craned her neck back, her full lips pulling down into a grimace. "First and foremost, I did not *attach myself* to him like a barnacle to the bottom of a ship. We are engaged by mutual affection. . . ."

"Indeed. It certainly sounded mutual."

"Second." She forced herself to go on, though she had turned flat white with rage. "Say more about the other thing. Quickly."

Audric tilted his head to the side, bemused. "But, madam, as you so helpfully instructed, it is better to not take interest in the affairs of strangers."

Clemency shook her head, the reddish-gold ringlets framing her face burnished brighter by the fire behind him. "Ah, but it sounds as if you are acquainted with Lord Boyle, in which case you are not a stranger after all."

"I see." For a moment, he considered toying with her for a while longer. But he had not come to Round Orchard to torment her. She seemed as ignorant of her fiancé's true nature as everyone else in the village. Audric had no wish to hurt innocents, and she had suffered enough indignation for one evening. "May I ask how long you have known the man?"

Her shoulders relaxing, her eyes losing their lustrous fury, Clemency walked a few paces to a nearby study table. She dropped down onto one of the chairs there, watching him intently. "You may. I was introduced to him last June, as the season ended. We began discussing a more permanent attachment at Christmas, though my father's health has made him something of a recluse."

"Then your time with him has been mercifully short," Audric said, nodding. It was no wonder the rogue had kept her interest this long, though he questioned whether Boyle could hide his true colors from her much longer. Judging by their exchange on the terrace, his mask was already beginning to slip. "I myself have had the misfortune of knowing him nearly five years."

"Five years!" Her eyes widened. "But he has never mentioned you!"

"No, I suspect he does not remember my name, and if he does, he never thinks of me. We are not friends, Miss Fry; I have known him for half a decade, known *of* him. Watched him deceive and dance his way around society, observed his wake from London to Paris and back again, ever one step ahead of the justice he deserves. . . ." Audric realized his right fist was clenched so tightly that his nails had nearly drawn blood. Closing his eyes, he reminded himself that she need not know everything yet. It was better, in truth, if she remained ignorant of many things.

"Heavens, is he a criminal?" she asked, a dove-like hand clutched over her heart. "But how could that be? He is a baron!"

Audric caught the full-throated laugh before it erupted. "Miss Fry, forgive me, but I very much doubt he is a true baron."

The poor thing had flattened herself against the back of the chair. Such a revelation could not be easy to hear.

"I cannot believe that. . . ." she murmured, tears filming her eyes.

"These are not allegations I would make lightly," Audric continued. "I have evidence, of course."

"Evidence!"

Audric jerked his head up and away from her at the sound of footsteps. They were hurried ones, and before he could say another word, a red-faced girl in an elaborate rose-colored dress swept into the library. She huffed and puffed as she peered inside the door, caught sight of Miss Fry, and yelped.

"Miss Fry! There you are!"

Clemency leapt to her feet and took a few unsteady steps toward the girl in pink. "I am here, Miss Pickford, is something amiss?"

"I'm afraid so." Miss Pickford grasped her bosom, desperate for air. "Your poor sister has fainted. Your mother says it is just the heat, but your family is taking her home now as a precaution."

"Oh . . . Yes. Yes, of course." Clemency spoke as if rousing herself from a dream. Her eyes flashed in his direction, but already Miss Pickford was leading her away. "I will come to Honora at once. Mr. Ferrand . . ."

Clemency paused at the door, one hand on the frame as she twisted toward him. It was impossible to read what lay hidden in her stare, but he had a strong feeling it would not be the last time he saw those beguiling gray eyes.

"Mr. Ferrand, you will excuse me," she said, making her curtsey.

He grinned and bowed to her. "Go to your sister, Miss Fry. Worry not, I will see to it that we meet again, and soon."

"It is all extremely mysterious and intriguing, Clemency!"

Miss Brock, thin as a reed and as sallow as one too, sat on the other side of Honora as the carriage rattled them home. Mrs. Fry, William, and Tansy were ahead of them on the road in the larger family carriage. Mr. Fry had not been well enough to attend, staying home in his study instead. By the time Honora was carried out and all the fussing was over, word had spread that Clemency had been seen in the company of Mr. Ferrand.

She had Imogen Pickford to thank for that. Honora's fainting should have been the bigger story, but nobody seemed interested. Instead, the whispers were about Mr. Greer's aloof cousin.

Miss Brock lived along the route back to Claridge, and with one spot open in their two-carriage retinue, nobody could find a reason to refuse her. Honora dozed quietly against Clemency's shoulder, her skin growing brighter and healthier, and her forehead less feverish.

"Mr. Greer received a letter last month from his cousin, inquiring whether he might come to the ball, and further that he wanted to take up a house in Round Orchard," Miss Brock continued as the carriage rocked them back and forth. Tiny webs of frost covered the windows, melting gradually from their breath. Ordinarily, Clemency ignored gossip, but now she was listening closely. The story after all did involve her. "That cousin is your Mr. Ferrand!"

"He is not *my* mister anything," Clemency reminded her. No, indeed, she should like very much to forget he even existed. Five minutes in his presence and her entire world had been turned upside down. Could his claims be true? It was so absurd, so outlandish, it simply had to be a trick. Turner Boyle not a baron . . . How could he possibly live a lie that big and improbable? There had to be a mistake, a misunderstanding. . . .

"It is likely he will take Beswick or Ashford, those are the only two available houses grand enough for a man of his fortune."

Clemency groaned internally at the thought of him settling permanently in Round Orchard. Beswick was not two miles from where the Frys dwelled. Now she would never be rid of him. She wanted only information from him, then she would be glad if he never turned those cunning and hungry green eyes upon her again.

"A man of means seeking to take up a residence near his family does not strike me as particularly strange, Amy," Clemency said.

"Oh! But it *is* strange! Mr. Greer has not heard a single word from his cousin in more than a decade. Mr. Ferrand's family came and went from England, but years ago; by all accounts, they simply vanished," Amy Brock continued. She had a high, squeaky voice, but Clemency had always found her endearing and, despite her vanity and gossipy nature, harmless. "He must be on the prowl for a wife!"

It was almost amusing to picture how her friend would respond if Clemency told the truth, that Mr. Ferrand had come to settle in Round Orchard only to destroy Turner Boyle's life. A fact she had not told Turner himself. Making it a sly little secret. *Big* secret.

Clemency blanched.

"Imagine it! Beswick or Ashford let again, both with such lovely ballrooms! And the grounds . . . With spring upon us, perhaps there will be a garden fete. The dances will make tonight's event look positively provincial!"

"Mr. Ferrand does not strike me as the type of man to host balls," Clemency told her with a dry laugh.

Amy sat up straighter, fixing her with a squinty stare. "Really? Then how did he strike you?"

Again, the truth must be withheld. They were approaching Amy's home, so at least she would not have to lie for much longer. Clemency puzzled over how to answer, and again she saw Mr. Ferrand in her mind's eye. Amy, with her love of the newest fashions, would approve of his appearance, his suit well cut, not ostentatious but made with expensive fabrics. She might even find him handsome, with his agate-green eyes and strong jaw, lean face and horseman's physique. To Clemency he could not be handsome, only a harbinger, a dreaded devil who had come to curse her with the mischief of knowledge.

The man you have attached yourself to is not who you think he is.

The words were burned into her brain. Turner had not come back to the house with them, choosing instead to stay at the Pickfords'. Clemency had gotten only a quick glimpse of her intended as they rushed Honora out the door, and she found the thought of being in his presence again challenging, to say the least. How could she not question him? Confront him? How would she keep such a secret until she heard the evidence and knew the truth?

"Shall I interpret your silence?" Amy Brock giggled.

"He is severe and very tall; he carries himself like a wealthy man but not necessarily a gentleman. I found him arrogant," Clemency finally told her. "And cold."

"Does he seem terribly French?" she asked.

Clemency smiled, wondering what that might entail. "No. I only noticed a subtle accent, and it was not harsh on the ear. And if you mean his arrogance, then perhaps."

"Well, that is all disappointing. By all accounts he is rather exotic. Still, I should like to be introduced, and make my own appraisal. Ah! But here we are. How is your sister?"

"Better, I think," Clemency said, taking Honora's hand and holding it gently in her lap. "Good evening, Amy."

"Good evening, Clemency. Give my love to your sister when she wakes."

The carriage door opening and closing allowed in a wintry visitor, and Clemency shivered, drawing Honora's shawl higher up her sister's arms. Suppressing a yawn, Honora stirred.

"Is she gone?" she asked without opening her eyes.

"You took ill at the ball, so I will not scold you for leaving me alone to entertain her," Clemency teased.

"You seem out of sorts," Honora murmured. "Even with my eyes closed."

"You're mistaken. I am perfectly all right."

Nothing more was said. Honora dozed and Clemency gazed blindly out the window, seeing and perceiving nothing, locked in her own thoughts, coming to the conclusion that she would probably never be "perfectly all right" again.

When the carriage arrived at Claridge and slowed up to the doors, Clemency roused her sister and helped her down and across the crisply crunchy gravel to the front doors, one of which was helpfully and unexpectedly propped open by their father, waiting there with a cane and shawl, a concerned pout on his pale lips as the two girls ducked inside.

"To bed at once, I think," he said, touching Honora gently on the shoulder. "I can rely on you not to keep her up all night with wild stories from the dance?"

"Of course, Papa," Clemency assured him, painting on a weary smile. "Besides, it was a dull evening at best. I'm sure I cannot think of a single memorable moment."

"I'm sure." He was a smart enough man to smirk at that and roll his eyes, but he relented and escorted them to the stairs, saying his good nights and leaving Honora in Clemency's care. The two sisters did as he asked, going straight to their bedchambers, but after Clemency was washed and changed, and her hair taken down and put into fabric curls, she sneaked into Honora's room through the small door that adjoined their rooms. When they were little, they stayed up nights whispering to each other through the crack, feeling very clever and roguish indeed.

Honora's dark hair was swept over one shoulder as she brushed it. Their maids had been dismissed for the evening, leaving the girls to gather on Honora's bed in the comfortable glow of a few dwindling candles and the dusting of starlight allowed in by the still-open curtains. The room smelled sweetly of beeswax and rose water, and the sprigs of dried marigold and thyme tucked into the cupboard drawers to keep their linens fresh.

"Something has happened," Honora observed quietly while Clemency took the brush from her and sat at her back, raking the bristles through her sheet of silken hair. "Will you not tell me? You shall have to become a far more convincing actress if you wish to fool me and Papa."

For a moment, she considered keeping the secret all to herself, but if she trusted anyone in the whole world completely, it was Honora. Her elder sister had ever been a confidante and guardian, and Clemency would burst if she had to go on without telling a single soul.

"Oh, Nora. I don't know what to think or do. Or what to believe!"

"Dearest, what do you mean?" Nora spun a little, and Clemency dropped her hands and the brush into her lap. "What happened?"

"So much . . . So much, I hardly know where to begin!"

Clemency sighed and shrugged, then let her shoulders sag. She felt tired enough to sleep for an age. "I know now why Turner has cooled."

"And?" Honora pressed. "What did he say?"

"That I am . . . insipid and smothering. That he liked me better when I was indifferent to him. I knew it. He wanted the challenge of winning my heart, not my heart for its own sake."

Honora gasped. "No. How could that be true? What man would not want his beloved to return his affection? Then he has broken it off between you, or you have broken it off . . ."

"No. No, nothing has been decided," Clemency said, each word making her feel stupider. After the way he had spoken to her, how could she go on pretending it was an understanding and not a farce? Yet she needed him, needed his money and standing. *If* it existed.

"That is not all," Clemency continued. "Mr. Greer's cousin came to speak to me privately. I was not fit to return to the dance after speaking to Turner, and so I hid in the library, but this man sought me out."

"Mr. Ferrand?" Honora asked. "The one Amy seemed so excited about?"

"The very same." Drawing in a shaky breath, Clemency collected her thoughts before continuing. She felt nervous and tender, as if her entire body had become one big bruise. "He has had some previous dealings with Turner Boyle, though he did not elaborate, but the implications are grave."

"How are they acquainted?"

Clemency shook her head, rustling the scraps of fabric tied into her red-gold hair. "I am not certain, but Turner must have done something despicable to the man, for Mr. Ferrand is determined to see him destroyed."

"Destroyed!" Honora tucked her feet up onto the bed and turned toward her fully, taking Clemency's hands in hers. "Yet he gave you no reasons?"

"One," she whispered. Her throat was closing up around it, around the ugly allegation. She didn't want to speak it aloud. "He claims . . . He claims that Turner Boyle is not the man we know, or purport to know, that he is not even a baron. But I looked into the man's eyes, and I suspect he would accuse Turner of far greater evils."

Honora was struck speechless. Her mouth hung open as she squeezed Clemency's hands. Then she frowned and exhaled through her nose, taking back the brush and running it swiftly, anxiously through her tumble of dark hair. "No. That cannot be. Papa gave your match his blessing, and Papa is an excellent judge of character."

"But would he know?" Clemency replied. "If everything we know about Turner is a fiction, then he must have taken great pains to make the story believable. I doubt Papa actually investigated the Boyle lineage. No, Nora, think. We have all taken him at his word. We had no reason not to."

"Then you believe Mr. Ferrand?" her sister asked, cocking her head to the side. "Lord, he must have been persuasive."

"I do not believe him," Clemency hurriedly assured her. "Before we were interrupted I demanded proof, of course. I shall wait to receive it and then make up my mind."

"Sensible of you," Honora said with a laugh. "I for one cannot counsel you to believe a man of such short acquaintance, or one with such a dark agenda. After all you have spent adequate time in Boyle's company, surely you would have noticed if something was awry?"

Clemency picked at the lace hem of her nightgown and sucked in her cheeks, ashamed. "You should have heard the way he spoke to me tonight, Nora. You might think differently if you had."

"Men lose their tempers," Honora told her, sounding more like a mother than an older sister. "I should know; I was married to one for nearly two years. Edwyn never raised his voice, but he had his moments. They were always troubling, those moments. Once, I dropped a necklace that belonged to his mother; there was not even a scratch upon it after inspection, but Edwyn did not speak to me for days. It seemed a cruel punishment for such a small crime. When such things happened, I always wondered to myself: Do I know this man or have I committed myself to a pleasant image?" She sighed and looked momentarily lost. "Perhaps it is the pressure of your impending nuptials, the confines of marriage might frighten Boyle."

It was becoming plain that Honora would remain firmly on Turner Boyle's side. And that might be for the best. Clemency had come seeking her sister's opinion, and now she had it. It was wise, she concluded, to wait until she knew more; rushing to judgment would cause only heartache. And Honora was correct—surely Boyle could not construct a title out of whole cloth?

"My sweet Nora." Clemency crawled off the bed, then leaned over and kissed the top of Honora's head. "Your weakness is that you see the good in absolutely everyone."

"There are worse faults," Honora replied, setting the

brush on the bedside table and beginning to braid her hair into a plait for sleeping. "See the good in yourself, dearest, and trust it. In your heart you know the truth, with or without Mr. Ferrand's proof."

"I assure you I do not," Clemency said, then sighed as she let herself through the short door joining their rooms. "My heart is all puzzlement."

When the door was latched and her own room lit with only a single candle, Clemency climbed under the thick blankets of her four-post bed. She traced the shapes on the tapestried canopy, her mind as jumbled as her heart. Honora had never given her bad advice before, and truly, it was absurd that Mr. Ferrand should be believed when Clemency had no guarantee of his credibility. He wanted her help and her trust, but he had done nothing to earn it. By contrast, Turner had, at least for a while, shown her courtesy and favor, and loved her well before her own loudly felt feelings imperiled their marriage. By that alone, Turner had the advantage. He would keep it, she decided, closing her eyes, unless undeniable proof of lies came to light.

There. That settled it. Clemency pretended to be satisfied and told herself it would probably all come to nothing. She vowed to go to bed thinking of ways to be a calmer, more contained woman, a proper English wife for Turner. Perhaps she might take up the pen and continue where Miss Taylor left off. Yes, she could be quiet and tolerable behind a desk, head bent over the page, lips sealed as she churned out warnings more urgent and convicted than Miss Taylor's. She would find ways to be disobedient where she could.

Clemency realized sleep would not be swift in coming. Going to the window, she opened the curtains and ushered in the moon and starlight, then sank down against the cool glass, picking up a book left there in a pile with several others. It was her copy of *Evelina,* by Fanny Burney, read and loved almost to tatters. She opened to the marked place and read.

It seldom happens that a man, though extolled as a saint, is really without blemish; or that another, though reviled as a devil, is really without humanity.

What would Boyle prove to be? Saint or devil? She shook her head and decided not to think of him for the rest of the night.

And further, she would not, she promised herself, think of Mr. Ferrand's cutting green eyes.

5

"Audric! You have returned so soon! And here I expected you to dance until dawn, brother."

Delphine roused herself from her chair by the fire at his entrance. Their room in the Heathfield boardinghouse was the most luxurious on offer, with two bedrooms adjoining a spacious enough central chamber, with the amenities for dining and sitting. The most handsome feature in the room was the large stone fireplace behind his sister. At the dining table, his valet, Ralston, had been playing cards against himself. Ralston also stood, rigid and blank-faced, with raven black hair pulled into a tail, his coat simple and clean, and his boots immaculate.

Audric couldn't help but feel a hitch in his heart when he saw his sister. Leaving her always pained him, for her health was so variable, and he constantly feared that he would walk out the door and return to find her lifeless in her bed.

But Delphine was alive, of course, and watching him with a pretty, bemused smile. He laughed and crossed toward her, shucking his greatcoat and handing it to Ralston as he passed. "Ah, you know me so well, *poupette*. Sit now, do not trouble yourself."

"Please. I despise that name." She did as he asked, and Ralston brought a second chair to face hers.

"Thank you, Ralston. We will not need you just now." Dismissed, Ralston saw to Audric's coat and then bowed, leaving them alone with the crackle of the fire and the muted voices coming from the dining hall below. It was good to give him a little time off, to enjoy himself at cards or to indulge in a pint with the other men of his class patronizing the inn.

Dropping down into the cushioned seat across from Delphine, Audric sighed and rubbed his temples. "Forgive me, Delphine, I have had a difficult evening."

"Indeed. On one of your quests. The others I have tolerated, but you know I do not like this. Do not say another word about it, please, it gives me a headache. Instead tell me of the gowns and sweets. Tell me about the lovely things, brother, I cannot bear any darkness tonight. Shall I have tea brought up?"

"No, no." He waved her off. "I should soon be abed." As if to taunt him, the noise seeping through the floorboards grew louder. The punters were raucous indeed that night. "Curse it. We must get out of this infernal place. Do you not find it drafty? Our new accommodations will be ready tomorrow. It sounds tolerable enough. Beswick allegedly has a serviceable view of the river."

Tolerable, serviceable, but nothing compared to their country home, Fox Ridge, in Reims. Its equal was not to be found in Round Orchard, or indeed in all of England. He spent less and less time at Fox Ridge, feeling it was too full of ghosts. No matter where he went, or what portrait he passed, he felt the unswerving, disapproving gaze of his dead father. Yet Delphine always looked so at ease there, in her natural element, surrounded by the elegant furnishings chosen by their mother. Both of their parents were gone now, and it fell to Audric to care for his younger sister.

He grimaced. Lord, but he had done a terrible job of it. He had not protected her as he should, but that was all different now. His aim—his only aim—was to make her life as comfortable and safe as possible. Finding the right place to wait out their stay in Round Orchard was a start.

How long that would be, he could not say, but he planned for the worst and hoped for the best. It all depended on how quickly he could bring Miss Fry around to his way of seeing things. He rubbed his temples harder, disliking the way her gray eyes danced in front of his vision, as if burned there.

"Brother?"

He snapped his eyes open, staring into his sister's comely face. Five years of convalescence had not been enough to heal the traces of sickly paleness that still clung to her like morning mist. She had their mother's doe-like brown eyes and the thick, lustrous black lashes that they both shared. Her hair matched his, dark and full. While a measure of vigor danced there in her gaze, she was a frail girl, with twig-thin shoulders. No matter how often her dresser came, she seemed constantly to swim in her frocks, sinking into them as if wasting away before his very eyes.

"Lovely things," he murmured, hoarse. Delphine nudged his foot with hers. "There were many fine white dresses, with the long trains and large sleeves. I think that is the fashion now, yes?"

"It is," she said, sounding disappointed. "But I so prefer colors."

There was one extraordinary sapphire-blue gown, but Audric avoided telling her of it. After all she had demanded that he not bring up his schemes, and the woman wearing that frock was part of the plot. He didn't trust himself to describe the gown without somehow giving himself away.

"Harrop Hall is quite grand. I might compare it to the Baudins' estate."

"Oh, but I adore their home. I so wish I could have come with you, Audric. You must realize it is terribly unfair to leave me behind all the time," she said, pouting. "I would have worn a crimson gown, just to shock them all!"

He snorted softly and grinned. "When you are recovered, then you can attend as many balls as you like and host as many as you like. I will happily finance them all."

"We do not have any friends here to invite," Delphine pointed out. She shrugged and looked toward the fire, the flames bouncing in her wide, glossy eyes. "And I will never be recovered."

Audric squeezed his eyes shut. Leaning forward, he rested his elbows on his knees, searching for the right words. The cholera had nearly killed her, but what came after was somehow worse; the slow, inexorable decline of her joy, her once-bright candle dwindling to a meager suggestion of flame. He suspected now it was more a malady of the spirit than the body that ravaged her. And he did not, in truth, know if she would ever heal completely. It felt as if they had visited every doctor on the continent, and they all had plenty of answers but no cures.

A fortune had been spent in the pursuit of her well-being, and Audric would spend it another hundred times more if he must.

"Do not speak that way," he finally said. "The house will soon be arranged and you can leave behind this drear place. That will cheer us both." At that, Delphine brightened and Audric clung to that tiny spark. "You may furnish it however you like, or keep what is already there, or do as you please. I know how you prefer a pastoral view, and now you shall have a river of your very own."

Delphine nodded, her melancholy forgotten. "I should like very much to read by the river, and there will be so many birds to enjoy! But not to shoot, Audric, you know how much I loathe hunting."

"Whatever you wish, sister," Audric said, climbing to his feet. He found himself abruptly exhausted and turned away toward his bedchamber to cover his yawn.

"Audric . . ."

"Yes, Delphine?" He paused outside the door, longing to fall into bed.

"I would like to hold a ball one day," she said, sitting very still by the fire.

"Of course, and you will, *poupette*."

She wrinkled her nose. "And friends. I should like to have some."

"You will."

"Audric . . ."

Turning, he leaned against the door, skewering her with his best "Now what?" older brother glare.

"What happened tonight?"

He had expected her to chide him, perhaps, or to make another small, charming demand, but this question required the complex maneuvering his tired brain struggled to provide. The hesitation and silence, however brief, only made Delphine squint and study him more closely.

"That little muscle in your jaw has not stopped moving since you walked through the door," she added primly. Audric touched his face, rubbing the place she meant. He hadn't noticed, but then, he also didn't doubt her observations; Delphine knew him too well for that.

"So?" she prompted. "What happened?"

Audric grumbled at her prodding, then muttered, "You distinctly asked me not to discuss the plans that brought us here, Delphine."

His warning tone did not dissuade her. Delphine simply shrugged and returned her attention to the fire. The victory was written all over her face. "Then I will not ask who she is," she said softly. "Or how beautiful she must be to provoke a response from the unflappable Mr. Ferrand."

A brisk morning walk was the most reliable cure on earth, according to Clemency Fry. As she strode across the empty, wildflowered fields northeast of Claridge, she felt quite the changed woman. The cool air sweeping down from the river to the north was the final ingredient in the tonic that brought her mind and heart relief. A bit of reading and a long night's sleep had done her immense good, and having slept on her sister's recommendations, she found them even more sensible in the renewing light of a quiet Saturday.

The world looked brighter, and though Clemency had not found perfect clarity, she had at least left her bed to find that the world had not ended.

Mrs. Barnes, their cook, had even baked her favorite rolls, glazed with ginger butter, and served with the precious rose congou tea sent by Tansy's family. Clemency could drink buckets of the gently floral tea with just a hint of cream, but she had savored her one allotted cup while her mother gave them an excruciatingly detailed recollection of the ball they had all attended. Her added commentary was occasionally amusing in its outlandishness, but Clemency's mind hovered elsewhere. Nobody noted her, all attention paid to Honora's health and general state of being after her fainting spell the night before, and Turner Boyle did not join them, leaving Clemency to linger over her breakfast in relative peace.

He was not far from her thoughts, of course, but the night's sleep, comforting breakfast, and now galvanizing walk through the fields had somewhat dulled the urgency of the whole affair.

Sordid affair.

No. She refused to allow Mr. Ferrand access to her mind at all. Until his "evidence" materialized, Clemency lived in a Ferrand-free universe.

The day's sunlight had melted the frost, leaving the grass slick and cold. Clemency carried a dark shawl and rubbed it across her chilly arms. Her hem gradually became sodden as she marched through the flowers and weeds, but her pace kept her warm, and at last she pulled the bonnet off her head and held it in her gloved right hand as the land dipped, rolling down toward the thin blue ribbon of river that separated the north fields from the next property. Across that river lay a great house near triple the size of Claridge, but with so much land it could not even be seen from those fields. The house itself sat atop a high, wooded hill, the abundance of

cypress and rowan trees clustered around it lending it a private, secretive air. It could be seen clearly only from the drive
and the frontal approach, it being otherwise concealed from
the public like a coquettish beauty, wary of prying eyes.

Claridge, though by no means a known Sussex destination, nonetheless held a special place in her heart. It felt like
the brown brick beating organ of her life, at the center of all
her happiest, most cherished memories. For its size, the garden was quite large, and the envy of their neighbors. Apple,
pear, and plum trees grew wild on the property, her father
decreeing that they should be left untamed and not pigeon-
holed into an orchard. Soon the blossoms would come, and
then the fresh tarts. . . .

Mrs. Barnes would have ample fruit to make compote for
their morning rolls, and then, later, when the apples were
ready for harvest, William might visit of a Sunday and fetch
out the old presses and make them all a spiced cider to drink
over cards. Clemency smiled but then worried the brim of
her bonnet with both hands. By the time those apples were
picked and squashed, she would be married.

"Oh dear," she murmured, stunned at the realization that
her wedding was swiftly approaching, and that she would be
locked into a life of ill-suppressed passion and anger, protecting her family's future by giving up her own. Soon she
would be Boyle's entirely, unless this Ferrand character provided ample proof of villainy. Then she might make a
choice . . . No, her mind was already made up! Of course it
was. Only . . .

Clemency stopped at the bottom of the hill, blinking rapidly into the sunshine, her vision unaccountably blurry. The
river came into sharp focus, sparkling and enticingly chilled,

and in a daze, she moved toward it. A bit of energizing water on her face would bring her around, she thought. As she hurried toward the river, she couldn't help but break her own rules and think of Turner. Where was he in that moment? Was he thinking of her? Was he devising some way to escape her? Could he be with another woman?

Kneeling, she laughed. That was a ridiculous thought. Hysterical. She sighed and set down her bonnet, then carefully leaned over the water, pulling off her right glove and cupping her hand, dipping it into the river and shivering at the bracing temperature.

Thus precariously posed, Clemency heard the thunder of approaching horse hooves and jerked her head up. The noise was so overwhelming, she thought perhaps she was in imminent danger of being trampled. The sun blinded her for a moment, and she gasped, sensing, in a panic, that the sudden movement of her head had doomed her to fall.

She saw the black mare charging toward the opposite bank of the river, and then Clemency screamed, plunging into the freezing water.

6

And it had been such a promising morning too.

Audric leaped from the saddle the instant his horse could be halted, almost tumbling into the river with Miss Fry's same clumsiness. It could be examined later, when she was not actively drowning, whether he played some small part in startling her, and subsequently upsetting her balance. Regardless of how the thing had been done, Audric resigned himself to fixing it.

He cast off his green velvet riding coat and waded into the shallows, finding the water quickly rose to his midthigh and went no farther. Thrashing in the weeds not far from him, Miss Fry appeared, popping above the surface like a jostled buoy. Her simple muslin dress had been soaked through, then darkened with river mud, her hair a reddish-blond snarl falling over her face as she sought blindly for safety. Only the dark shawl twisted around her form offered modesty, and, he thought slyly, he was almost sorry for its presence.

Among the sundry plant matter and mud coloring her gown was a concerning blossom of red near her elbow, large and growing larger.

"Do not fret about so," he chided her, reaching confidently and pulling her to the bank where his horse waited. "You are quite safe now."

"I do not *feel* safe. Oh, but my arm . . ." She began to fall over again and Audric intervened before she could sink back into the river, scooping her up into his arms and hoisting her onto dry land.

"Let me see," he said, trying to examine her elbow when she was standing steadily once more.

"I cannot see anything!" At last she managed to toss the sodden hair out of her face, then slicked the moisture off her cheeks with the flat of her palm. "*You.*"

"Accusations and unpleasantries may begin shortly; allow me to examine your arm."

With great reluctance, Miss Fry grew still, then began to shiver violently as he tore open the thin fabric of her sleeve. At that, she yelped, then shuddered more, her teeth rattling like a military snare. She tried to wrap the unfolded shawl around herself, blanching.

One thing at a time. Her chill could be addressed next. Audric clamped his hand around her wrist, leaning down to take a closer look at her elbow. A gash had opened up, running jaggedly up her forearm. Tearing away the already shredded lower half of her sleeve, he twisted the fabric and wrapped it tightly around the wound, tying it off to stem the bleeding.

"That will have to suffice for now," he muttered.

"Is it terribly gory?"

Audric frowned, then glanced down at her, noticing a faint smile on her pale, damp face. "I am afraid so, madam. Fit, in fact, for only the most macabre novel. Undoubtedly we shall have to amputate."

Snorting, she stomped away from him and back to the edge of the river.

"I wouldn't suggest a second go," he called after her. "You were soundly beaten the first time."

"My bonnet," she said, pointing across the offending strip of water. "And my glove."

Audric opened and closed his mouth a few times in shock and annoyance. But Miss Fry simply twisted at the waist, and while he was confident her look of bewildered innocence was entirely fake, it was also profoundly affecting.

"You are bleeding profusely, Miss Fry," he pointed out, coming to join her. "I do not think your *accoutrements* are of the highest priority at present."

"But I love that bonnet," she said with a sigh. Then, naturally, she did what any precocious, clever girl would do and turned those sparkling gray eyes on him, using them like a torch to burn his protestations to ash. "And you are the reason, sir, that I am now parted from my *accoutrements*. You startled me, then took me to this side of the river. The whole debacle is obviously your fault."

Audric bristled, but his irritated looming did not move her in the slightest. It was tempting to climb on his horse and ride away, and let her sort out the bonnet, glove, and flesh wound, but he remembered himself—he needed this brazen young idiot to help him. Without her cooperation, the full beauty of his revenge could not be realized.

Puffing out a breath, Audric stormed to the river, waded back into the icy water, and sloshed his way to the far side, retrieving her bonnet and glove, and gallantly returning without dragging them spitefully through the mud.

"Your items, madam," he said with a theatrical bow and

sarcastic tone. "Now, may we please retire to some place warm before my legs grow so brittle they break?"

"W-Why of course," she replied blithely.

Audric swallowed a snarl and bent to grab his coat, continuing his bid for sainthood by draping the garment over her shoulders. Wordlessly, Miss Fry wrapped it tighter about herself, the size of it swallowing her up.

"Thank you," Miss Fry said. "For my things and the coat. Not for surprising me so rudely."

"I did not . . ." Audric bit back his retort. Was his plan worth suffering this indignity? He closed his eyes and thought of Delphine's melancholy little face and decided that he could damage his pride a while longer for her sake. "We can litigate this later, Miss Fry. Beswick is a neat ride up the hill there, and the hearth beckons."

He saw something like confusion or calculation flicker across her face, but only the devil would know what the minx was thinking. Now that her hair had begun to curl again in a soft frame around her face, and the bloom in her cheeks swelled, he almost regretted giving her the coat; the wet muslin had clung to her in an admittedly alluring way. Now she more resembled an impudent turtle, her head poking out of his immense coat while she considered her reply.

"Very well," she agreed at last.

Chuckling, Audric couldn't help but cock an eyebrow at her demure manner. "What," he teased, "no saucy response?"

Already she had begun walking toward his horse, her words whipped back to him over her shoulder by the wind. "Do not tempt me, Mr. Ferrand."

She tried to pull herself up into the saddle unassisted, but she winced the moment her injured arm bent in the attempt.

"Allow me." Audric needed apply only the scantest amount of strength to hoist her onto the black mare. Some skill for riding must have been part of her education, for once she was up on the animal she adjusted her angle, sitting sidesaddle with her weight shifted toward the pommel. Riding with her nestled against his chest and lap would be a special kind of torment, no doubt she was already thinking up a storm of pert remarks to hurl at him while they trotted the mile back up the hill.

But to his surprise and confusing disappointment, she said nothing once he had joined her. Miss Fry kept her seat admirably while cradling her wounded arm, huddling under his coat, and clutching her hat and glove, and she also kept her silence. Audric decided that was a deliberate tactic too, meant to draw attention to the icy tension that grew swiftly between them, and though they were almost as close as two people could be, there was no mistaking the firm wall building itself between them.

When halfway through the journey it became clear she would not speak, Audric broke the silence himself. "Do you know Beswick well?"

Miss Fry roused herself as if out of a dream. She turned her cheek toward him, her hair sweetly fragrant of soap. He had not had the pleasure of viewing her in profile for an extended period, and Miss Fry at that angle was as handsome as any ivory cameo.

"It is the nearest estate to my family's," she replied. Raising her good arm, she pointed back the way they had come. "Just across that dastardly river? That is Claridge; that is where our property begins."

Audric had to laugh. "Then I bring glad tidings, Miss Fry. We are to be neighbors."

She went rigid, the pink in her cheeks fading. Again, he sensed her choosing her reply cautiously. "Glad indeed. Beswick is a magnificent home; it is time it was let and had life in it again."

"You do not object, then, to the proximity?"

"I do not know you, Mr. Ferrand, and so I cannot muster any specific objections," she said.

His curiosity piqued, wanting to see where this might go, Audric slowed the horse's pace. He navigated them expertly through the dense trees standing sentinel on the expansive grounds.

"You are wearing my coat, Miss Fry. I think you know me a little."

At that, she smiled brightly, and he had to remind himself sharply that this woman, however clever and comely, was only to be a pawn in his schemes. One could admire her but absolutely go no further.

"I suspect our acquaintance will advance if, and only if, you provide the evidence we discussed last evening," she told him, watching him from the corner of her left eye. "Otherwise, propriety demands that I freeze you out. You have after all made outrageous claims about my intended."

"Ah." Audric could not find fault with her answer. Any woman of good breeding would shun him if he was lying. *If.* "Our shared interest."

"A subject I expect you can speak on at length."

The house showed itself at last, first just a glimpse of silvery stones through the heavy cover of trees. Then the roof appeared above the leaves, and the elevated southern veranda with its plethora of wide stone steps sketched itself in. It was almost ludicrous of him to take the place, especially when he and Delphine and their servants wouldn't even fill the bottom floor. But taking Beswick was an important move, and it sent a deliberate message to his enemy: I am not going away anytime soon, I have the means and motivation to unmake you.

Fear me.

"I need only say a little," Audric told her with a shrug. "But it is much better said when we are dry, and at the fire, and you are not bleeding into my coat, Miss Fry."

She lapsed into her stony silence again, and it did not unnerve him that time. Let her keep her blessed ignorance awhile longer, let her think on her doomed relationship in peace, for soon she would have cruelly little hope to cling to.

The estate, empty for more than a year, looked as if it had known only the company of ghosts. The grand halls lay cavernously empty, the walls barren, an echo booming through the house at each step, the only inhabited room a small salon in the east wing. Some fine, polished chairs had been brought in and put near the charming fireplace, and a single pink chintz sofa pushed beneath the tall, thin windows.

As she followed Mr. Ferrand through the house, navigating toward that single comfortable room, Clemency imagined the curtains, carpets, statues, portraits, and tiny comforts that would turn the austere, mausoleum-like estate into a proper home. Utterly desolate, it was hard to imagine the place could ever be cheerful or warm, and normally a family would have their furnishings sent ahead to populate the house and make it fit for living before the owners ever arrived. When they reached the east salon on the first floor,

Clemency assumed the scant furnishings had been provided by whomever had come to rent the place to the Ferrands.

"Oh." Clemency faltered to a stop just inside the salon. There was nobody there, and Mr. Ferrand strode ahead. It had just occurred to Clemency that she had never inquired after his family at all. Amy Brock had mentioned his potential hunt for a wife, but Amy was not known for having perfect information.

"Oh?" he prompted. He was looking for something, or someone, walking diagonally to another door leading south.

"May I ask who will be joining you here at Beswick?" she asked.

Mr. Ferrand's brow furrowed as he stared out the open door. "My sister." Then he bellowed, "Hello? Hello there?" and the sound threaded its way around the empty galleries of the house.

Clemency pressed farther into the room, drawn by the enticing warmth of the fire. "No wife?" she asked, adopting a breezy tone. "No children?"

Footsteps could be heard clapping toward them at a rapid rate.

Mr. Ferrand propped his knuckles on his waist and swiveled toward her. "No," he said shortly. His face had gone red with frustration.

"Your sister, then," she said, warming her hands. The cut along her forearm throbbed, aching terribly whenever she moved her right arm. "I see."

"I daresay that is hope I hear in your voice, Miss Fry."

She rolled her eyes at the flames. "You are mistaken, sir, and forgetful. I may soon be married, remember?"

"For now."

Before Clemency could reply, a footman arrived through the door where Mr. Ferrand waited. He was an older gentleman and dressed for labor in a plain mustard-colored jacket and dark trousers, no doubt already hard at work turning over the house in preparation for its new inhabitants. A dusty white wig sat slightly askew on his head, and he corrected it as he hurried into the sitting room.

"Might there be bandages and clean water about? This lady has injured herself in the river, and the wound must be tended to at once."

The footman bowed and turned around without a word, off on his mission.

"Efficient," Mr. Ferrand said wryly, tucking one hand under his chin and watching the man go. "Perhaps I should hire him on permanently."

"I have often wondered what these great homes look like when unoccupied, and who maintains them," Clemency mused. Soon, she thought, she would be mistress of her own fine house and the details would matter. Though of course, it would fall to her husband to make the more important decisions, and it would be right for her to simply trust in his judgment and live wherever he chose. Likely London before they found a suitable place in the country when the season was out. And given their last interaction, it seemed clear that Turner Boyle wanted to be the one to make those choices, and have Clemency at his side, obedient and submissive.

Clemency wrinkled her nose.

"There is a small staff that lives on the grounds and tends to Beswick, though now that I have taken it, my own staff will begin the transition. So far I find that the previous staff have done a more than adequate job, perhaps the most qualified will agree to stay on with us. Mr. Ferrand told her, wandering to the fire, where she made room for him. They stood side by side, both of them holding out their damp hands.

"Will you give up your previous home entirely?" Clemency wondered aloud.

Mr. Ferrand shook his head. "The staff from my place in London will come here, the family seat in Reims will go unchanged."

"So many houses . . ."

He smirked down at her, proud as ever. "We have not even touched upon my properties in Paris and Marseille, shall I give a full accounting?"

"You shall not," Clemency said, glancing up at him. In the bright light of day, absent the romantic glow of the ball, he appeared different to her, more severe, less refined, the shadow of a beard already threatening to darken his jaw, despite the morning shave. His nose was somewhat too large and hawkish, dominating his face, nearly obliterating the effect of his emerald eyes. The breadth of his smile and jaw balanced everything, and Clemency was noticing that he had a tendency to hold his lips to the side in a tight half-smile that might mean anything or nothing at all.

A puzzle box of a man. His coat smelled strongly of juniper and leather, though that same perfume clung to him too as they stood closely side by side.

Not altogether unpleasant, she allowed, and a combination, like his unusual features, she would not easily forget.

The footman reappeared, crossing to them stiffly, eyes wide and wary, showing concern that he might have interrupted something private. Mr. Ferrand broke away from the hearth and intercepted the servant, taking a roll of linen bandages, a small hand towel, and a bowl of steaming hot water from him. The footman dismissed himself, again silently, and again to the seeming satisfaction of Mr. Ferrand, who smiled and gestured to the chairs not far from the hearth.

Clemency indulged him, retrieving the chairs one by one, a job better left to the footman with her injured arm, but she did not call him back, using her left hand to drag the chairs to the lovely glow behind her.

"You are scratching my floors, Miss Fry."

She dropped the second chair unceremoniously, loudly, and flopped down onto it. "Had I the use of both arms, I should have made a gentler job of it."

Mr. Ferrand's lips squished together tightly. He lowered himself into the chair across from her, dwarfing it comically, his legs almost like a stork's as he perched there and loomed over her. "And I suppose you will blame that injury on me too?"

"Who else?" Clemency stuck out her arm and bent it, showing him the cut.

"And where was your destination this morning, Miss Fry? I cannot imagine it was the bottom of the river," he murmured, dipping the hand towel into the hot water and then pressing it carefully to her arm. She hissed but did not jerk away. "Oh, it will sting."

Clemency inhaled through her teeth. "I did not have a destination in mind, I merely wanted to enjoy the fine weather. It is not uncommon for me to take a novel into the fields and lie by a tree for hours."

He was not, as other gentlemen might be, appalled by this minor confession.

"Novels?"

"Oh, yes. I read widely," replied Clemency. She couldn't help the faint smile that crept over her lips, even just speaking of books soothed her. "Burney and Edgeworth and Austen, Radcliffe and Hamilton . . ."

"I'm afraid that is not reading widely, Miss Fry. That is reading women," he said with a chuckle.

"I will not apologize for my taste, sir."

"Mm, nor would I expect you to." His brow furrowed again as he concentrated, unrolling the linen bandage once the wound was cleaned and the blood drips wiped from her forearm. "Do you often walk into town?"

"Where is this line of inquiry going?" Clemency narrowed her eyes.

Mr. Ferrand shrugged lightly, then wound the bandage snugly around her arm. She couldn't help but notice his long, elegant fingers; they wouldn't be out of place on a musician or painter. "You wanted proof of your beloved's treachery; I promised to provide evidence."

Clemency sat up straighter, interested. "And just how does my going into town prove your ridiculous claim?"

"Does *Lord* Boyle go into town with any frequency?" He couldn't help but say it in a mocking way, emphasizing Boyle's title with visible rancor.

"He does."

"And does he keep a house in Round Orchard?" Mr. Ferrand asked.

"No, when he is in the country he stays with his friend Mr. Connors."

The bandage tied off neatly, Mr. Ferrand sat back, his fingers knit together, resting between his knees. It was a shockingly casual pose, but after being carried by him, riding practically in his lap, and receiving his medical care, Clemency was willing to overlook it. Especially if he was arriving at the point. "Do you know Mr. Connors well?"

"Not at all well," Clemency replied. In fact, she did not like Mr. Connors, for he drank too much at every dance and had more than once splashed his vomit on some poor, unsuspecting lady's shoes. "Again, where is this line of inquiry leading, Mr. Ferrand?"

A slow, chilly smile eased across his face, and Clemency was again struck by how easily he turned from gentleman to hunter. "Today's excitement has spoiled your garment, Miss Fry. It must be replaced, *n'est-ce pas*? New fabric must be ordered, fabric that I am sure your intended would willingly finance. . . ."

Clemency cradled her arm to her chest, withdrawing. Her gaze fell to the floor. She could not remember the last time Turner Boyle had gifted her anything of note.

"Come now, Miss Fry, a few yards of muslin or silk are nothing to a baron. Mere trifles. He must have an extensive line of credit already established." He paused, and Clemency held her breath, knowing an unkindness was coming, and wishing she could avoid it. "Unless, of course, you prefer that I handle the bill?"

She shot him a black look. "Whatever you are trying to prove, you will be disappointed."

"I think not."

"Barons can be destitute," she pointed out. Clemency quickly cringed internally. If he was, in fact, an impoverished baron, then marrying him to protect the interests of her family made far less sense.

"Do you believe him to be destitute?" Ferrand asked.

"I do not," Clemency said. "He has never spoken of financial strains."

"Then, it will be a thing of no consequence," Mr. Ferrand replied, standing with a sigh and returning to the hearth. "Were you my bride-to-be—"

Clemency stood up abruptly. "Well, I am not, sir." She had heard enough, been insulted enough, and absorbed enough insult on Boyle's behalf. Making her curtsey, she shucked his coat and let it fall where it may.

"Shall I fetch the footman to escort you?" he asked, not even bothering to look at her or return her courtesy.

"No, sir, I am more than capable of finding my own way."

Clemency was no longer cold, her face hot with shame and anger as she stormed out. The scent of his coat had soaked into her gown, and the smell of it made her light-headed, almost giddy, and as she navigated the empty halls and strode out the door, she hated herself for it.

Her anger kept her warm for the long walk home. If Mr. Ferrand were a gentleman and not a devil, he would have insisted she take a carriage or at the very least his horse. That he had *offered* was insignificant, he should have *insisted*.

The very idea that Turner Boyle could not afford a bit of silk and ribbons and thread for a new gown was laughable. It had to be. It *had* to be. She was not abandoning Miss Taylor and all her crucial ideals to marry a penniless icicle who loathed her. Clemency stormed her way back to Claridge turning that idea over and over in her head. When she reached the river, she diverted, going north until she came across a small footbridge that allowed her to safely cross.

"The suggestion . . . The nerve . . ." Clemency had almost mashed her bonnet into an unrecognizable ball of straw and fabric by the time she arrived home. Fortunately, she was spared an interrogation, finding that her parents were both sitting in the garden, conversing quietly. Clemency avoided them, skirting the edge of the hedges and ferns hemming in the back garden and going instead to the open door near the kitchen. Inside the house, she found most of the rooms devoid of life, the curtains, linens, and carpet stripped, all of them brought outside to be cleaned and hung, and then put away for the warmer seasons. The distraction of turning over the house for spring and summer afforded her the secrecy she wanted, and soon she had dodged up to the second floor and into her bedchamber, nobody the wiser.

Through the small door between her and Honora's rooms, she could hear her sister singing to herself softly, probably at needlework or drawing.

Clemency forced herself to check her appearance in the looking glass near the window.

"Dreadful," she murmured, aghast. She had never looked so dirty, strange, and forlorn in all her life.

"Clemency? Is that you?"

She swore under her breath. Honora must have heard her come in. There was no time to clean herself up or even concoct a smart enough lie. She simply called back, prepared to loop Honora deeper into the conundrum that had become her life.

"I'm here!"

The fairy door opened a moment later, and Honora's dark head of curls appeared. She, like Clemency, was dressed in a light, ivory muslin dress. A silk shawl trimmed in turquoise fringe hung from her elbows. As she glimpsed her sister, Honora squeaked.

"What has happened to you?" she whispered, rushing toward Clemency and carefully touching her bandaged arm. "Heavens, but you look bedraggled, sister."

"That irritating Mr. Ferrand startled me when I was near the river; I fell in and cut myself on a rock."

Honora took a step back, her brow furrowing. "Mr. Ferrand? What was he doing so close to Claridge?"

"Oh, Honora. It is a disaster. He and his sister are taking Beswick; they will be living practically on top of us."

"That does complicate things," Honora said, wincing. "Shall I fetch Mariah? You should really have a bath."

"Yes, I must clean myself up." Clemency began pulling the pins and ribbons out of her ruined curls, while Honora hurried out into the corridor. "It is not midday yet, there is plenty of time to take the walk to Round Orchard. Perhaps Papa will even let us take the carriage."

Honora leaned over the bannister in the hall, calling down for help. Mariah was summoned, and soon Honora was with Clemency again, helping her undo the tiny buttons down the back of her muddied dress.

"Round Orchard? Today? Surely not. You should rest, Clemency, you're covered in blood!"

"You're exaggerating," she replied tartly. "And anyway, there is no time for resting. After I dropped into the river, Mr. Ferrand brought me on his horse to Beswick to be bandaged, and of course he had more ludicrous proposals to make. . . ."

Once a hip bath had been brought to her room and filled with steaming hot water, a dash of goat's milk, and a scattering of flower petals, Clemency sat soaking while Honora curled up on a cushion and tried her best to comb through the snarls in Clemency's hair. For her pains, Clemency apprised her of all that had occurred at Beswick.

"And you intend to follow this man's directions?" Honora was asking, pulling on Clemency's reddish-blond curls so hard it made her cry out for mercy. "I thought we had agreed that he is not to be trusted."

"But what if there is merit to his accusations?" Clemency replied, gingerly holding her wounded arm above the surface of the water. "What if I discovered the truth of them too late, and I had married and gone to live with a charlatan! This could be my chance, Honora, to be free of a marriage I do not want, for if, God help us, Boyle is destitute, then there is no reason for me to sign my heart away."

"True . . . True . . ." Honora sighed, combing her hair more gently. "And I suppose there is no harm in trying to spend a small bit of his money. After all when you are married, he will be expected to finance such things. If he cannot afford to pay for a muslin, then he cannot provide you and your children with a life of any comfort."

"Precisely."

"And I can tell you wish for me to accompany you on this task. . . ."

"Of course, Nora, I wouldn't deny you the satisfaction of proving Mr. Ferrand wrong. That would please you, wouldn't it? I can tell that you do not like him, insofar as you can dislike anyone." Clemency tilted her head back, giving her sister a wide, smug smile.

In retaliation, Honora flicked some of the murky water at her face. "I do not like troublemakers. It seems to me as if this Mr. Ferrand was put into our lives only to upend things. I rather prefer a steady state of things."

"And you shall have it again soon, sister." Clemency finished scrubbing the grime away from behind her ears and reached for the warm sheet hanging an arm's span from the bath. "We will clear up this entire misunderstanding, and all will be set to rights."

"Well . . ." Honora set the brush down, standing and going to the open window, leaning out, the birdsong so clear and bright it almost sounded like high summer. "Not all to rights. You will still be marrying reluctantly."

Clemency grimaced, standing and discarding the wet shift she had been wearing in the bath. She took the clean sheet and wrapped it around herself, mindful of her sore arm. "What matters is that his fortune will allow me to take care of all of you. I will find ways to fill my time, and we will hate each other; many such marriages exist. Only . . . it is never the life I imagined for myself. Spinsterhood appeals far more."

Leaving the window, Honora crossed to the cupboards near the basin and pulled out a fresh chemise and stays for her sister, then handed them across. Their eyes met, and Clemency could see her sister was on the verge of tears. "That is not the life I would choose for you. I would choose love for you, sister, a true and lasting love."

"The whole of England knows I am spiteful toward matrimony," Clemency reminded her. "My season was a disaster. No, my actions have led me to this path, and now I must walk it. At least I will hold my head high, even if every step down that road is agony."

Half of the village had sweatily crammed itself into Tindall and Batt's on that fine Saturday afternoon. Clemency had trouble navigating through the shop without constantly bumping her throbbing arm. Valiant Honora did the best she could to clear a lane, but they were at last forced to gain ground inch by inch, browsing silks and cottons and notions at a snail's pace.

"What a lovely coincidence!" Amy Brock's narrow, prim face materialized between two shelves. It was a modest shop, but well-stocked for the size of the village. Mr. Batt took sales while his wife made herself useful to the circulating customers. Mr. Tindall was rarely seen, making alterations and repairs in a cloistered back room.

A trio of tall windows looked out onto the dirt main street of the village and the carts of merchants who came to sell sweets and kites to strolling families.

Amy crammed her way through the crowd, joining them near the windows and a few upright displays of tempting new ribbons. She had come adorned in a pink-and-white-striped frock with a lace fichu tucked around her neck, a profusion of silk flowers decorating her moss-green bonnet. Despite her frail appearance, Amy always seemed to have an air of excitement and vigor, even on cold, cloudy days. As it was bright and fine out, she was even more energetic.

"Did you hear? You must have heard! Beswick is let! It is just as I predicted—Mr. Ferrand and his sister have taken it. Can you even believe it? You are to be neighbors! How glamorous! Ah, but you truly do have all the luck." Amy pretended to pout, but she did not have a jealous bone in her body.

"How fortunate," Honora said politely, inspecting a spool of periwinkle ribbon.

"We may get our ball after all, hmm?" Amy nudged Clemency, giggling.

"Indeed, we may," Clemency muttered. She glanced around the shop for something that might grab her attention and save her from discussing Mr. Ferrand further. No doubt her dunk in the river and subsequent ride to Beswick with Mr. Ferrand would be discovered by the gossips eventually, but she intended to enjoy every minute before that came to pass. "What do you think of this for a new walking gown?"

Clemency placed a single finger on the bolt of sprigged muslin, and it was enough to draw Amy's attention away from the new additions to Round Orchard.

"Just delightful, perfect, really!" Amy reached out to touch it for herself. "And so soft. My, but it must be rather expensive. . . ."

Honora shifted, and Clemency simply smiled.

"I think I will have it," Clemency declared, and as if summoned by magic, Mrs. Batt was there, sensing a potential sale like a hound sniffing out a fox.

Once the yardage was decided and Clemency had chosen accompanying buttons and a white satin ribbon, the total was tallied, and their party ushered to the back of the increasingly warm shop. Ordinarily, Clemency would simply request that the fabric be added to her family's general bill, but not this time.

"Do you think Miss Ferrand is a fashionable woman?" Amy was musing, tapping her gloved fingers on her chin as she considered it. The three young ladies lined up at the counter, where Mr. Batt busied himself bundling up the fabric and trim, folding it inside a lovely, crisp paper. "With a fortune like that, it would be a shame to have no taste . . . I wager she is unbearably elegant."

"Miss Fry?" Mr. Batt prompted.

"Might you put this on Lord Boyle's credit?" Clemency asked sweetly. Mr. Batt stared at her, his face an unreadable mask. His nose had been broken in the war, and he made it a habit to smile broadly, offsetting his intimidating look, but his salesman's grin had vanished. "We are soon to be married," she hurried on, realizing that perhaps this seemed like an overstepping of boundaries on her part. "And he assured me this would be a gift."

"Right, I'm sure he did, miss," Mr. Batt grunted. He plucked nervously at his apron, then an eyebrow, then lowered his voice. Their exchange was beginning to draw attention. "But that man's coin is no good here, never has been, because I've never seen it. My apologies, miss, but after what he owes in the village, I'd be a fool to take on more."

"Nonsense!" Amy just had to say, garnering even more unwanted attention. "You cannot mean *her* Turner Boyle. He is a baron, sir!"

"Amy, be silent," Honora hissed.

The shop had gone suspiciously quiet. By tomorrow, the entire village would know that her intended did not pay his bills on time or at all. The gossips would send a plague of whispers to sweep through town tomorrow, making it the only topic of conversation at afternoon tea. No, the spectacle she had made of herself would be the topic *du jour*.

"How . . . How . . ." Clemency bit down on her lower lip, feeling a hot flush of humiliation rush over her cheeks and neck. Someone behind her tittered. Honora and Amy stood rigid beside her, but she could imagine Amy probably had her mouth wide open in shock. "I see. My mistake, Mr. Batt. Would you please put these on the usual account, then?"

His smile returned slowly, a little sadly, his eyes warming to her as quickly as they had cooled. "A'course, Miss Fry, glad to."

Clemency had only the vaguest memory of leaving the shop, feeling every pair of eyes boring into her as she went. Eventually she realized Honora had taken her by the arm, shielding her from some of the curious gawking until they were out in the fresh air again. Clemency sucked down a frantic breath, not realizing until that moment how close she had come to suffocating on her shame.

"I am convinced he will have an explanation," Amy chirped, seemingly impervious to the staring and whispering. "He comes and goes so frequently, perhaps the bill simply slipped his notice."

"Perhaps," Honora bit out, even her politeness strained. "I think I should take my sister back home now, Amy—"

But she wasn't done speculating. "Still, how odd that he would send you there to pick out a gift and then not provide for it. Well. The minds of men, mm? They are utterly unknowable to us."

A cart carrying firewood rumbled by.

"Utterly unknowable," Clemency muttered. "And utterly disappointing."

"I beg your pardon, what did you say? That carriage was so disrupting." Amy beamed at her, adjusting her green bonnet with a sweet laugh.

"Clemency had a bit of a fall this morning on her walk," Honora intervened, tugging Clemency away, down the road to the west and toward the lane leading to Claridge. "It seems to have rattled her more than we anticipated."

"How awful! Let me help you both home—"

"No," the sisters said in unison. Honora swiftly cleared her throat and patted Amy fondly on the hand. "That will not be necessary. I am quite capable of taking her on my own."

Amy frowned, squinting at them, the sunshine falling directly into her eyes as she watched them shuffle away. "Oh! But you will not have to! Is that not your family's carriage now? And there is William!"

And so there he was. The carriage came charging up the road toward them, their brother hanging out the window, whipping a hat around in a circle. The dust flared and then settled, and once they had stopped, William and Tansy spilled out, red-faced and shining as if they were immensely drunk.

"*Girls*. Girls! There you are! It is the most remarkable thing!" He scooped them into an embrace, Clemency sore and disoriented, inhaling through her teeth as he squished his arm against her cut. Tansy's bonnet had almost fallen off completely. She righted it, laughing uproariously, joining their little circle of family merriment. In her left hand she clutched an opened letter, waving it around like a flag.

"Do not keep us in suspense, William," Honora chided, searching between him and his wife for answers. Even Amy came to see what had happened, lured by the commotion.

"It's the *Villefort*!" Tansy shrieked.

When nobody responded with the correct amount of enthusiasm, Tansy rolled her eyes and tossed her head, then thrust the letter toward Honora. "My father's ship! It has returned safely from the West Indies, and her sister ship is expected to arrive in good condition!"

Honora had already flattened out the letter, reading and mouthing the words at speed. Her voice rose when she reached the relevant passage. "It is with all the joy in my heart that I write to you, daughter, for with this bounty of silks and spices, our good name and fortune are restored." She looked up from the letter in a daze. "Tansy . . . Oh my dear, what news! What glorious news!"

"Felicitations," Clemency stammered, stunned. "This is . . . How wonderful for you both."

"And so we must celebrate," William roared, taking Honora by the arm and swinging her around for a jig right there in the street. "You must come too, Miss Brock, and your family. We shall have you all tomorrow to Claridge, after church, and we will toast the changing winds of fate!"

Clemency still felt the hot sting of shame prickling at her throat, but news of this caliber could certainly be a balm. Her eyes drifted to Honora, who had stopped spinning around with William. Clemency's mind raced to keep pace with reality—Tansy's fortune belonged primarily to William, and now he might finally have the means to keep Claridge in the family, and even provide larger, more enticing dowries for her and Honora. More than that, it freed her from the financial chains binding her to Boyle.

Freedom.

The relief of that victory did not last long enough to be savored, for she could not forget the bitterness buried beneath the sweet. The man she had loved, that she had joined herself to, that she had nearly *married,* had been keeping secrets from her. And if Mr. Ferrand was to be believed, and now perhaps he should be, those secrets were crucial indeed. Clemency did not share Miss Brock's charitable view of the situation; there was no good excuse for a man of Boyle's alleged means to have established such a low reputation at a village modiste. Perhaps this explained why he had never purchased a home of his own in Round Orchard; it was not, as he'd stated, that he preferred to stay with Mr. Connors, but that his debt prevented a purchase of any significance.

Dark secrets. How could she ever trust her judgment again? Indeed, she could not. And that was all right; she could now, perhaps, safely swear off men forever.

While her siblings herded her toward the carriage, Clemency glanced back at the shop, feeling as if the girl who had walked through those doors to buy fabric no longer existed. The Clemency who emerged back into daylight was someone different. Something different. A woman of stronger stuff, meaner stuff, who would not be fooled again.

7

A crisp, cold gale followed Audric into the village. Darkness had only just fallen, the Sunday evening church bells tolling their last as he moved with the bluster down the empty cobbled street. Eventually it dissolved into more of a dirt path that ran the length of a mile through the center of commerce. It was a tiny place, roughly half the size of Heathfield, with the standard English country provisions—cheesemonger, church, cobbler, stable, modiste, miller, bakery, tavern, and vegetable stands. Its most attractive feature was the surprisingly spacious assembly hall built directly across from the charming square with a round stone well and felt bunting hanging from the posts of an outdoor stage.

A few candles burned in the windows as Audric strode by, though only the tavern did any business at that time of night. The echo of the church bells faded as Audric reached Tindall and Batt's. Distant male laughter leaked from the nearby tavern, a film of fiddle music washing over the chilly silence, carried along on that sharp wind.

As he rode the distance from Beswick to Round Orchard, he worried a strip of fabric in his pocket. He had kept the bit of bloodied sleeve that had once served as a bandage, it having fallen by the wayside while he dressed Miss Fry's cut with a fresh wrapping. It was morbid to keep it, and unhygienic, but something compelled him to stash it. It seemed to soothe his anxious mind to fiddle with it between thumb and forefinger as he rode, a little unseen ritual in the pocket of his coat.

While his mind ought to be occupied with the innumerable details of letting a new house, instead he thought constantly of her. No woman outside his family had ever dared speak to him the way she did, with so much cheek and so little fear. He frightened most people, which usually he found an advantage, but it also meant that women found him unapproachable. His father had cultivated an earned reputation for severity and stoicism, a reputation he imparted to his son. Happy memories of his father were vanishingly scant, their only shared passion the hunt. What would his father say now if he knew Audric spent his time helping the spurned, insulted, and abandoned women of France find the men that left them in ruin? He had become an instrument of revenge, a man to be feared by liars and cheats. Perhaps his father would be proud, though the far more likely alternative was that his father would find the pursuit ridiculous—men had appetites that women did not, in his father's opinion; that women suffered the indignities of those indiscretions and not the instigators was simply the way of the world.

No, he was not his father. The elder Ferrand hunted for the kill; Audric hunted—beast and man alike—for the temporary ease it gave his soul. He could sink his mind into something else for a little while, distract himself from his sister's pain.

Away from his loneliness.

Given his silent, ferocious nature, few mothers targeted

him for their daughters, a mercy most other men of his four-and-thirty years would not be given. Delphine had once overheard a pair of girls whispering about him at an assembly in Paris, describing him as *un peu satanique*.

Delphine thought it hilarious, of course, but it bothered Audric more than he cared to admit. Did women really find him vaguely satanic? If so, that made Miss Fry's behavior all the more intriguing. He never had the impression that she found him scary, only—perhaps rightly—exasperating.

More than that, he sensed in her a fellow hunter. Huntress. She enjoyed their verbal spars and delighted in outwitting him, that much was clear.

Again and again he returned to a single thought: The so-called Lord Boyle did not deserve a woman as brash, handsome, and infuriating as Clemency Fry. Their entanglement had begun to sincerely rankle him, an offense to the very idea of marriage as an institution and love as a broader concept. This wrong would be corrected, and while Miss Fry was almost certainly too much for any sensible man to want or handle, Ferrand included, she did not deserve the infamy of being connected to someone like Boyle.

What an apt name the scoundrel had chosen, for he was exactly like a boil—unsightly, exigent, a thing to be lanced and popped, nothing more than an oozing carbuncle on the arse of society.

At last, he reached his destination and dismounted.

The two-story shop no doubt housed apartments on the second story, which meant Tindall or Batt was guaranteed to be somewhere within. He hoped they weren't part of the clamor coming from the tavern, as this business was best conducted in private.

Audric smiled as he lifted his leather-clad hand and rapped three times on the door. Just as he had expected, Miss Fry had come to shop for new fabric and discovered that her husband-to-be was a well run dry. He had only to send his man Ralston into town to get a whiff of the day's gossip, and sure enough, Miss Fry's name was on the lips of every busybody. Ralston had a talent for fitting in anywhere and was paid handsomely not just for his valet services, but for his frequent forays into espionage on Audric's behalf. The other intriguing story involved Miss Fry's sister by marriage, Tansy Bagshot, and news of some windfall. That served Audric too, a stroke of luck that would benefit them both.

"We're closed!" A gruff voice boomed from inside.

Audric knocked again, and again. He had waited years to put his plans into motion, he could be patient awhile longer. At last, the door flew open, revealing a red-faced short man with a healthy beer gut and thinning hair.

Before the man could shoo him off, Audric bowed and swept off his hat, giving the full gallant treatment. "I beg your pardon, sir, I know the hour is inopportune. Do I have the pleasure of speaking to Mr. Batt or Mr. Tindall?"

"You can speak to the door, sir. We are closed."

Audric wedged his boot in the door subtly and offered the man a slow smile. "How disappointing. Ten minutes of your time would be worth as many pounds, but if you insist . . ."

"Just a moment, there. Slow down." The man's eyes glittered as he held the door open wider. "What sort of business have you come on, Mr. . . ."

"Ferrand. Audric Ferrand, at your service, sir. I am here to discuss a debt and to clear it. It has come to my attention that a Lord Boyle has accrued a sizeable bill and failed to pay it." Audric withdrew a billfold from his greatcoat and let the man see just how many pound notes waited within.

"Come in, come in, Mr. Ferrand." The man gestured, suddenly all smiles. "Mr. Tindall is at the tavern, as is his custom, but I deal with the books, anyway. Come now inside and be quick about it, that wind's as harsh as an ill omen. Fanny!" he cried to some unseen woman within the shadowy shop. "Have tea brought down, bring it to my desk!"

Mr. Ferrand tucked his hat under his arm and followed the man inside and to the right, where the darkened shop was lit with only a few dwindling candles.

"Thank you, Mr. Batt. Again, I apologize for calling so late."

Mr. Batt waved him off, bustling through the shop and to a large desk in the back right corner of the store. A small chain guarded the way behind it, and Mr. Batt unhooked that and then disappeared for a moment, squatting down to find something, the sound of paper rustling rising from behind the desk.

"We don't stand on ceremony here, Mr. Ferrand, not when a hefty debt can be paid. And it *is* hefty. . . ."

"I do not doubt it."

Fanny appeared, a birdlike woman with a lace cap and iron-gray curls, a pair of spectacles as wiry as her arms perched on the end of her nose. The tea tray rattled a little as she carried it, and he noticed Fanny holding her thin lips together tightly in frustration. Audric retrieved the tray from her and placed it on the desk.

"Oh, thank you, sir," she murmured, glancing away shyly. "Sewed night and day for thirty years, now these hands struggle to hold a pin."

"It is no trouble, madam. I hope we did not disturb you overmuch," Audric replied.

"Not at all." With care, she poured the tea, gave a curtsey, and turned to go, her husband giving her a muffled thanks from behind the desk. Audric had no intention of taking tea, but he picked up one of the cups and held it to appear accommodating.

"Well now." Mr. Batt stood again, slamming down a leather-bound ledger. "This gentleman is a popular subject today."

Audric nodded gravely and heaved a sigh for added effect. "My friend has expensive taste and shallow pockets. I suppose those habits are now known to the whole of Round Orchard; it will deeply embarrass him."

Mr. Batt rubbed his chin thoughtfully. "Aye. He's been a thorn in our sides long enough, 'tis time we were paid what we're due."

Setting down his teacup, Audric leaned onto the desk, then produced his billfold again. "I could not agree more, Mr. Batt. Indeed, it is just such a reckoning I have come to propose. You see, I am willing to wipe out his debt at this shop, but I believe my good friend should be taught a lesson."

His eyes roamed subtly to the ledger. It was not hard to divine which line in the books belonged to Boyle, for many times it had been circled as if in a panic. He calculated a rough estimate, pretended to wince, and slid forty pounds across the desk.

"This is more than is owed," Mr. Batt murmured, beady eyes widening at the sight of the money.

"I understand his intended suffered some shame on his behalf this afternoon, and I should like to make a gift of her purchases. Perhaps you could also include whatever is currently most fashionable? I don't know, fabric and bits and bobs, whatever pleases your professional eye? Audric couldn't tell if he was listening or if he had been struck dumb by the stack of pound notes.

"O-Of course, sir. Anything you like, sir." Mr. Batt bowed awkwardly behind the desk.

"Excellent," Audric said, taking a small card from his pocket and adding it to the stack of money. "Please include this note with the gift."

"No trouble at all, sir." He paused, eyes flicking from the pound notes to Audric's face and back again. "How is it that you know the man, if I may ask?"

Shrewd, Audric thought, but not shrewd enough.

"We shared the same society in Paris, though it seems a lifetime ago now," Audric explained, hoping it sounded wistful. "We both have a passion for horses and the more . . . unmentionable delights Paris has to offer."

He winked.

Mr. Batt tapped his nose and gave a knowing chortle. "Right, right. Gentlemen about town, eh? But you mentioned a proposal?" Mr. Batt carefully took the money and stuffed it behind the desk quickly, as if afraid Audric might change his generous mind.

Greedy, greedy . . .

"There could be ten pound more for you in it," he continued, watching Mr. Batt flush with excitement. "I ask only that you confer with the other merchants in the village. As I said, my friend must be taught a lesson in responsibility, and I think it's time his debts were called up. All of them."

"Ha!" Mr. Batt gave a short, uproarious laugh. "Are you trying to give the man an episode, Mr. Ferrand?"

"Me?" Audric slid his billfold back into his coat with a casual shrug. "Surely not, there simply comes a time when a man must confront his place in the world. I assure you, Mr. Batt, I would never dream of giving the estimable Lord Boyle more than he deserves."

As Clemency stood at the window, a light rain had begun to fall outside. The scent of woodsmoke and damp filled the house, remnants of a day spent with the windows and doors flung wide open. They had all assembled in the Painted Salon, named for the attached corridor where portraits of and collected by the Fry family were displayed. Sherry and port had been poured, and Honora sat at the pianoforte, playing through her many memorized études while everyone digested and bathed in Tansy Bagshot's enthusiastic glow.

She looked like a candle, slender and bright, illuminating the entire room with her smile while she bobbed her head a little drunkenly to Honora's music.

Clemency gazed around at her family, feeling as if she were somehow apart, set behind a thick screen, there but translucent, a gossamer figment of a person. Nobody had brought up the awkward moment at Tindall and Batt's during supper, for Tansy's news was far better conversation material. Naturally, it interested Clemency too, as a financial turn for William could free both her and Honora from the burden of marriage. Clemency had begun to suspect that Honora's disinterest in courtship might be permanent, and that she would rather remain Mrs. Hinton forever, even if her husband was no more than a ghost.

Honora's husband had been struck by a carriage and killed over a year ago, not long after Christmas. She had more than exceeded the appropriate period of morning, yet she never so much as glanced at a man when they attended church or parties.

Her sister had always been a quiet, solitary creature, and more and more, Clemency liked the idea of growing old with her, just the two of them confined to Claridge, happy, forgotten women. She smiled to herself, imagining Honora's probable horror at the idea—no, Nora would insist she go out into the world, try for love, even if all the men Clemency had the displeasure of meeting were trouble in one way or another.

Holding her full glass of sherry, Clemency wandered into the shadowy corridor housing the paintings. It was a wide, airy space, and the recipient of many of her mother's overwrought floral arrangements. Still, it made for a pretty combination—the riotous explosions of blooms juxtaposed with the statelier, subdued oil paintings of men and women stiffly posed in their finery. Honora began wandering the melodious paths of Handel while Clemency came to stand in front of a portrait of her grandmother. Margaret Fry was not by any means a beautiful woman, but the artist had captured her spirit, a mischievous gleam in her eye that had been passed down to Clemency's father and, she had been told, to Clemency herself.

She tapped the nail of her forefinger restlessly against the sherry glass. They had expected Turner Boyle at dinner, but he never appeared, his chair sitting conspicuously empty, everyone else ignoring it while it seemed constantly to mock Clemency. Perhaps word of their humiliating experience in Tindall and Batt's had reached him and he was refusing to attend out of spite. She had spent all afternoon preparing her speech, rehearsing the sharp words she intended to use, slicing him to ribbons once they had a private moment to speak.

She could not play the meek and accepting woman, not even for a handful of days. Ludicrous, then, that she had thought herself capable of changing completely for Boyle.

Unlike Honora and Amy Brock, Clemency did not think the incident a misunderstanding. A gentleman paid his debts, so what did that make him?

Honora's playing ended abruptly, commotion erupting in the sitting room as everyone leapt to their feet. A visitor had come. Clemency wandered to the archway leading back into the salon and froze. Her stewing must have summoned him, for there was Turner Boyle, fresh out of his hat and coat, his boots slick with rain, a few wet, ginger curls falling in his eyes. He brushed them away and rushed to congratulate Tansy.

"What excellent news," he said, beaming at both William and Tansy. She hiccupped and pressed the back of her hand to her glee- and drink-reddened cheeks.

Honora's wide, terror-stricken eyes slid from Turner to Clemency.

"Come in, come in," William was saying, ushering him toward the sofa. Their father had long ago retired, leaving William to be gallant and obliging. "Warm yourself, take some brandy, Honora was just delighting us with her playing."

"Yes, of course." Turner did as he was told, but quickly his gaze found Clemency where she lurked in the shadows between sitting room and gallery. He gave her the strangest smile, apologetic, maybe, or ashamed. "I do apologize for my lateness," he said, Honora beginning to softly strike the keys again. "The road near Foster's Gate flooded so we were very delayed returning from Heathfield."

He touched his hair again, and Clemency scowled. *Liar*.

"Foster's Gate flooded?" William asked with a laugh. "With so little rain?"

Yes, interrogate him. Show him for the snake he is.

"The weather turned earlier over the north pastures I think," Turner told him smoothly. Had he been caught out in the rain on his horse for that long, he would have been soaked through. Nobody else noticed, and conversation again turned to happier things. Was this how he glided smoothly through his deceptions? Too amiable, too handsome to ever really sustain a critical thought?

"We were just discussing arrangements for the season," Tansy said, glancing at William. "In a week's time we will depart for London, to stay with my father and see if he has need of us. Of course, Clemency stayed with her aunt, Mrs. Drew, last time, and their house might be grander, but I so prefer to have her near."

"London has been much on my mind too." Again, that odd smile crossed his lips, and he dragged his gaze over to Clemency. She turned her back and merged into the dark corridor. "If you will excuse me . . ."

Clemency made a fist with her empty hand and squeezed, then repeated the motion three or four times. Suddenly, her mind was a blank. She needed to remember all the clever, cold things she wanted to say, but now her thoughts betrayed her. His footsteps fell heavier on the inlaid tiles of the gallery, and he came near enough to share his warmth.

"Clemency . . ."

That was a new tone of voice. A *contrite* tone. She ignored him, staring up blindly at the portraits, pretending to be engrossed in something or other.

"I do hope you are willing to listen to my explanation."

"Why are you late?" she asked, putting on a neutral air. She had no interest in her drink but sipping it casually did seem like the right thing to do to complete the picture of a bored, unmovable adversary.

"Foster's Gate—"

"Could not possibly have flooded," she interjected. "You hardly have a speck of rain on you. Try again, and try harder."

At that, she expected him to lash out, or at the very least walk away from her. Their last exchange had been a tense one, but Turner seemed like a completely different person. Out of the corner of her eye, she saw his narrow shoulders slump forward. She almost pitied him. Almost.

"I am late because I went to settle things at the shop," he told her in a desperate whisper. "Will you please look at me?"

The irony was too delicious.

"No, I don't think I will. A look might be awfully *smothering*."

"Very well, I deserved that," he muttered. "I did not . . . I did not conduct myself properly at the Pickfords'. I know that. I'm stupid, all right? Stupid and humbled. Will you accept my apology? On my honor, I will never speak to you that way again. It was . . . It was rude and unacceptable, and I am terribly, terribly sorry."

As apologies went it was quite good. Better if he had been on his knees, but Clemency could have a heart. She gave him the quickest look, then returned to surveying the art. "I was humiliated at the ball," she said icily. "And I was humiliated again today."

"I know . . . I *know*. I wish I had a better explanation for my behavior of late, but everything has been in such a tumult. Those debts . . . It is not my spending that is the problem, Clemency, or my lack of funds. A damned generous spirit has landed me in these dire straits. It's Jack, you see, he—"

"Mr. Connors?" Clemency whirled to face him, nearly splashing sherry down his shirt. She knew little of the man, only that he and Boyle were dear friends, so much so that Boyle preferred to stay with Connors while in town instead of letting his own house. "What does he have to do with this?"

"Jack is . . . He is not always wise with money," Turner told her, his cheeks flushing. He almost adjusted his hair, then stopped himself. His eyes shimmered in the low light. Was he actually going to *cry*? "I allowed him to use my credit around town, a mistake I will not make again. He has been the source of my misery and moods, and I have left his company. I should never have taken it all out on you, but he has made my life taxing indeed as of late." Turner sighed and shook his head. "After settling my debts, I rode to Heathfield to take a room. I wanted to have it done, you see, to prove to you that I am serious about leaving his company."

Clemency squinted. Jack Connors was a notoriously flamboyant and stupid man, which also made him a convenient scapegoat. This revised story, however, did make more sense than the last.

"I wonder that you did not ask my father to stay here at Claridge."

"After the way I treated you, dear Clemency, and with his poor health, I would not presume." He closed his eyes for a long moment, composing himself. When he looked at her again, it almost made her heart clench. Looks like that had bewitched her over the summer, and they were potent indeed. "Say you can forgive me, please—I cannot bear to know that you think ill of me. I was so stupid. Stupid, *stupid*."

"What I think of you is *your* doing," Clemency replied, tipping her chin back. His self-flagellation was annoying, not enjoyable. "You cannot expect me to simply forget the awful things you said. That was but two days ago! Am I to believe you are now a different man entirely?" He turned away, silent. "How many Turner Boyles am I to encounter this week? Tell me now so I might prepare."

"Give me a chance to make amends," he pleaded. Swiftly, he reached for her right elbow, ignorant of the bandage there, his hand clamping down hard enough to make her see stars. Clemency hissed, jerking away. "Lord, are you hurt?"

"I . . . fell," she whispered, retreating toward the portrait wall. She downed the sherry to try to mask the pain, but it felt like he had torn the wound open anew. "Blast, it may be bleeding again." She twisted her arm, contorting, trying to see if crimson had leaked through the ivory silk of her sleeve. "Ferrand ruining my other gown and now this—"

His name was out of her mouth before she could consider the consequences. And now that bell could not be unrung. It was like she had cast a spell. Turner Boyle's embarrassed flush disappeared, replaced by a ghastly pale, as if just the name "Ferrand" had sapped him of all life and left him an upright corpse.

"What did you say?" She almost couldn't hear his whisper over the beating of her heart.

Well. She couldn't take it back now, could she? He was the liar here, not her.

"Mr. Ferrand," Clemency said, pretending not to notice his bizarre reaction. "He is taking Beswick, he startled me on my walk, and I stumbled into the river." She was speaking too quickly to be casual, but she charged ahead. "That was why I needed more fabric, my favorite walking gown was mangled, I bled all over the sleeve and tore it."

"Y-Yes," Turner stammered. "Yes, of course. Your sleeve. New fabric. What appalling luck. But you are feeling well now?" He passed a shaking hand over his face.

His behavior was now too obvious to reasonably ignore. Clemency held her arm more loosely, studying his face. "Well enough, though it still stings. Are you acquainted with Mr. Ferrand?"

"Was he . . . I mean . . . who?" His tone aimed for breezy and fell short by about a mile. "No—or rather, I could have heard the name in passing. Is he new to town? Jack may have mentioned something about it. Or we may have been introduced at White's. . . ."

Either way, his lying was plain enough. Clemency let him drone on about other far-fetched ways they might have met, watching him dig his grave ever deeper. It was almost impressively clumsy, which suggested they really had known each other in some capacity. Mr. Ferrand had claimed Turner might have no knowledge of him, but apparently even the arrogant Mr. Ferrand could be wrong.

"Do you know," Turner said, stopping himself at last. He gave an airy, hoarse laugh and managed to give her a sparkling little smirk. His agreeable, attractive boyishness had returned. "Now that I speak of White's, I do so miss London, and the season will be upon us soon. Could we not go to town? We could join your brother and his wife, as it seems an opportune time. And you must choose a wedding gown from London, dear, I am certain your mother will agree—"

He probably would have offered eight hundred more reasons if Clemency had not delicately put up a hand to shush him.

She had no interest in London at the moment, but she also had no interest in listening to Turner ramble on and on. The mention of Mr. Ferrand had left him unhinged, and she intended to begin her own sort of investigation. She stalled for a moment, choosing her response carefully. Unless she could begin to verify some of Turner Boyle's stories, she had no intention of spending more time in his company. He had wasted enough of her time already. If Jack Connors really was the source of all his financial and social woes, then a bit of snooping was in order.

All these things could be understood, but she needed time.

"Well?" Turner reached for her hand, taking it carefully, and Clemency forced herself not to recoil. If this was to be smartly done, he must not suspect her true motives. "Let us away to London, and I will apologize in high style."

"I . . . suppose I could be persuaded," Clemency replied shyly. Over his shoulder, she saw Honora watching them, her notes a little louder and harsher as she silently begged something of her sister. "Can you not go ahead and make the arrangements for us? I have promised Wednesday tea to Miss Brock, and she is always cross with me when I break our engagements. Is that agreeable?"

"Most," Turner almost cried out. His entire demeanor changed, his cheeks ruddy once more, his shoulders shivering with pent-up energy, as if his skeleton might hop out of his skin. "*Most* agreeable. Ah, but I will have that brandy now, as there is even more to celebrate! This will be ever so good for us, Clemency, you shall see. This is exactly what we need before the wedding, I am convinced—the delights of the city will put us both to rights. I promise all will be well, after all you are marrying a baron."

Turner Boyle bowed and kissed the back of her hand, and after he had strode excitedly away, Clemency could not help herself, she rubbed her skin vigorously against the side of her skirts, wiping that kiss away.

8

The bundle of silks and ribbons arrived just as Clemency was on her way out the door. She was not expecting a delivery, but her name was written on the note tucked under the crisscrossed twine, and the boy who had run it up to the house scampered off before she could ask him any questions.

"What has come?" Honora asked, appearing behind her.

Clemency closed the front door, pulling off her bonnet and veering to the left, into the little informal family sitting room where the women often trimmed hats or read. A sprig of lavender rested on top of the note addressed to her, and Clemency slid it out from under the twine, smelling it as she set down the packet on a folding table near the fireplace.

"I am as surprised as you are," she said.

"You must open it! I hope it is something lovely."

"This is the paper Tindall and Batt's uses," Clemency observed, peeling open the wrapping to reveal a generous yardage of fanciful striped pink silk and muslin with delicate little roses in the weave. Some of the fabric she had ordered on Saturday was there too, with ribbons and buttons to match.

Honora gasped and ran her gloved hand reverently over

the pink fabric. "It appears you have an admirer, dearest. Perhaps your intended is apologizing in earnest?"

"Perhaps," Clemency said with a chuckle. She would be impressed indeed if this was Turner's doing.

"But after all that has happened," Honora continued, watching Clemency unfold the note. "Could you really love him again? Can a gift erase the terrible way he made you feel?"

"No," Clemency replied. "But it will be more tolerable to be married if he at least loves me and buys the occasional pink silk."

"You say these things, Clemency, but I know you do not mean them. You are not a cold soul, try as you might to appear such."

"No, Nora," Clemency said, sighing. It had been so long since she had seen Turner's hand. Even that made her heart twinge. Once, his penmanship filled her chest with fluttering wings. She ought to know love. *No, you are finished with all that now.* "You understand almost every part of me; the only parts I keep hidden are the ones that would disappoint you, and those parts are callous and withdrawn, but right now I must confess that they seem the truest parts of me."

Honora crossed her arms, scrutinizing Clemency with narrowed eyes. "Well? Who is it from?"

Clemency held up the heavy brown paper and looked to the bottom for a signature. Even if there were likely only two candidates for sender, somehow she had immediately convinced herself the second one wasn't a possibility. Her blood turned wintry in her veins.

"It is . . . it is from Mr. Ferrand," she muttered. "How disappointing."

And improper, though she was hard-pressed to discard such an odd gift. Honora rolled her eyes and flounced to the nearest overstuffed chair. "For how much you claim to despise Mr. Ferrand you certainly do speak of him often, dear sister."

"It is only his loathsomeness that makes him worth discussing!" Clemency cried. "Now hush and let me read."

Honora allowed her that, tucking her chin onto her hand and staring out the window at the fine day being wasted while they dawdled inside.

Miss Fry,
Had enough? If so—if you fancy revenge—seek me out at your earliest convenience. I trust you know where to look.

Regards,
A. A. Ferrand

"Is it a declaration of love?" Honora teased, batting her full eyelashes and springing to her feet.

More like a declaration of war. Clemency lowered the note, aware of the sour expression her sister could plainly read.

"Would you think me awful if we postponed our walk?" Clemency murmured.

"Is something the matter? You've gone very pale." Honora joined her again, taking Clemency by the shoulders and inspecting her. She pulled off her glove and touched Clemency's forehead.

"I am quite well, I assure you," Clemency said. "But I must speak to Mr. Ferrand directly. It's a matter of urgency."

"Then I will walk you as far as Courtney Lane and pester you all the while."

Clemency smiled weakly, tucking the note into the velvet satchel dangling from her wrist. The fabric and ribbons could be sorted out later. Taking her sister's arm, they swept out the front door and into the damp bite of a spring morning. The whole world smelled of fresh, wet grass and slick stones, and the budding flowers lining the path to the drive looked ready to burst into bloom at any moment. Clean linens billowed on the line to their left, Mariah clipping up new wash as they passed. A pair of wood pigeons hopped along a low branch that dipped over their heads, a natural roof over the hedges that framed the path.

For a long while, their shoes crunched rhythmically over the gravel as they left behind Claridge, Clemency wishing they could take the far faster route through the fields, but knowing she would arrive covered in grass smudges, her hem soaked with dew.

Mr. Ferrand's note hung heavy in her mind, painting a dark cloud over the sunny weather. Revenge. Was that what she wanted? It left her feeling confused and flustered that she did not know at all what she wanted. She had relayed Turner Boyle's amended attitude and apologetic pleading to Honora the night before while they made themselves ready for bed. Honora, of course, took it as a hopeful sign, but Clemency wasn't convinced. What was happening to her? Just days ago she would have given anything to have Turner demonstrate such tenderness and affection. Now she could view it only with suspicion.

She *had* to view it with suspicion. His emotional about-face was simply too sudden. What might bring it on? What had changed? Clemency walked faster and faster, Honora huffing to keep up. What had transpired between the ball and last evening? He had not known of Mr. Ferrand's arrival until she said it, so it had to be something that came before. His debts were found out, and then Tansy and William had shared their good news. . . .

Clemency nearly jerked to a stop. Maybe the answer was simple. Simple and despicable. William's financial solvency meant a larger dowry for her and Honora. Turner had gone from berating her and calling her a sphinx to begging for her forgiveness, which was utterly explicable if he needed money. On Friday evening, when he treated her abominably, she had none. On Sunday evening when he wanted to whisk her off to London, she had some. Perhaps he had been planning all along to abandon her for his own amusement, when it pleased him to humiliate her, but now she had value.

"*Bastard.*"

"Sister?" Honora choked out. They had just reached the lane that sloped down toward the edge of Round Orchard.

Clemency tore herself away from her own jumbled thoughts. "Yes?"

"You swore."

"Oh . . ." Clemency tugged at the ribbon holding her bonnet on, finding it itchy. "Forgive me, this whole business with Mr. Ferrand has me quite out of sorts."

"I have been meaning to say . . ." Honora pulled in a deep breath, trying to slow their pace as they took the shaded side path that skirted the village. "As your sensible elder sister I'm afraid I must tell you, these interludes with Mr. Ferrand will not go unnoticed forever. An ignorant onlooker might draw . . . unfavorable conclusions, dearest," Honora said, biting down nervously on her lower lip. "You know I would never think you changeable. . . ."

"Maybe you should," Clemency replied, a touch crisply. "My mind is changing all the time. I will not be ashamed of it. What good is a mind if we do not fully employ it?"

"You can still employ your mind when married," Honora insisted.

To a possible scoundrel.

"And whatever we know the truth to be, others will form their own opinions," she finished. "Books have done this to you, haven't they? Put these ideas in your mind. I know you think love and marriage are fanciful but true independence is even more so. Just . . . think on it, Clemency."

"I am, Nora, I assure you, I am. And all will be clearer soon," Clemency told her. "That is why I must speak with Mr. Ferrand. In fact, today I intend to make up my mind once and for all."

By the time they reached Courtney Lane, they had devised a plan for the striped pink silk. They would need a bit more lace, it was decided, and Honora parted ways to go retrieve just that. It would be a charming gown, fit for London assemblies, with Vandyke points at the hem and a very wide neck, with a fitted under dress in a contrasting, simpler cream cotton.

Clemency did not have a head for such things, but Honora promised it would be breathtaking. The undertaking of this sewing project filled her sister with excitement, and Clemency was glad they could part speaking of happier things. She knew that soon, all that goodness and light would be gone, for she dreaded what awaited her at Beswick.

Approaching the great house from its circular front drive certainly left an indelible impression. Clemency somewhat preferred the quirky charms of Claridge, but there was no denying the stately, imperious silhouette of Beswick, standing tall and square and symmetrical against a backdrop of deciduous grandeur. Architecture and nature in harmony, the one complementing the other. A number of laborers were out trimming the verge, and the topiaries were being reshaped while a line of carts filled the drive, carrying the Ferrands' furnishings under thick brown blankets.

The doors were flung wide open while porters worked in a steady stream to fill the home with the trappings of a genteel family's life.

Clemency slipped in among them almost unnoticed, but a tall, pleasant-faced man with long black hair had been striding through the foyer and stopped the moment he laid eyes on her. He bowed, then approached with his hands out to his sides, as if afraid to startle her away.

"Mr. Ferrand is not expecting me," Clemency spoke up, pulling the note out of her bag and showing it. "He wrote, and he claims it is somewhat urgent. You may tell him Clemency Fry is calling."

"I am afraid, miss, that the gentleman is not at home," the man said. He had a strong accent, Welsh perhaps, and kind brown eyes. Though his face seemed gentle, he was as broad and well-muscled as Mr. Ferrand. "He is expected back soon, if you care to wait."

"Ralston? Ralston?"

A soft, pretty voice echoed through the still, empty house. It came from above, somewhere beyond the exquisitely polished staircase curving up the left side of the foyer. It had been done in lacquered black wood and marble, matching the diamond pattern of the tiles on the floor.

"One moment, miss, please."

"Of course."

The man, presumably Ralston, disappeared up the stairs, leaving Clemency to shuffle awkwardly to the side, out of the way of the hardworking porters. She wondered who the lady's voice might belong to, though Mr. Ferrand's sister was the obvious conclusion. Would she be as infuriating and arrogant as her brother?

"Nonsense, Ralston! I am more than capable of entertaining her until Audric arrives. . . ." The lilting, sweet voice returned, and then, a tiny, frail creature appeared at the top of the stairs. Miss Ferrand. She was dressed in dark, almost matronly blue, the wrap-style dress nearly drowning her birdlike frame as she descended the steps. Ralston hurried after her, huge by comparison, looking like a giant lumbering after a pixie.

"But Mr. Ferrand made it very clear that—"

"I am mistress of this house while he is away, Ralston, that is also very clear," the young woman said. For her diminutive stature, she had a forceful way about her. That was not surprising. She floated over to Clemency, every bit *la dame très gentille,* complete with silent footsteps, that Clemency had never managed to become. She imagined a stack of books on the girl's head, and knew they wouldn't wobble at all. Still, when she came close, Clemency saw a darkness under her eyes and a thinness to her skin that spoke of illness.

"Men!" Miss Ferrand exclaimed, giving a divine curtsey. "How exhausting they are. You are our first neighbor to come calling, and I must thank you for it. Miss Fry, was it?"

Clemency returned the curtsey, though with far less effortless grace. She liked this young woman immediately. "Indeed, Clemency Fry. If I am at all intruding—"

"Of course not, I am consumed with doing absolutely nothing, as you can see," the girl said with a smile, and the family resemblance was clear, even if she did not share the vivid green eyes. "Ralston and my brother will not allow me to lift so much as a book to help. Is that not so, Ralston?"

Ralston blushed to the roots of his raven hair. His eyes danced away nervously as he ducked his head. "'Tis so, miss."

"And it is all very gallant of them." She had a girlish laugh, and Clemency could not tell her age. She might have been fifteen or five-and-twenty. "Ralston, take us to the river view, please, and find someone to bring tea. You must call me Delphine, and I will call you Clemency, unless you object. Which you can! Oh, but I do not often host alone; it must be obvious. . . . I am so appallingly out of practice. *Mon Dieu*."

"I cannot imagine being mistress of such a large place," Clemency said, trying to put her at ease as Ralston led them through the place. "You are doing just fine."

"It is too large," Delphine agreed with a shrug. "Audric— Mr. Ferrand, that is—always insists upon these castles and palaces and places that we could not possibly hope to fill. Half the house will sit empty and then he will complain of a draught."

"That does sound like him," Clemency murmured.

Delphine turned wide brown eyes on her. "You know him well?"

"Not at all well," she hastily replied. "We . . . are recent acquaintances." Clemency fumbled for a respectable reason to call, her mind racing as Ralston navigated them through the labyrinthine halls of Beswick and to the south veranda overlooking the park. "Your brother rendered me a service the other day; I fell into the river just there," she said, pointing. "And he fished me out of the water. I wanted to . . . to thank him for his assistance."

"Indeed, that is Audric all over. *Sauveur suprême de la femme!* As we cannot be expected to save ourselves, mm? I am sure it was his pleasure to play the hero for you," Delphine said, laughing again. Her amusement turned to discomfort, as she coughed raggedly for a while after, and Ralston offered her a handkerchief. Taking it, she smiled and waved away their concerned looks. "Do you know, in Paris he made me attend *Don Giovanni* three times. Three! Such torture. It is a wretched story, filled to the brim with murder and disguises, but he has a dramatic heart, one fit for the opera . . . but what am I saying? Forgive me for rambling so. You fell into the river! I hope you were not harmed."

Delphine whirled around to face her, and Clemency calmed her with a light shake of her head. "Only a scratch on my arm. Your brother bandaged it for me."

"The savior! Ha. That was good of him," Delphine replied, waiting until Ralston had pulled out a wicker chair for her on the veranda. A canopy of leaves and birdsong soared over them, the shade keeping the creeping sun at bay. The chairs and table had been decorated with expensive silks from the West Indies, orange and red, as bright as the wild-flowers dotting the fields below. "*Bien sûr,* it is also good of you to call on us, Miss Fry—Clemency—what an unusual name that is, if you do not mind my saying so."

"My mother has a flair for the dramatic," Clemency said, accepting the chair Ralston offered. "Do you think your brother will be long?"

"Is my company already tiresome?"

"On the contrary, Miss Ferrand, I only worry that I am trespassing on your kindness and making a nuisance of my-self while you are not yet settled in your new home," Clem-ency replied. She turned her face to the light breeze rolling toward them from the river. Somewhere in the distance, Claridge hid among the trees, and she wondered if at night they could see the candles in their windows blinking like dis-tant eyes of fire.

"You must push such worries from your mind," Delphine told her. Though the day was warming she had bundled a heavy shawl around her thin shoulders. She too seemed to enjoy the splendor of the wind off the fields. "As I said, I am glad of your coming—it is quite troublesome to make friends, as I know nobody here."

"And what do you think of Round Orchard so far?" Clem-ency asked. Ralston returned, bringing their tea. It was somewhat unorthodox, but she did not comment on it. He had brought a blanket for Miss Ferrand, folded over one arm, and he placed it on her lap carefully. It struck Clemency as strangely intimate, and she stuffed her face down into her teacup to keep her eyes elsewhere.

"I have seen so little of it, I hardly know how to respond," she said with a sigh. "I like Beswick well enough, and this view is rather striking. And so far I like you, Miss Fry, and if there are other young ladies of quality here, then I think Round Orchard will have many charms indeed."

"If you are hungry for information and acquaintances," Clemency said, watching Ralston retreat a safe distance away, "then I can introduce you to my sister, Mrs. Hinton, and Miss Brock, and several other amiable ladies. It is not Paris or London society, but—"

"I hope they are not!" Delphine cried, half-interrupting. She smirked and picked up her teacup with two trembling hands, steadying it, her cheeks pink, while Clemency pretended not to notice her fragility. Her accent was stronger than her brother's, more distinctly French. "I miss the fashions of Paris and little else. Conversation is blood sport there, oh, but I do not have the stamina for it. My heart is sewn firmly to my sleeve. No, I think my constitution is better suited to a place like this." She trailed off wistfully, then glanced toward Clemency. "I should like to meet these ladies you mention. Indeed, I should like very much to have new friends."

"Then you shall have them." Clemency wasn't sure what had gotten into her. She had not meant to become so friendly with Miss Ferrand, but she could muster only pity and interest when she looked at the girl, as pale and pretty and breakable as a porcelain doll. One, it seemed, that had been locked away from society for too long. Whatever her ailments, she did not deserve to be shut up indoors all day. A woman would go mad, especially in a huge, echoing monstrosity like Beswick. An odd little bird, this girl, but friendly and clever too.

Out of the corner of her eye, Clemency noticed Ralston

snap to attention. An instant later, Mr. Ferrand came charging out the door, bringing with him the crackle of a lightning
storm as he strode toward them through pockets of leafy
shadow to bow to them, standing a handsbreadth from his
sister.

He had clearly just come from riding, his hat tucked under
one arm, his dark curls pleasantly mussed, the familiar green
coat that Clemency had draped over her shoulders now but-
toned tightly across his chest.

"Miss Fry. Delphine."

Before the women could speak a word, he noticed the
dense mantle blanketing his sister.

"Are you chilled?" he asked, at once solicitous, hovering
over his sister and adjusting the shawl higher up her shoulders.

"Do not fuss, Audric. Miss Fry and I were just discussing
all that is to be found here, and she has vowed to bring me
into Round Orchard society!"

Clemency would not phrase it that way exactly, but she
smiled and took another sip of the very excellent tea. The
cream probably came from the same cows, but somehow it
tasted fresher.

"Has she? How quaint. May I steal Miss Fry for a moment, Delphine? There is a matter I wish to discuss with
her." His green eyes swept across the table to Clemency, and
she felt her jaw tighten with . . . something. She told herself
it was anxiety. A nasty little voice suggested instead it was
excitement. He had been right about Boyle's finances, and if
Mr. Ferrand had been smug before, she could not imagine
what he would be now.

"A matter? What matter?" Delphine looked back and

forth between them, sitting up straighter. "Oh, I will not snoop in your affairs, brother, but do not detain her long. You may have saved her from the river, but she has saved me from the pain of boredom."

Clemency stood and fought the urge to fidget. Coming around the table, Mr. Ferrand nodded subtly toward the wide promenade that ran the length of the back of the house. They walked side by side, leaving behind the tea table and Delphine, who continued to drink her tea softly, Ralston crossing to join her and bend down to whisper something in her ear.

"Mr. Ferrand—"

"Miss Fry—"

They both broke into tense laughter. Clemency pursed her lips and kept her eyes trained on the woods to her left. Feeling his presence was more than enough, looking at him would only unnerve her to the point of tongue-tied stupefaction.

"That gift of silks was not necessary," she said softly, her voice hoarse. "But it was . . . generous. Thank you."

He was quiet for a moment. "And how am I to interpret your coming here? Are you at last ready to listen to me? Are you prepared to believe?"

They had gone a polite ways from the tea table, and Clemency paused, turning slowly to face Mr. Ferrand, her back resting against the stone bannister of the promenade. "Something . . ." She sighed, frustrated. The speeches she had rehearsed failed her. "Something is amiss, that much I believe. He came to me last night, the picture of contriteness, I might add, and when I mentioned your name—"

His face darkened, and suddenly Mr. Ferrand was angrier than Clemency had ever seen him. None of her cheek or sass had ever made him look ready to bite his tongue in half. He reared back, then closed his eyes tightly, gesturing vaguely with his hat. "I never asked you to keep my name out of this, so I have no right to scold you . . ."

"Mr. Ferrand—"

"Were you testing him? Or were you testing me?" he snarled. "Am I now to assume you are working against me?"

"No!" she almost shouted, offended.

But Mr. Ferrand ignored her, pacing a tight line back and forth in front of her. "I considered you many things, Miss Fry, but never stupid."

In his rage he had begun to perspire, and he reached into his pocket for a handkerchief, taking one out and dabbing at his shiny face. Something small and soft, white and dark red, drifted out of his pocket, falling to the ground. Clemency stooped and snatched it up before he could notice, pulling the little scrap of fabric taut and recognizing it at once. It was a piece of her sleeve, torn and bloodied, and it looked as if someone had twisted it errantly, like one might twirl a lock of hair.

Mr. Ferrand froze. Clemency searched out his eyes, holding the scrap of sleeve up for him to see. Anticipating him, she jerked it away before he could grab it out of her hand.

"I considered you many things, Mr. Ferrand, but never sentimental."

"Are you laughing at me?" he whispered, eyes burning.

"No," Clemency replied simply. She offered the scrap back to him, and he took it with a ferocity that left her breathless. "Nor am I working against you. It was a mistake, my saying your name, I assure you it was not said with any agenda."

He blew out a breath through his nose and nodded, his rage seemingly quelled. "It was bound to happen sooner or later. And what was his response?"

Clemency had to smile, recalling the sheer terror that crossed Boyle's face. "Boring excuses, lies, but then he suddenly became so desperate to leave one might assume he soiled himself."

Mr. Ferrand gave a bark of laughter, startling a few birds out of a nearby tree. "And what else? Did he say anything?"

"He tried to deny knowing the name," Clemency told him. "Clumsily, I might add. Very clumsily. And then he suggested we leave for London. He has gone ahead on his own, and I told him I would join him soon."

"Yes, yes, of course. Good." Mr. Ferrand nodded, his eyes far away as he made some private calculation. "He wants to get you away from me, away from what I have already told you. And he wants to flee his debts."

"He blamed them all on Jack Connors, the man he was lodging with," Clemency said. They began to walk again, this time at a more leisurely pace. She felt comfortable, unexpectedly so, as if she were strolling with a friend and not a lunatic who had dropped out of the sky and into her life like a cannon.

"Your man is never responsible for his own mistakes and faults."

"He is not *my man*," Clemency snorted.

"Very well." Mr. Ferrand paused again, but this time he

regarded her with a small, secret smile. "Our man, then, if you like. Our quarry."

In the strained silence that fell between them, Clemency tried to understand the confessional urge that rose in her like a hiccup. It couldn't be suppressed. Mr. Ferrand had been right about Turner Boyle, and she wanted to know more. She couldn't help herself, she had to. She had to know the depths of the darkness that swirled around the man she had loved. A single drop of poison had fallen into the well of that love, but had swiftly spread. Mr. Ferrand did not press her, and for that she was thankful. For once, he afforded her the polite silence and the time to find her words.

"There is . . . I have a theory."

Mr. Ferrand leaned back against the house, crossing his boots at the ankles, propping one elbow on the back of his left hand. "Indeed? I love theories."

"What if I told you that the ebb and flow of 'our man's' affections seem to follow the ebb and flow of my family's fortunes," Clemency began, knowing she ought not to share such private things with a half-stranger, but also knowing that nobody else would understand it like he could. "That he proposed when all seemed quite secure, then grew cold during our financial hardship, and now his heart changes once more, just as our hardship ends."

"If you told me that," Mr. Ferrand replied with equal care, "in the strictest confidence, of course, then I would answer that you are perceptive. And you are learning. And you are correct."

Clemency had already supposed it to be true, but his response, and even just her saying it aloud, made it feel real, and terrible, and unbearably shabby. Honora would never accept such things unless she heard it from Turner Boyle's mouth directly, but Clemency felt the truth of it in her soul. He wanted her money and nothing more, and if the Bagshots' ships had fallen to piracy or storms, then their fragile understanding would probably be over within the month.

Marriage. A foolish, fantastical notion. Miss Taylor had guided her well from beyond the grave, or tried to, at least. Maybe being unlovable could be a freedom, that she could now, permanently, be unshackled from the dream of a lasting romance.

She spun around, scrunching her face into a ball until the desire to cry passed.

"Miss Fry . . ."

"I'm quite all right," she murmured, forcing herself to face him again.

Mr. Ferrand pushed away from the wall, taking a single step toward her. When it was clear that she would not burst into tears, he asked gently, "Do you remember what I told you at the ball?"

"You told me many things, sir."

"A proposition," he said. "I had a proposition for you. We were interrupted before I could explain it fully."

Clemency pulled back her shoulders, concentrating closely on his words because it was easier than thinking about the sick, venomous feeling in her stomach. "You wanted to dismantle his life," Clemency recalled. "Ruin him."

"And do the details interest you now?" he asked.

She gave a mad giggle, hardly believing the sound that came out of her mouth. "Does it involve a duel? A rapier through his guts? If so, you have my wholehearted consent, sir."

"Not as clean as that," he said with his own dry chuckle. Mr. Ferrand took out his handkerchief again and offered it to her, and Clemency realized only then that tears had started to creep down her cheeks.

Pressing her lips together, she accepted the cloth and touched it to her eyes. The silk square had his leather and juniper scent, and the faint perfume of his sweat. She felt suddenly light-headed, and she wondered if he would catch her if she fell.

"It begins with his bills coming due," Mr. Ferrand continued, that predatory hunter's gleam coming into his eyes again. This time, Clemency was not wary of it. No, indeed, it ignited her. "All of them at once. That I have seen to already. It continues with a journey to London; you will follow him there and you will pretend to know nothing, and you will let him crawl back into your good graces, sickening as that may sound."

Clemency narrowed her eyes and began to speak, but Mr. Ferrand took another step toward her, and laid his forefinger over her lips, silencing her. His skin was cool and dry, calloused. She stared up into his eyes, not shy, but trembling and afraid. She did not know if she trusted him, but in that moment, foolishly or otherwise, she damn well wanted to. His hand slipped over her jaw, cupping her face, his thumb grazing her gently parted lips. What the devil was he doing? Was he going to kiss her? Did she want him to?

She feared very much that yes, she wanted him to.

"You will let him think he has won his prize, that his future is secure, that you will promise to pay all of his mounting debts, ignorant of the landslide of humiliation he would heap upon you." Mr. Ferrand's voice dropped to a deadly whisper, and Clemency could not tear her eyes away from his. "And then I will be in London, and I will court you, and he will be powerless to stop me ripping away everything he ever wanted or thought he had. I will break his bank, his heart, and his spirit."

Through the finger touching her lips she could feel the pounding pace of his heartbeat. Hers raced just as fast. When he pulled back from her, Clemency felt the fear drop away, a veil torn from her gaze.

"We."

Mr. Ferrand raised a single brow in inquiry. Honora's warning from that morning floated back to her—that people would whisper and talk, that Clemency might suffer irreparable harm by playing such games, but only reckless action would soothe a scorned heart.

"We will do those things. He will be powerless to stop *us* from ripping away everything," Clemency corrected. He did not argue. Instead, he kissed her.

His hand slid deeper across her face, holding Clemency to him. Her breath became his, a pact and a secret and a want shared between them. She had not intended it to happen, and she suspected Audric had not even meant to do it. But how, then, were their lips pressed together? He tasted faintly of tobacco, and his lips were shockingly soft. Inviting. All of this was an invitation, a proposition, a covenant sealed with dangerously rising heat.

Audric broke first, moving her suddenly away. He frowned and shook his head.

"Forgive me—" he began, but Clemency offered him her

hand, swiftly and surely, as a man might. This was a deal after all, their arrangement.

"But there will be no secrets between us, and you will tell me everything I want to know," she demanded, also as a man might. "Everything. If that is your proposition, Mr. Ferrand, then I accept."

9

Ordinarily, the emptiness of the Wimpole Street townhouse in London would not bother Audric. That he even noticed the oppressive quiet was strange. Bewildering, really. He enjoyed solitude, sought it whenever he was not seeking some irredeemable roustabout on the streets of Paris or Calais, but a restless unease gripped him within an hour of waking. Over a bracing cup of coffee, he watched the neighborhood wake up while a heap of croissants went untouched on the desk behind him. Only the staff awaited him at Kilby House, though Delphine and Ralston would join him in London soon, after taking a much gentler journey by carriage.

Audric had nearly killed his horse racing to London. Working off Miss Fry's information, he could not allow Turner Boyle to slip the net, and he worried that the man, now pinned under a mountain of called-up debt, might grow desperate enough to flee England altogether. His poor horse had suffered, and Audric would not allow himself to consider it had anything to do with that kiss.

That damnable kiss.

When his mind wandered for even an instant, he thought of her. Clemency. She stoked such fire in him, odd and absurdly bossy but desirable, nonetheless. It was some remnant of childhood, he assured himself, a trick of the brain. His father had been so domineering and unbending, expecting absolute obedience from their mother. It was not unthinkable that he should find himself attracted to a woman that would make his father's hair fall out in shock.

He did not hate his father, but under no circumstances did he want to become him.

That was all it was, that kiss. And that fire. Just a desperate attempt to distance himself from a fate he refused to entertain.

Boyle was the true matter at hand. Whether he sought to leave the country or call upon more friends for cash, it did not matter—it could not be allowed, not when Audric's plan was otherwise unfolding flawlessly.

Nothing, it seemed, had changed on Wimpole Street since his last visit—the same fashionable couples held the same fashionable addresses, the same fashionable carriages clip-clopped down the same cobbles, and the same fashionable stores carried the same fashionable wares. Most of the townhouses were near identical—white brick lower entrance levels with arched doorways, a darker brick façade rising above, flower boxes in the windows providing a striking touch of color and cheer. But the familiarity of it did not provide much comfort—he missed his sister, and her laugh filling the halls of his home. Stranger still, he found he constantly missed Miss Fry's company too.

She made things considerably more interesting, even if she also made them considerably more precarious.

There it was again. That kiss. Those enchanting eyes . . . No.

He drained his coffee and turned to contemplate the rolls

on his desk, his loneliness and his disquiet robbing him of all appetite. Mercifully, Lee Stanhope arrived, rescuing him from the somewhat pitiful fate of eating a hot croissant alone in an empty house.

"What have you found?" Audric asked, striding around to the front of his desk, dispensing with any formal or informal greetings. That was not the sort of relationship he had with Lee Stanhope. A former Bow Street Runner, Stanhope could find a white cat in a snowstorm or an honorable man on the floor of Parliament. Henry Fielding himself had been the man's mentor, and Stanhope had been regarded as something of a prodigy. He had retired young, after a bullet wound shattered his knee and left him with a pronounced limp. Now he was in the business of secrets, the expensive kind, and Audric paid him handsomely for his services.

"He's still knocking about Grosvenor Square, Lord knows how he's affording it," Stanhope said, nudging the door shut with his cane. He made his way across the plush red-and-gold carpet, a wrapped packet of papers tucked under his right arm.

"I pay *you* to know, not the Lord," Audric muttered, leaning back against his desk and crossing his arms.

With a crooked smirk, Stanhope rubbed his chin. "He has nothing on my contacts."

Short and wiry, Stanhope stood about a head shorter than Audric, but even maimed he was brutal in a fight. He kept company with boxers when he wasn't cultivating secrets and digging for information. Small, quick eyes darted about the room under his shaggy brown hair, a dimpled chin lending him a roguish air. There was nothing stylish about Stanhope, yet he exuded easy sophistication, his credentials and his capability more impressive than any jeweled cuff links. He handed the package to Audric and then helped himself to a croissant, tearing into it like a man starved.

"Denning Ede," Audric read, tearing open the packet and glancing over the top page. It was an old lease, presumably one for wherever Boyle was staying. "Denning Ede . . . Why do I know that name?"

"Because he never shuts his mouth. Loudest Tory in London," Stanhope said around a mouthful of roll. "Rescued Lord Ardmore from a particularly nasty scandal with a duchess last year. That lad would've wound up disinherited or worse, but Ede makes a few visits behind a few closed doors and suddenly Ardmore has a career in Parliament again. Disgraceful horseshit, if you ask me, but not unimpressive. And anyway, he's always kissing up to the Runners, so you didn't hear any of that from me."

Audric frowned, glaring down at the lease. "And do we think his lordship knows Boyle's secrets or is he just another victim?"

"Remains to be seen," Stanhope replied. He reached over and tapped the bundle of papers in Audric's hands. "I have a friend at White's that will bring it up discreetly. Ede won't talk to me, but he might spill his guts to another lord."

Audric flipped to the next page, where Stanhope had scribbled hasty shorthand notes. Legible, just barely. Stanhope started in on his second croissant while Audric digested accounts of Denning Ede and Boyle making public overtures toward a widow called Mrs. Chilvers. "This woman . . . How is she involved?"

"Could be Boyle's next swindle. She does seem the type. Spinster, wealthy, pretty enough, not much family to speak of—were I a half-cocked crook looking for a credulous mark, she would be it."

"My God but he works fast," Audric said with a sigh. "Not four days in town and he is already scouting Miss Fry's replacement. He must be looking for someone richer, or stupider."

"And how is she, eh? Was my information accurate?" Stanhope had every reason to be smug. He had been the one to pick up Turner Boyle's scent in Round Orchard, following the trail from assemblies in town where whispers of a potential engagement to Miss Fry had lingered. After that, he had compiled a thorough dossier on her and her family, describing a young woman of middling fortune but better-than-average appearance, whose public disdain for marriage made her a tempting challenge for Boyle's act.

"She is everything you described," Audric replied, clipped. *And far more.* "We should watch him carefully when it comes to this Mrs. Chilvers, I will not have him cheat and ruin another innocent while we stand idly by."

"Assuming she is his target and not his ally. . . ."

"Assuming that, yes. I suppose it would be far wiser to assume nothing in regards to Boyle; he will be a slippery foe now that he has been alerted to my presence." Audric was about to turn his attention to the next page in the stack Stanhope had brought him when a sudden fear gripped him. He went still, his eyes looking ahead but not really *seeing*.

"Sir?" Stanhope prodded.

"This is my greatest hunt yet," Audric murmured. "If we fail . . . but we cannot. There is too much at stake. We cannot miss a single detail. Boyle will be my final quarry, and either my greatest success or my utter ruination."

Clemency muttered under her breath, pricking her finger for the third time in as many minutes. To her right, bent over the hem of their shared focus, Honora shot her a warning glance.

"Have a care, sister," Honora said with a laugh, a dark curl hovering in front of her eyes. She brushed at it with annoyance. "I will not have you bleeding all over this silk, not after the hours I have poured into it this week."

Four days had passed since her eventful visit to Beswick, and she had seen nothing of Audric, receiving only a brief, dashed-off message explaining that he was on his way to London, and that he would make contact with her once she arrived the following week. Perhaps foolishly, she had hoped Delphine might extend an invitation or call at Claridge, but the Ferrands remained silent. She had been distracted ever since, her thoughts coalescing around the singular feeling of Audric's finger pressed to her lips. Clemency was not one to enjoy being silenced by anyone, yet she returned to that moment again and again, not with anger but with curiosity.

Her mother, also present to work feverishly on Clemency's new London gown, had noticed the gift of fabric from Mr. Ferrand, and then the message of his that arrived a few days later. The quality of the paper and the practically Gothic black wax seal sent her into a conniption that showed no signs of stopping.

Ordinarily, Mrs. Fry would not sit and sew with her daughters, but lately she had been conspicuously present, joining them to cut flowers, trim hats, and now assist Honora with her needlework. She had developed a bothersome passion for the minutiae of Clemency's days, the timing of which was not the least bit subtle.

"He is so distressingly rich," their mother was saying, ignoring Honora's warnings to Clemency. Just like Clemency, Mrs. Fry seemed to be in her own world, lost no doubt, in visions of "distressing" wealth. "But a better age for Honora, I think."

At her side, Honora went pale, her needle flashing faster through the cloud-soft pink silk.

"You know I have no interest in marrying again so soon," Honora demurred softly. "And besides, it is quite plain that Mr. Ferrand's attentions are elsewhere."

Clemency, with what she considered extreme benevolence, waited until her sister had withdrawn her needle to jab her with an elbow. "It is neighborly politeness and nothing more," Clemency assured them both. Indeed. It was common, was it not, to share a coiled, smoldering kiss with neighbors? Just a friendly gesture. Clemency winced, for whenever she remembered the sensation of kissing Audric, her face flamed impossibly.

Irrespective of her confident tone, neither listened. They did not seem to notice her blushing either. In fact, Mrs. Fry, dressed for winter in a mountain of shawls despite the spring warmth (she always, always had a chill) adjusted the lace cap covering her strawberry-blond waves and clucked her tongue.

"A lady can change her mind, you know," she was saying, directing her gaze to Clemency. "I recall a time not so long ago when Lord Boyle did not appear to treat you with appropriate affection, my dear."

At that, Clemency almost stabbed herself again. So her mother *had* noticed Turner's chilly demeanor. That she had never said a word about it until a richer prospect came along only made Clemency's heart sink to her toes. Was money all anyone thought about? Her intended? Her mother?

"You despise the French, Mother, remember?" asked Clemency, trying to concentrate on the bit of ribbon she was tacking to the puffed sleeve of the gown.

"Not when they have five thousand a year!" Mrs. Fry exclaimed, cackling in a way that suggested her daughters were to knowingly join in. They did not. "I would heartily let you marry a potato if it had five thousand a year."

"Now there is an image," Clemency replied lightly, though a darkness lingered in her soul. It was odd to hear a man she was coming to respect reduced to a tawdry number. She rather thought kissing a potato would not fill her with such flutterings and tremblings. "I should wonder what Father would say to a potato. Do you think it would make a pretty proposal?"

"A very down to earth one, I should think," Honora teased.

Clemency smirked, brushing off her mother's exasperated sighing.

"The pair of you . . ." Mrs. Fry set down her needle and thimble and stood, sweeping dramatically into the hall. They had been at work in the cozy little room where Clemency had gone to inspect the bundle sent from Mr. Ferrand. Despite being in the hall, she could be heard perfectly as she lamented: "My daughters. A perfectly handsome widow who is content to wither away alone, and the finest beauty in the county resigned to marry a mere baron!"

"Mother!" Clemency nearly shouted. Honora did not seem nearly as shocked or offended. "Mr. Ferrand has no title at all, you must at least be consistent in your prejudices."

Mrs. Fry pressed her lips together tightly as if holding back tears. "I must do nothing of the sort!"

She whirled by Mariah, who had returned with hot water for the tea. The two young ladies shared a silent, furious stare. It was not until their mother had clomped out of earshot that Honora spoke up again, only in a whisper.

"It is not so bad to wither," she said, her shoulders sloped suddenly as if she were caving in. "And I do not *feel* withered. Do I look it?"

"Do not listen to her," Clemency bit out, too angry to sew a single stitch. "You have suffered enough heartbreak for two lifetimes, Nora, you have earned whatever life you prefer."

At that, her sister slowly smiled. "My heart is mending, though it should heal faster under calmer circumstances."

"Then you must come with me to London," Clemency told her, swiveling to face her sister. Honora was the true seamstress of the family, able to knock together a simple muslin morning dress in just a few days. Finishing a more elaborate pattern like the ball gown she was presently sewing for Clemency required only a bit more time.

"Only one or two temptations exist for me in London, but I will think on it," Honora said as she shrugged. "Though that reminds me, I wondered if you might call on a friend for me while in town. We were not long acquainted, but a letter hand delivered by you, dearest, would be charming indeed. Would you consider it?"

"Of course! It would be my pleasure to be your courier."

"Ah, you say that now, but the moment you set foot in the city you will be bombarded with invitations and obligations, balls, and teas, and long afternoons in the park. If you cannot find the time to call on her I will not be offended." Honora finally paused in her work, setting her hands in her lap and giving Clemency a long, meaningful look.

"And?" Clemency raised her brows. "Out with it, what admonishment is brewing there in that sisterly brain of yours?"

"In some ways I do wish to accompany you, dearest, but only to protect you."

Honora knew little of what had transpired at Beswick during her last visit, and Clemency felt a guilty knot tangle up in her stomach. With her quick mind and knack for observation, Honora must have noticed that she was holding something back. Something like a brief, ill-advised but still life-altering kiss. But she couldn't drag her sister into it, and more . . . Clemency's cheeks grew shamefully hot. She was not proud of what she had agreed to—tricking Turner Boyle until he could have his comeuppance was not the sort of behavior Honora approved of. And how could she? Clemency herself hardly approved of it. A shadowed, annoying, truthful corner of her heart told her that it was wrong and that she was acting this way only because her pride had been wounded. But whenever she tried to remove herself from it all, whenever she entertained writing both Turner and Audric and cutting herself off from both of them, her mind rebelled.

Her heart knew better, her mind did not. The kiss lingered. She only wanted Turner Boyle to feel as she did when he humiliated her at the dance—small and foolish, and perhaps even afraid.

Was that so bad?

"You have nothing to fear, Nora, and nor do I," Clemency said, taking her hand and patting it reassuringly. "After all I will be with William and Tansy, and whenever a question arises I will ask myself what you would do in my place."

"That is a thoughtful fiction you have just told me," Honora replied in a whisper. Her eyes grew distant, and she picked up her needle again, withdrawing from Clemency's grasp. When she returned to her sewing, it was with less enthusiasm than before. "I wonder, sister, is it a fiction you are also telling yourself?"

10

The rear left wheel on the carriage cracked six miles north of Ide Hill, leaving William, Tansy, and Clemency stranded beside a vastly green and depressingly empty pasture. The wet mist of morning had never dissipated, trapped beneath a threatening gray canopy of clouds, the view in every direction a little muzzy, the feel of the day itself sinister, cold, and damp. They had left their lodgings at Tonbridge behind at half-past six, and while rain threatened they had made good time on the road to London until the wheel gave out, wedged into a deep, rocky hole, splintering when the horses lurched forward at the crack of the driver's whip.

Presently, William and their driver, Mr. Dandle, stood outside in the chill fog inspecting the damage. They had managed to push the carriage off the road and onto the edge of the pasture, where it sat, the horses stamping and idle, while the men discussed what to do.

Clemency craned her neck to watch them, forehead against the glass, Tansy chewing the edge of her finger on the bench across from her.

"Mr. Dandle will need to unhitch one of the horses and go for aid," Clemency said with a sigh. "I do not think we shall be moving again for hours and hours."

"What an ill start." Tansy pouted. She darted across the seats suddenly, huddling close to Clemency. "Oh dear. You do not think there are many highwaymen in Kent, do you?"

Clemency smiled and pulled off her bonnet, setting it in her lap and preparing for a protracted wait. At least Tansy was amusing company, and she had packed several books that could easily and pleasantly dissolve the hours. Somehow, she doubted Tansy shared her enthusiasm over the prospect of protracted reading time. "I think we should die of boredom, Tansy, long before we die at the hands of criminals."

"Let us pray that you are right. I must say, I am glad we are traveling together," Tansy said, smiling as she leaned back on the seat, rolling her eyes up to stare at the ceiling. "Otherwise I should be stranded alone in this carriage with nobody to comfort me. Sometimes I think your mother's poor nerves have spread to me like the pox!"

The men outside had stopped talking, both of them turning north to face the road. Clemency squirmed for a better vantage but could not see what they might be observing. Her breath fogged the glass as she spoke.

"I see the bravery to set sail on adventures of commerce and fortune does not run in the blood, then," Clemency teased.

"No! Not at all. And anyway, I have my mother's constitution. She always hated the sea; she could never keep her feet even on a ferry."

"I think someone is coming," Clemency said, at last spying the object in the distance traveling swiftly down the road toward them. "Another carriage."

"We are saved!"

"If they stop . . ." Clemency unlatched the door and helped herself down, while Tansy squealed with fright behind her.

"You must stay inside! What if those are the highwaymen? You mustn't leave me all alone in here!"

"They would be very fashionable robbers, indeed," Clemency called back. She gestured for Tansy to join her but her sister-in-law would not budge. Shrugging, Clemency shut the door and wedged her bonnet back on her head, tying it tightly against the blustering wind. Then she trudged over to where William and Mr. Dandle stood waving to get the oncoming coachman's attention.

"Ah. Clemency. Yes, do stand there, perhaps the enticement of a damsel will encourage these folk to stop," William said. He smirked at her, his right fist propped on his hip, holding his long, black coat open while Dandle waved his hat above his head and shouted.

"I shall prepare to swoon," Clemency said, chuckling. "As all damsels must."

The approaching carriage had to belong to someone genteel, for it was not so shabby as one used by the post or for paying passengers. Well-polished and trim, the carriage rattled toward them with a team of four matching black horses. As it drew closer, Clemency frowned, for it looked rather familiar. . . .

"I'll be damned," William cursed, shouting happily. "That's Jack Connors."

Clemency went rigid. Jack Connors did not have an enviable reputation in Round Orchard. He was considered a vagabond and a drunk, only his money protecting him from real social scorn and snubbing. Her direct interactions with the man were limited, as he usually kept to himself with the gentlemen at assemblies and balls, debauching in billiards rooms where no lady dared to tread.

"Do you know him well?" Clemency asked.

The carriage slowed, the driver noting their distress and reining in the horses accordingly. A spray of gravel arced across the pebbly dirt road, and Dandle hurried out in front of the horses to direct the other driver away from the hole that had caused their misfortune.

"Not really. Well enough to ask for assistance. Jack Connors is a useless sort of man, unfit to run a house, unfit to manage tenants, fit only for drinking and gambling, but he can be amiable. Certainly he is harmless," William replied. He took off his hat and fixed his tangle of golden curls, which had grown damp from standing in the mist. He had their father's tall, thin frame and soft, pot-bellied middle, but his face remained handsome, and he projected a protective authority that always soothed her.

"He and Turner Boyle could be quarreling," Clemency added in a low tone. William shot her a glance from his height, his lip curling in annoyance.

"That is hardly reason to ignore us," William replied. "Rendering aid is the gentlemanly thing to do."

"I'm simply warning you," she said, also growing annoyed. "If he seems chilly, there is a reason."

"Be quiet and pleasant, then; I do not fancy freezing to death here while Dandle rides for aid."

Clemency scoffed and turned away, retreating a few steps behind her brother and Dandle to fidget with her gloves. Out of the corner of her eye, she watched Connors's carriage swerve to the opposite side of the lane. The driver pulled down a woolen scarf from his mouth and called to them.

"Is there trouble?"

The door swung open a moment later and Jack Connors appeared. He was dressed in a heavy green coat, an ermine draped haphazardly around his shoulders. He had a collier's body, thick as a stump, a square head, and quick, small eyes that fixed on each thing in turn, suggesting a measured wit that Clemency sincerely doubted he possessed. His black hair was kept very short, making his big, protruding ears more noticeable.

"Trouble?" Jack Connors echoed, hurrying over to them. His eyes lingered on Clemency and he frowned, as if trying to remember where he had seen her before.

"Wheel is shot," William said, approaching and taking the hand Connors offered in friendship.

"Well, it's William Fry, what a chance!" Connors guffawed boyishly. Stupidly. Clemency berated herself for being so mean, but she considered him an accomplice to her intended's deceptions. She wondered how a man with a reputation for not holding his drink had managed to remain friends with Turner Boyle without throwing a punch.

"Are you traveling alone?" William asked, stepping back while Dandle and the other driver attended to the broken wheel.

"I am, I am," Connors replied. His gaze kept flicking to Clemency in a way that made her squirm. "Up to London. Some, um, some business there."

She tried not to roll her eyes. How incredibly vague. And could it be a coincidence that the man who had accused

Connors of stealing from him and then stormed off was also recently removed to London? She made her face into a steely mask.

"I have here my sister and my wife, and if there is room for them, I beg you take them on," William explained, gesturing to Clemency and then the carriage. "We are also bound for London, and I would be in your debt for any assistance—"

"There's room enough for the whole party," Connors replied. "Your man can ride ahead for the parts, then meet us in Croydon, and there you can resume as planned, or hire a new carriage. Of course, you're welcome to join me for the remainder, but I would not presume . . ."

"Thank you, sir, truly," William said, beaming. "Let us to Croydon, and firm up our plans there. Anything, I say, to be out of this cursed damp."

Connors nodded and swept his hand toward his own carriage. "Hear, hear."

William leapt to open the door to his carriage and help Tansy down, and Clemency wandered a few steps away, wringing her hands and pacing. They needed the help, obviously, but the prospect of being stuck in a small box with Jack Connors for hours on end did not exactly please her. She heard the gravel behind her crunch as he came to her side, and Clemency pasted on a neutral smile, turning to regard him with a polite curtsey.

"Mr. Connors," she said, blank. "Thank you so much for your kindness."

"It is no trouble, Miss Fry, and lucky that I happened by."

He offered his arm and reluctantly she took it, trying to hold herself as far away from his hip as she could. They took the walk to his carriage in silence, but she knew a man bursting to speak when she saw one. He seemed to hum with unsaid words, his jaw set and tense as he offered the flat of his palm while she hoisted herself into the carriage. It smelled like a brewery inside.

Clemency flattened herself against the opposite door while Tansy was fetched, and while William and Connors had a word with the drivers.

"How lucky," Tansy cooed, nestled down into her heavy shawl across from Clemency.

She was about to suggest that Tansy join her on the same bench when the men returned, cutting her off, Jack Connors settling his bulk onto the seat next to her. It was suddenly very difficult to breathe. A million questions sprang to mind, but fortunately, William instantly launched into talk of what the neighboring farms could expect, and the local predictions for when the summer weather would properly begin. It afforded her the perfect opportunity to stare out the window and say nothing.

By and by, Tansy fell asleep, the afternoon whittled away by the two men conversing over the dull, serious things men of little acquaintance had to discuss. As the sun slipped to the horizon, even William succumbed to his drowsiness, his head falling onto Tansy's shoulder while the two of them dozed, leaving Clemency and Mr. Connors in a taut, unfriendly silence.

"Time for tea, or well past it," he said, puffing out an anxious breath and pulling a small bottle of sherry from inside his coat and uncorking it.

"You favor a potent brew, sir," Clemency murmured, still gazing out the window. She knew then that, wedged into the seat beside him, there was no avoiding conversation. Briefly she had considered pretending to fall asleep—she did feel tired. Not just because of the long journey and the many stops on the road from Round Orchard to London, but weary in her bones. She felt tired of being caught between Boyle and Ferrand, for she was wise enough not to fully trust either of them. Even if Mr. Ferrand now sought to bring her into his scheme and pretend that they were equals in the execution of it, she did not believe for an instant that he had told her the full truth. There was something sly in his eyes, as ever present as the danger she saw lurking there.

Jack Connors chuckled and did not disagree with her.

Clemency shifted uneasily. She had lived on unsteady feet since her last interaction with Audric—a sensation like walking on constantly shifting sands. Half of her dreaded arriving in London, the other half of her eagerly awaited their next encounter. No matter how she tried to distract herself, her thoughts always returned to the pressure of his finger against her lips. It was as if with that single touch he had sewn a stitch to her skin, and it tugged and tugged, reminding her not only of his existence, but of the great distance between them. The farther he went, the more the pain of that pull seemed to be.

Something brushed her sleeve. Clemency sat up straighter, turning to find Jack Connors was offering her the bottle, the glass still shiny from his mouth.

"I did not think to find you so hospitable, sir," Clemency said softly. She took the bottle from him, regarding it. She knew nothing about sherry, but the label looked expensive.

"Ah," he said and fixed his small, intense eyes upon her,

heaving a drastic sigh. "Because of our . . . shared acquaintance?"

Clemency drank quickly from the bottle, hoping that her brother was well and truly asleep. He would be scandalized to see her swigging alcohol like a pirate. But if she was to get any information at all from Jack Connors, she needed to earn his trust. God only knew what Turner Boyle had told him about her. Clemency handed him the sherry bottle and choked down the liquor; it burned and made two points of heat flare on her cheeks.

"You do not appear overly cross with him," Clemency observed. "Strange."

"We bicker and bicker, but it is always resolved come morning," Connors replied. He gave a sad, bitter little laugh and stared down at the sherry in his hands. "Only . . . for once, he was not there come morning. I am sure this is all just a misunderstanding. Turner has a tender heart; he feels it all so deeply. . . ."

Clemency blinked. Were they discussing the same man? The man who had snapped at her and called her a sphinx? Where was his tender, deeply feeling heart then? She bit back those questions, fighting against the burn of the sherry in her throat, picking her words with care. Mr. Ferrand had warned her, in a note that arrived at the house upon his departure for London, that the way forward demanded a degree of delicacy and finesse.

We have lost the advantage of surprise even if we have the scoundrel on the run, he had written. *A cornered beast is desperate, and fights to the end with tooth and claw. Turner Boyle knows I am coming for him; therefore, we cannot af-*

*ford even one more mistake. You do not know him as I do,
he will vanish if pressed too far, and then, neither of us will
have our satisfaction.*

Audric thought himself very clever and sharp; Clemency
could be clever and sharp too.

"I had no idea you were so close," Clemency remarked
lightly. That seemed to make him relax, and he gave another
huffing laugh. "Almost like brothers. And if so, yes, brothers
will quarrel, but all is forgotten and forgiven."

"*Brothers.*" He drank more of the sherry. His nose had
the permanent, splotchy red of a career drinker. "No, not
brothers. Then . . . then, he did not often speak of me?"

*In fact, he spoke of you only once and to make a hideous
accusation.*

Distant bells of warning chimed in her head. *Delicacy.*
She turned toward the window again, determined to maintain an air of casual indifference. "He mentioned a disagreement," she said, coy. "Some gentlemen's business, but that
was his reason for returning to London. He may not have
given me the complete picture of the situation; it is surely not
anything a woman should concern herself with."

"Certainly not!" His voice shook with anger. She heard
him slurp down more sherry. "It was only a misunderstanding. All over money, of course. So predictable. So vulgar!"

The carriage rattled more violently, bumping them back
and forth. Clemency heard him swear under his breath and
assumed he had spilled some of the drink on his coat. She
sensed he wanted to keep talking, and simply looked down
at her gloves, letting him swig and work up the courage.

"We are neither of us smart with money, that is for sure,"
he muttered bleakly. "How his debts could all get called up at

once . . . Just an unfortunate turn. It will get handled, of course. Of course, it will get handled, but— My apologies, we should talk of something else."

No, no, no . . .

"You owe me no apologies, sir," Clemency said gently. "Your concern for him is touching, really. I know so little of his family—it is heartening to think Lord Boyle has such a devoted friend."

Jack Connors pinched his lips together, then nodded, rubbing the side of his head as if a headache was coming on. "Yes. I am a most devoted friend. And I worry for him. I worry for him so. That is why you see me now, why I am going to London at all."

Clemency offered him a plying smile. "To resolve your misunderstanding?"

"And to aid him however I can." Connors clicked his nails nervously along the edge of the sherry bottle. He drew up his shoulders, pushing out his chest. "He needs to know there is no enmity between us, that I was and remain his stalwart ally." Then he turned to face her, reaching clumsily for Clemency's hand and finding it. He jerked it onto his lap, sandwiching her hand in his palms. "And he must know that he is in danger. That you are both in danger."

"Me? Us? In danger, sir?" She licked her lips, letting her mouth drop open in maidenly shock. "What sort of danger?"

Connors glanced at William and Tansy, verifying that they were both still sound asleep, swaying together to the rhythm of the carriage wheels over the road. Outside, the sun had plunged below the horizon. Jack Connors stared into her eyes, the dark surface of his glinting with fear.

"I should have realized sooner . . . Damned drink, I should have stopped, maybe then I would have realized . . . but regret will not help him now. Or you." Connors stumbled over his words, jumping from thought to thought incoherently. "He told me a frightening tale. When first he came to stay on my property, he told me: Jack, if a man by the name of Ferrand ever comes here looking for me, you tell him that I am not here. That you have not seen me in years. Tell him that I am dead. Dire, it all seemed. Most dire."

Clemency frowned, realizing this inebriated oaf might have accidentally maneuvered her into a trap. Many now knew that she was an acquaintance of the Ferrands, and to lie about it to his face might risk too much. But the alternative, to slip up and give away just how close she and Mr. Ferrand had become . . .

We cannot afford even one more mistake.

"I know of the Ferrands," Clemency squeaked. "Mr. Audric Ferrand and his sister, Delphine. They do not strike me as dangerous people. A little French, perhaps, but—"

"No. *No.*" Jack Connors squeezed her hand so hard she yelped like a kicked spaniel. He shook his head again and gave a strangled laugh. "That man is out to smear Turner, and all because of some ridiculous, ages-old flirtation! It should be water long under the bridge, but Ferrand is cruel and bored and singular, and guards his sister's heart with Ladon's fury. I hear she hardly leaves the house, for he is more jailer than brother."

"Flirtation? I . . ." Clemency's hand went slack in his grasp. In a way it was the most obvious explanation for Ferrand's rage. But he had spoken of lies and secret identities, and Clemency had been utterly fixated on how those things affected *her*. And yet she had met Delphine, and the girl said nothing about it. But as Connors said, Audric kept Delphine in that big, empty house, how much did she really know about the people of Round Orchard? Did she even know about Clemency and Turner?

"Childish stuff," Connors continued, sputtering. "Just the expected follies of youth! Ferrand has made a mountain out of nothing!"

"What manner of follies?" Clemency asked, narrowing her eyes.

"Oh. Oh!" It seemed he had remembered that she was, in fact, connected to Turner. "Nothing untoward, I assure you, Miss Fry. The Ferrand girl fell in love with Turner, but he did not return her affection. She was heartbroken, but they were children! He hardly even remembers it; I don't think it occurred to him that she, or the brother, would hold such a grudge."

No, Clemency thought darkly. *Men rarely do consider such things.*

Clemency pulled her hand free of his grasp, trembling. "Thank you, Mr. Connors. I am warned."

"Good," he murmured, taking up his bottle again. "That is good."

Clemency swiveled toward the window, hiding her furious blush. If this was true, then she had sworn to help a man she had completely misjudged. That did not outweigh the obvious lies Turner had been telling her, but it concerned her deeply. She was to help Audric, be his partner, and all the while he was keeping these things from her.

Who haven't I misjudged?

The answer, then, was to stand alone. To trust nobody.

Clemency leaned heavily against the door, grateful for the cool kiss of the glass against her overheated face. Something was amiss . . . *Many* things were amiss. Delphine Ferrand had not struck her as a lovesick girl pining for some distant, unattainable gentleman. If anything, she seemed only frail, gentle, and young. Clemency reconsidered what Connors had just told her—*they were children*.

That seemed unlikely, given that Delphine appeared younger than she, and Turner older. How could they have been children together? She bristled. More lies. Lord Boyle had no doubt found Connors an easy man to deceive—how would he ever keep the stories straight while soaked in brandy and sherry? He wouldn't question the little details, oh no, but Clemency would. She would have to be smart indeed to stay ahead of both Turner Boyle and Audric. Neither of them were telling her the truth, and she was tired of being the unwitting pawn.

She watched a twinkle of lights sparkle down the road, winking at her between the trees. Croydon. They would soon be able to stop and rest, and Clemency could untangle her thoughts in the comfort of a warm, solitary bed. She wished fiercely that Honora had come, for only Nora would give her the kind of sensible, measured advice she needed.

A leaden weight fell on her shoulder. Clemency squeaked and twisted to see Mr. Connors slumped next to her, fast asleep, curled up around his sherry bottle like a boy snuggling his toy bear. Carefully, she found the cork where it had fallen on the floor and wedged it into the precariously tipped bottle.

Clemency yearned for her sister. For London. For solid ground. And she told herself she did not yearn to see Audric again, but that, she sadly knew, was just another lie.

11

"What do you think?" Tansy asked brightly, holding aloft two nearly identical muslin frocks. "Papa has invited me to tea with Lady Margaret Veitch, and I simply cannot decide. Ooh, can you believe it? To be seen with her ladyship, and at her home in Mayfair, no less!"

Clemency inhaled, hard-pressed to get a word in, and Tansy immediately silenced her again, whirling in a fantastical circle, the two dresses flaring out like wings as she spun. "And Papa is convinced she wants to hire our fleet for an exclusive contract. Dearest, it seems sure our luck has changed, the winds are blowing our way, and I am ever so glad you are here to experience it with us. Finally, don't you think? Finally! We so utterly deserve this."

Tansy flung the muslins back onto her bed and hurried to Clemency's side. She sat at the writing desk near Tansy's window. Two dainty pink curtains wafted lightly, blown by the gentle spring breeze, carrying with it the scent of baking bread, smoke, lady's perfume, and horse manure, an odor specific to Gracechurch Street, in Clemency's experience. William and Tansy would take their own larger London house soon, though construction to expand the property left it currently uninhabitable.

"They are both delightful," Clemency assured her. "And you will look striking no matter what you choose."

"Do you think so?" Melting a little, Tansy knelt on the worn carpet, tucking her side against Clemency's legs. "I am so nervous. I have never met someone of her rank before . . . what if she is snobby and scary, and I say something stupid without meaning to?"

"Just remember yourself, Tansy," Clemency counseled with a laugh. She did not share Tansy's fear of the aristocracy. Perhaps her interactions with Lord Boyle had soured her against the gleam and shine of it all. But then again, according to Mr. Ferrand, he was not a baron at all. And anyway, Lady Veitch sounded like something one hacked up while ill. Shrugging, Clemency adjusted the lace cap covering Tansy's dark curls. "Remember who you are—the daughter of a fine and successful man, and the wife to . . . well, to William, and he is quite good, I suppose. Despite the lopsided head."

"You're a horrible tease." Tansy giggled, popping back up to her feet and returning to the bed, and the devilishly difficult decision before her. "Hmm . . ." She murmured to herself as she regarded both dresses.

Clemency's eyes slid to the two letters burning on her lap. Her fingers itched to tear them open, but she knew better than to do so with Tansy there. The Bagshots' two-story house on Gracechurch Street was cozy and clean, the rooms a bit poky and cramped, but kept in a way that made one feel instantly at ease. There was no pretension or attempt to seem more than they were—a rising merchant family who had struggled and eked out every coin they earned. Clemency admired it, their subtle style, their acceptance of just who they were and how they had made their way in the world.

Mr. Bagshot still lived at the house, of course, his office and warehouse not far away. Mrs. Bagshot had passed some years ago, and only Mr. Bagshot, one of his brothers, and the staff lived in the townhouse. Yet a woman's touch was everywhere—the furnishings chosen by Mrs. Bagshot maintained and revered, as if her memory lived in the sofas and blankets and paintings.

Clemency was staying in Tansy's childhood room, while she and William occupied one of the larger suites. Mr. Bagshot and his brother were not at home when they arrived, detained by business at the wharf.

That was just fine with Clemency, for she longed to be alone in the feminine nook of Tansy's old room, dried flowers hanging from the eaves, a fresh bouquet of lilies on the desk, the view onto the street allowing for ample daydreaming and people watching. . . .

And there were the letters, of course.

They had been waiting for her on a silver dish in the downstairs hall, just below the mounted ship's wheel, salvaged from the first vessel the Bagshots ever commissioned. Clemency had quickly thanked the butler offering the silver dish and tucked the letters away. She recognized Turner's hand on the top one, Audric's on the one below.

Clemency shuffled the sealed letters on her lap anxiously, realizing that just like Tansy, she found herself torn between two impossible choices. If only her options were as benign as two pretty dresses. At last, she decided she could wait no longer, and cleared her throat softly, drawing Tansy's attention.

"The right one," she said, grinning. "I think the lace on the hem is finer."

"Yes! That is the answer." Tansy scooped the gowns into her arms and nodded, running over to brush a sweet kiss on Clemency's cheek before retreating to the door. "Do not grow too fond of your solitude, I shall be back before you know it for your thoughts on shoes and gloves!"

"I am your faithful servant," Clemency told her gently. With a giggle, Tansy bustled out the door, mercifully closing it on her way out. "Oh, thank God," she whispered, practically tearing the first letter in half in her zeal to unfold it.

She spread it out on her lap, but it was only a short note. Boyle had stayed briefly with a friend but felt the accommodations were lacking and would instead be joining them all at the Bagshots' Gracechurch townhouse. Clemency went pale. That was bad. She had come to London with the intention of studying Turner's past, his lies, his connections . . . now he would be practically on top of her every moment of the day. How would she sneak away to meet with Mr. Ferrand? How many stories would she need to concoct to explain her frequent absences? She had assumed he owned at least a townhouse in London of his own; that he apparently did not gave Mr. Ferrand's accusations only more weight.

"Arriving tonight," she muttered, squeezing her eyes shut. "I should have known it would not be easy. Always more complications . . ."

Tossing the letter onto the desk, she opened the next, cracking the heavy black wax seal. It was not stamped with the now familiar Ferrand crest, but she recognized the wax itself, like something out of Lathom's *The Midnight Bell*.

Miss Fry:

Please send word the moment you arrive in London. We have much to discuss, and even more to plan. Events are unfolding rapidly, more rapidly than I care to admit. Should you cross paths with our quarry before we meet, I beseech you: Treat him with all deference and kindness, dote upon him, and do nothing to arouse his suspicion. An unpleasant prospect, I know, but give your most convincing performance.

Now that he is aware of my presence, he will be watching us as closely as we are watching him. I have enclosed directions to my home, but be discreet. If you call, be certain that you are not followed and wear a dark veil.

Burn this letter after reading.

The note was left unsigned, but its author was obvious enough. How typical of Audric, giving her nothing but curt orders. Had she been foolish to feel warmth in that finger he pressed to her lips and in the kiss they shared? Maybe it was all imagined.

Sighing, she committed the address to memory and strode to the fire, tearing the letter into tiny pieces before scattering them in the hearth. Afterward, she found herself standing much where Tansy had been, in the ruminating place, not knowing whether she should close the curtains and rest awhile, or bathe and dress at once, and ask Tansy's driver to take her to Grosvenor Square.

Of course he lived there. He probably lived down the

street from the lofty Lady Veitch. They were certainly best friends. She did not like when her own thoughts took a mocking tone, but it was hard to resist—Audric felt himself so superior that he could command her this way and that, and not even sign his name at the bottom of a letter. The paranoia of it all was rather oppressive, she thought. Oppressive and unmistakable, for she dreaded seeing Turner Boyle again, especially if she was expected to play a part, and simper, and lie to his face.

The idea of it, of having to flirt and bat her eyelashes while quashing her disdain, made up her mind for her. She was bone-weary and desirous of sleep, but there was plenty of daylight left. Trudging to the closet, she picked through the clothes she had brought, searching for something adequately dark and morose, something to suit her equally dour mood.

It wasn't fair. She ought to be able to just avoid them both and take in a show, do as she pleased, but staying in would assure her a night of dealing with Turner. Going out alone was unthinkable, and therefore she stood pinched between the two men that had become the Scylla and Charybdis of her social life. And interior life. She did not dare suggest the word heart. There was no room left in her mind to consider anything else, her thoughts, obnoxiously, strayed ever to her problems, and more specifically, ever to Audric and his annoyingly kissable mouth. She didn't understand him. Why hide Delphine's feelings for Lord Boyle? It seemed like the perfect way to appeal to a woman's sympathies. In fact, knowing that Lord Boyle had toyed with Delphine's feelings would make Clemency only more inclined to help Audric with his scheme. She liked Delphine.

There had to be an explanation for such an omission.

The charitable part of her said that he was trying to spare his sister embarrassment, but the increasingly cynical portion of her brain insisted there was something more. . . . Something he very much did not want her to know.

Well. She would not find out more about it by avoiding Mr. Ferrand or his sister. And she would absolutely not resign herself to an evening of flattering the strange and unknowable Lord Boyle. She unearthed a black lace fichu from the top shelf of the closet and held it up.

"What will I tell Tansy?" she said, sighing as she stood and walked to the slightly warped looking glass propped near the window. Clemency draped the black lace over her face, and found it made her gray eyes even more startling. She looked dangerous and tempting, and she told herself it would be a diverting role to play. A nervous prickle began in her stomach, a warning, perhaps, or a little sparkle of excitement.

Her eyes brightened with an idea. "Honora asked me to deliver a letter to her friend here in town," she practiced, shocked and unnerved by how convincing, how natural it all sounded. "She said it was a matter of some urgency, but I promise to be home before dark. Just leave a bit of cold supper upstairs for me; it will be no trouble at all."

The house at Grosvenor Square was less grand than Clemency expected. In fact, it was downright modest compared to the soaring monument to wealth and ostentation she had imagined. She told the driver to wait, and vowed she would not be long, then pulled out her veil and draped it over her face, watching as a wigged servant darted out from the town-house door to help her down.

"Thank you," she said softly, brushing off her skirts as she stood staring up at the Ferrands' London home. The family had become a puzzle to her, and this place was just one more piece. It was difficult to fit along the rest, the opposite of Beswick's sprawling grounds and castle-like profile. Indeed, this townhouse, while certainly nice and claiming a fashionable address, blended in among the other slim, white-stone buildings with their gated, shallow yards and nondescript walkways. Nothing distinguished this one from the next, and Clemency could only hope she had remembered the address correctly as she followed the wigged man up the stairs and into the warm foyer.

Here too, she found the home clean and tidy, sparsely furnished, a decidedly masculine air to the dark red patterned rug and lacquered tables. A few stuffed stag heads were hung on the wall opposite the door, a sturdy table beneath for calling cards and the post.

A mirror was to her right, the only visible touch of opulence, for it was immense and perfectly clear, not a ripple to be seen, something that had been purchased at great expense.

Clemency caught her reflection and gasped. She hardly looked herself, dressed not in her customary light blues and pinks and whites, but in a deep burgundy wrap-style dress, the only dress she had brought dark enough to match the delicate black veil draped over her head and hair. The combination made her appear older and certainly more mysterious, and had she seen this reflection as a stranger, she would think unfavorable things, and make assumptions about where that woman was going and whom she was going to meet.

Her heart beat a little faster, and she couldn't quite decide if she liked this new guise or feared it. Her thoughts swirled, especially the idea that she was becoming someone else, someone more like the daring authors and thinkers and heroines she admired, willing to stake their very reputations to follow their hearts. Was that so bad? She was ready to eschew love and marriage forever, so she could at least look the part.

That confusion was quickly obliterated, as from around the corner leading deeper into the house, came scratching and scrambling, and then two hulking, shaggy dogs charged toward her, their paws the size of saucers. She reeled back in surprise, clutching for her chest, pulling off her veil as she did so.

"Talos! Argus! Come, you ruddy beasts!"

Clemency recognized the voice, but it was not Mr. Ferrand's. A man hastened around the corner, catching the dogs by their collars and keeping them from leaping on her skirts. Ralston, the dark-haired man she had met at Beswick, had come to her aid. He blinked at her and then smiled, taking a moment to study her face.

"Ah! Miss Fry, welcome," Ralston said, wrestling with the jolly, drooling dogs. They were wolfhounds, massive and gangly, and they soon lost interest in tackling her and instead turned to licking and nuzzling Ralston's hands.

Behind him, a small figure entered the foyer. The wigged man who had helped Clemency down from the carriage had just been on his way to fetch someone, but now there was no need. Delphine Ferrand beamed at her, bird-fragile and pale in a soft, billowing dress of cocoa brown silk.

"Miss Fry! What a lovely surprise, though Audric said we

might expect you," Delphine said, holding out both her hands for Clemency to take. She eased by the dogs, who whined up at her. "My brother's dogs, they are cumbersome and a nuisance but sweet; I promise they will do you no harm, only beg for attention and the occasional belly scratch. He never takes them hunting; they are now more spoiled children than animals."

Clemency let Delphine take her by the hands and maneuver her away from the foyer, around the corner, and into a spacious sitting room that overlooked the street. This too was modestly appointed, though comfortable enough. A roaring fire greeted them on the opposite wall, and the furniture huddled near it.

"Is your brother at home?" Clemency asked, trying to sound conversational. "He bade me call when I reached London."

"How diligent of you, and still weary from the road! Fear not, he will be returning soon," Delphine assured her, gesturing to the tea and cards already laid out by the fire. With only Delphine present, she could only assume Ralston had been her partner for cards. "Again you must sit with me and wait, and make the customary talk of weather and road conditions and accommodations. . . ."

Clemency sat on the sofa, glad for the fire, and not at all bothered by the company. Ralston lurked in the hall, speaking softly to the dogs before letting them loose. They came, slowly this time, and curled up side by side before the hearth, their loving, glossy eyes trained on the new woman in their house.

"More tea, Ralston, I think, unless Miss Fry has a taste for something stronger?" Delphine picked up the two hands of cards and shuffled them back into a single deck. It was obvious she played cards often, for she handled them deftly, without so much as a glance at her hands.

"Actually . . ." Clemency considered the alien, mysterious woman that had gazed back at her in the mirror and felt a queer tremor pass through her from head to foot. What was London doing to her? And after only a few hours . . . Honora would be scandalized. "Brandy, if that is all right and not too daring."

"Brandy!" Delphine shrieked with excitement. Her whole face brightened, banishing some of the sallowness from her hollow cheeks. "Two brandies, Ralston. And do not be stingy."

"Miss Delphine, I do not think your brother would—"

"Forget my brother, Ralston, I am the lady of the house when he is absent." Delphine sniffed and raised her chin. Despite all their wealth, she did a very poor job of looking imperious. It simply wasn't in her nature, Clemency mused. "Two brandies."

Ralston shuffled off with a huff, and then the only sounds in the room were the crackle of the logs behind the grate and the soft *hush-hush* of Delphine shuffling the cards.

"Ralston and I have only just arrived ourselves," Delphine informed her. "Last night, in fact. That big, empty house made me feel like a ghost. Like I was haunting it. Dreadful. I may not love London society but it *feels* like there is so much happening all the time. It lifts my spirits. May I ask where you are staying, Miss Fry?"

"My brother and his wife are staying with her family on Gracechurch Street," Clemency told her. "It is not as lovely as all this, Miss Ferrand. Your home is beautiful."

Delphine raised her thin, dark brows. Ralston had returned, and he set down two crystal glasses of brandy, though to Clemency's eye they did not seem generously full. He retreated quickly, as if not to be scolded for exactly that.

"You are so kind, Miss Fry," she said, swiftly dealing out hands for cards. "But my brother oversaw the decorating of this place, and it shows. He has such sober taste. I should have done a better job, I will never know why he chose a plum-colored sofa, of all things. . . ."

Clemency carefully sipped her brandy and found the taste extraordinary. Between the hearth and the drink, she was sure her cheeks and neck were bright, shiny pink. "I quite like it. It is rather simple. Simple but inviting."

"Really? You are the only one to think so, I assure you," Delphine teased, eyes bright with mischief as she drank almost half the brandy in her glass in one go. She did not seem ready for it, sputtering a little as she dabbed her lips with the back of her hand. "I will absolutely not tell Audric; he will gloat and be impossible to live with. Do you play cards or games of chance?"

"A little," Clemency said, taking up her cards. "And not well."

"I rely on instinct," Delphine instructed her with a wink. "And of course in that regard, brandy is always useful. It has been such a long, long time since I have had the chance to enjoy a wicked taste of brandy and a wicked hand of cards with a woman close to my own age."

She sighed and called for Ralston to return and fill their cups. Clemency hurried to finish her first glass, finding that her head felt light and stupid, and her body heavy and bolted to the sofa. Her mother disapproved of ladies drinking, and so even at balls Clemency always behaved herself.

"My brother's wife is likely a better match for you," she told Delphine. "Tansy is diabolical when it comes to whist."

"Then you shall have to make introductions, Miss Fry, though I do not doubt you will be a charming partner also."

"That is much too kind," Clemency said with a chuckle. "And soon to be disproven. You will trounce me so easily it will be no fun at all."

"Oh, there is plenty of fun to be had in a trouncing," Delphine replied lightly. Ralston, for his part, did not seem happy about refilling their drinks, but he acquiesced, wearing a hangdog look all the while. The brandy was refreshed, and Delphine again partook with the eagerness of a girl suddenly unchaperoned. "The next game we play must be on Gracechurch Street, if such a thing would please you, of course."

Clemency hesitated, the cards nearly slipping from her grasp. Though Miss Ferrand seemed the exact kind of sweet, rich company Tansy would love to have, there was the complication of a certain Mr. Turner Boyle coming to stay at that very house. She sensed an opportunity to tease out more about the situation, and perhaps gain an advantage over Audric. He had omitted any mention of Delphine and Turner knowing each other, and now she had her chance to discover why.

"Only if you can withstand an onslaught of new company. It is a very full house at present," Clemency told her, pretending to study her cards, but really waiting to see how she might react. "Tansy's father and uncle reside there, and now William, my brother, has come, and of course I am there, as well as Turner Boyle. . . ."

The effect was immediate, and so was Clemency's regret.

Delphine went even paler than her normally ashy hue, her lips parting on a silent sound of shock. Her cards scattered to the table between them, and she jolted to her feet as if struck by lightning.

"Oh. Oh, I see. Now it all becomes much clearer. Damn you, Audric."

Delphine grew instantly cold and withdrawn, and hugging herself went to the fire, slipping the toes of one slipper under a dog's side, as if for protection.

"I have said something to offend you." Clemency scrambled to stand too, turning the same shade of plum as the sofa. *Stupid, clumsy, unfeeling fool* . . . "If so, it was not my intention—"

"So many things have now come sharply into relief," Delphine murmured, cutting her off. Her huge, wounded brown eyes traveled across the carpet and then up Clemency's entire form until their gazes met. "You are part of my brother's games. I should have assumed as much, but then I had begun to like you, and regard is so utterly blinding. I should know."

She showed Clemency her back, hunching, becoming impossibly small as she shook her head and leaned toward the flames.

"Forgive me, Miss Ferrand, I did not mean to wound you. I will go—"

"No." Delphine's head came up quickly and she twisted in profile, swallowing a sniffle. "No. Stay. I want you to stay; I do like you, and therefore you deserve to know just what it is you have stepped full into."

Something caught her attention behind Clemency, and a wave of horror passed over her face, then she mastered it and sneered. "There you are, brother. And just in time."

"Delphine." The warning in Audric's tone was unmistakable. He loomed in the corridor, watching them. "Do not say another word."

"I will say as many words as I please," she hissed. "Come. Join us, Audric. It is only fitting that you are here while I tell this *friend* of yours our truth."

Audric prowled the edge of the room, far more intimidating and feral than the two massive hounds curled up at Delphine's feet. He was dressed for the club, in a sharp black coat and snowy cravat, close-fitting tan trousers tucked into glossy, knee-high boots. His low-simmering green eyes flicked to Clemency, and a horrible quivering nausea traced over his face as he looked at her.

She felt suddenly trapped, and sick, and wrung out her hands, wishing she could bolt. But she felt bound to stay and sensed that leaving would hurt Delphine more than staying to hear what the girl wanted to say.

"What has he told you about me?" Delphine asked, her voice high and almost babyish. Mocking. "That I am ill. That I am frail. Has he told you what was between Turner Boyle and me? Only that was not his name when I knew him, was it, Audric? No, he was Morris Alston, a gentleman, or so I thought. We met at the opera in Paris. Normally my brother would accompany me to the performances, but I begged him to let me go with an acquaintance. She and her mother were far less watchful than Audric. It was five winters ago now, but it feels like a lifetime has passed . . . since . . ." She almost swooned but caught herself. Audric strode urgently as if to catch her, but Delphine put up a hand, keeping him at bay.

He stood near the abandoned table with the brandy and

cards, his shoulders bunched up around his ears as if he were coiled to strike.

"N-No, I will tell it all. I must. If you are to join Audric on this damned crusade of his, then let it be with eyes wide open," Delphine stammered. Clemency couldn't help but admire her; it must have taken immense strength, for each word seemed like an agony. "We courted in secret. He said we would be married, that he had claim to a fortune, that when he returned to Paris all would be settled, and our lives would begin."

At last Audric spoke, but only to growl, "She was sixteen."

"Yes!" Delphine cried. "A girl. A reckless, senseless girl. I loved him and I believed him, and of course none of it was true." She balled her hands into fists and a spasm gripped her, a tear sliding free down her cheek. "There was a child. I had survived cholera not long before that, and the babe . . . It nearly killed me. And now it is gone, for it had no father, and it did not deserve a mother that would look at it only with hatred and regret. Audric found it a loving family, or so he says. I do not know! How could I know? I do not even know if it was a boy or a girl!"

She whirled again to face the fire, a sob overwhelming her as she dropped her face into her hands.

Clemency trembled, and stared, and felt her body go numb as Audric went to his sister and held her. A hurt had been building inside her, and it was high as a wall now, brick by brick, indignity by indignity. She'd thought Turner Boyle very low indeed, but he had sunk now to a depth she had never thought to encounter in her life. Her simple, sheltered life in Round Orchard. The occasional voyage to London, but there only to clean and lovely assembly halls and gleaming ballrooms. And so she had led a narrow life, walking down a single hall, unaware of the paths snaking off it and into the darkness. That narrow life had made her an easy target for someone like Turner Boyle, but now she was building that hurt, brick by brick, and she would build it wide indeed.

How easily she could have been Delphine. How easily she might have fallen prey to Turner's easy, charming manner when first they met and he worked so hard to woo her. Clemency had sworn never to marry, and Turner had scaled even that high wall.

Delphine startled her, racing out of the room, brushing by Clemency close enough to ruffle her hair. Still, she could not move, frozen by the unfairness and the sorrow that felt potent enough to choke her.

"Are you satisfied?" Audric whispered, bent toward the hearth, his right hand braced on the mantel, a broken man, a silhouette of fire. *"Are you satisfied?"*

"Why did you not tell me?" Clemency whispered, hoarse. "You ask for my trust and yet you keep such things from me. I would faithfully guard such a secret! I should have known. What if he had tried to do the same to me?"

The mere suggestion of that made him wince and groan like a wounded animal. "It was not my truth to tell. It is a pain so deep and ragged and raw that I dare not even *think* of it, for whenever I do, it threatens to drive me mad. There is a howling in my soul, and it will not stop until the proper justice is had. Not the justice of courts and judges, but true justice. Poetic, unflinching, searing justice."

An urge to hold him as he sagged against the hearth rose

in her. She had never thought to see him a defeated thing, but all his arrogance was gone, and when he turned his head to look at her, his eyes still held the danger she had seen before, but now she felt it echo in her own gaze. Just to know what had happened to Delphine—just to glimpse that cruelty—made her want to be dangerous too.

"Delphine does not approve of your . . . crusade, she called it," Clemency said slowly. Carefully. He began to stand again, regarding her with hooded eyes. "Why not?"

"She says it is a reminder of all she suffered," Audric muttered, running a shaking hand through his graying black waves. When he spoke next, he sounded out of breath. "For years I have hunted other men like Boyle, men that use girls and drain them like that evening's claret and toss them away to let them shatter. Whatever justice the woman wants, that is what I give—a lashing, a thrashing, just a look, or a word, whatever is required. But Delphine would prefer we never speak of her suffering again. That it is eventually forgotten. She wants to move beyond it. But what she cannot see is that one does not move beyond such things. The world should not move beyond such things. The world should stand still, and gasp and weep, and have to look at their dear little sister sprawled on a bed dyed red with her blood. The world should have to witness the ripping of a child away from its mother and hear its cries, and watch as it is taken out into the cold, and pretend it is just a sack of flour and not a much-beloved nephew."

Clemency squeezed her eyes shut. "I am . . . so sorry. So, so terribly sorry," she said. Audric seemed to ignore that, his face slack and his eyes wandering. "And I am so, so enraged. Devoured by rage. Trembling with it."

His eyes snapped back to her, a squint leading her to believe he was seeing her in a new way. "You are not repulsed by our secrets?"

"I am repulsed, of course," Clemency replied. "But not by you." He said nothing, but nor did his eyes stray. "I want to help. I realize it is unfeeling to go against Delphine's wishes, but I want . . ." Clemency faltered a little, afraid of the words even as she burned to say them. "If it were me, I would beg for a brother brave enough to do as you are doing. Please, I want to hold your hand as the knife goes in."

12

It was only a matter of time before Delphine recovered and came to harangue him. Not that he believed himself undeserving of her scorn. She arrived like the presaging of a blizzard, the air in the room going still and flat, a moment of anticipation winding a knot between his shoulders, and then Audric heard the office door hinge squeak, and he let out a long-building breath.

"You should have told her everything," Delphine murmured, her voice ragged from the sobbing she must have done in her chambers. "If you wanted her to be a partner in your cruel business, you should have made the terms of her participation clear."

Audric was too cowardly to immediately face her. He stared instead out the window, the desk between him and it, his fists pressed into the hard surface, digging, hurting, to the point where the pain had become punitive.

"How could I tell her?" he asked softly. "When I can hardly tell it to myself?"

"Oh, yes, it is impossible to accept," Delphine whispered. She sounded exhausted, as if the sadness had broken like a fever, leaving her only weary. "And yet we must accept. And now she must too. It is all so terribly disappointing, Audric.

All of it. I thought you were courting her in earnest, and now I have to grieve that lie too."

The candles in his office had burned low. He stared at one not far from a stack of papers left by his bookkeeper. The flame flickered and danced, and burned its way into his sight, so that when he finally rose and stood straight and turned in profile toward his sister, the fire followed, a yellow smudge blighting his vision. He didn't know how to respond to Delphine—to deceive her further seemed inconceivably cold, but his own thoughts when turned toward Miss Fry were murky. In his mind, she stubbornly eluded labels like "friend" or "acquaintance." They had kissed, and he was not fool enough to declare it unwanted. He wanted her but understood their arrangement made any innocent, romantic notions unlikely. Clemency after all despised marriage.

He might remain a hunter ever eluded, and the thought stung. At least he would not become what his father had become to their mother—an ominous, looming taskmaster. A master, not a partner.

"Miss Fry is wary of men and marriage generally," he said. "One can hardly blame her. My only concern right now is your—"

"My what?" Delphine laughed and crossed the office to where he stood leaning against the desk. She took his hand and held it loosely in the warm weave of her ten fingers. "My safety? My happiness? I am as safe as I can be," she added, staring up at him. He still could not meet her gaze and winced when she dropped his hand and reached up to fix one curl of his hair. "And I am as happy as I can be. Look to yourself, brother. What about your safety and happiness? Take care, or you will wind up like Father, all alone in an

empty house, staring down a long line of loveless memories."

They rarely spoke of their father. Their mother, Elise, was
all but sainted in their eyes. She had endured so much in that
big, sprawling house along the river. Even alive, she had been
like a specter haunting Fox Ridge, a vanishing smear of sunlight against their father's encroaching night.

"That is too far," he whispered, ragged.

"Maybe," Delphine said. "Maybe someone ought to have
told him the truth too. He might have met a better end. We
might have loved him more."

Audric had always pictured their father's final moments
as an oil painting, curling at the edges as it burned. The
chamber where he spent most of his time had been consumed
by a sudden fire. The damage to the house was not extensive,
but their father's room was obliterated. He imagined his father sitting at his desk, hunched over, his black curtain of
hair parting only to reveal empty, staring eyes. He showed no
emotion, no regret, no fear, as the flames brought annihila-
tion.

When Audric walked the smoldering remains of that
wing, he had found melted glass in hardened pools all around
the bedchamber. He never escaped the sense that the fire was
not mere accident.

"I will look to my life," Audric promised. "But we must
look to revenge first."

"That cannot be so," Delphine chided. With a sigh, she
left him, sweeping back toward the door, the gray shawl
looped through her elbows and falling to her feet swishing
softly across the carpet. It reminded him of some haunted
specter glimpsed at the end of a long, dark hall. Like their

mother. Yet the gentleness that entered her voice defied that comparison, and she sounded young, and almost hopeful, and Audric tried to hold tight to that. "For my happiness is tied to yours, brother. Remember that. While you and Miss Fry are on this crusade of yours, remember that."

She lingered at the door, and Audric risked a quick glance in her direction. Her thin smile was long-suffering with sisterly affection. He owed her better, he knew, yet seemed terminally incapable of providing it. If he let go of the sputtering rage in his heart he knew it would make her glad, but how could he? What would he be, what would inspire him, if he doused that ever-burning ember?

"Are you angry with me, *poupette*?" he asked. Audric couldn't remember the last time he sounded so helpless or so small. Only Delphine was allowed to see him like that. "Please, do not be angry with me. Are you?"

"No," Delphine admitted, sighing at him again. "I have made peace with our disagreement. I know you cannot be dissuaded, and foolishly, I am almost pleased that you are no longer doing this on your own. When I think of you with Miss Fry it brings a smile to my face. What an unlikely pair you make."

That bolstered his spirits, just a little, enough to convince him it was safe to stop clinging to the desk and truly turn to look at her. She drummed her pale fingers once on the edge of the door, then began to glide away into the gloomy corridor. Of course, she could not do so without having the last word. She had more than earned it.

"Yes, it pleases me to think of you two together." Delphine's voice was fading, but still utterly comprehensible, and it made the hairs on the back of his neck stand up in alarm. "My brave but foolhardy champions. I wonder, Audric, if you know what you are getting yourself into with her. I saw something awaken in her eyes tonight; it shakes me to remember it. Strange, but I think you might truly deserve each other."

I am going to destroy you, Clemency thought, watching Turner Boyle sing a full-throated tenor rendition of *"No One Shall Govern Me,"* one hand flourishing on the words, while Tansy accompanied him artfully on the pianoforte.

Whatever happens to you, she further concluded, *you will have earned.*

She stood in the airy, vaunted beauty of Lady Margaret Veitch's drawing room, the rest of the company sprinkled about the room, arranged at intervals like subjects of a Titian painting. It would take a party of no fewer than forty to make the drawing room feel cramped. Instead, they were allowed to sit or stand wherever they pleased, and with so much space, one could almost feel solitude creeping in. The next closest person happened to be her brother, William, seated what felt like a street's length away on a pink-and-gold chaise longue nearer the pianoforte. Plaster angels soared above them, merry and rotund, and a chandelier dripping crystals presided over the music and tea-drinking. The whole house had a baroque feel to it, though Lady Veitch and her two daughters had done an admirable job of bringing the curtains and carpets and upholsteries up to modern style.

Tansy had apparently made quite an impression during her visit, winning them all an invitation to take tea with the widow and her daughters, Arabella and Adeline. Sir John Veitch, Clemency was told on the carriage ride over, had died fighting the French. He was, as it turned out, an *actual* knight and a member of the nobility. Lady Veitch had greeted Turner with an initially chilly demeanor. Clemency's heart had soared. But Turner quickly mentioned that his close friend Denning Ede sent his regards, and Lady Veitch's suspicions were all forgotten.

Clemency decided she would not be defeated, burning the name Denning Ede into her brain for later.

Four nights had come and gone since Clemency's secret trip to the Ferrand townhome. She had expected that over time, her outrage and despair would cool somewhat. The opposite proved to be true. While Boyle deemed it necessary to spend only the evenings at the Bagshot residence, the experience of existing within his orbit for those four evenings of cards, music, poetry recitation, and conversation stoked the searing fire in Clemency's chest higher and higher. That he dared smile in her direction, touch her hand, flirt with her, struck her as disgusting and ludicrous.

Yet somehow she did not find it hard to perform the role of Naïve and Trusting Intended. In fact, she was perfecting the part. Boyle seemed delighted by her quiet, pliant nature of late. He did not know, nor probably even suspect, that the wide-eyed, openmouthed gaze of wonder Clemency turned upon him was not one of doting affection, but one of constant, awestruck horror.

And now the villain was holding court, luminous in a suit he had stolen or borrowed. He was unbearably handsome, of course, his hair more radiant than ever, his eyes bluer than the queen's own sapphires. But Clemency was hardened against his beauty. She saw only a perfumed Lucifer, and any brightness in his eye or twinkle in his smile she immediately deemed nefarious. Whenever a look of excitement or joy flickered across his face, she assumed it was only because he was brewing up some new and horrid way to enrich himself. The song ended. It was one of her favorites, which Boyle knew, and he had thrown her mischievous looks throughout the whole ordeal, very pleased with himself indeed that he had managed to remember a single thing about her tastes.

Perhaps it was unfair to compare him to the devil. At least Lucifer had at one time been an angel.

What have you ever been, she thought, *but selfish?*

"The absolute bastard," Clemency muttered.

"Sorry?" Tansy was suddenly at her elbow, appearing there like a lacy apparition. She had no idea how the woman had traveled from piano to her side in a mere blink.

Clemency spun toward her, composing herself, stretched smile at the ready. Yes, she was becoming good at playing this part. "I said what amazing plaster," she chirped, batting her lashes and pointing to the bouncy cherubs above them. A few columns were littered about the space too and wound with real, vibrant ivy.

"Mm. Lady Veitch has the most finessed style; do you not agree?" Tansy asked, loud enough for the widow herself to hear and smile, and nod, and fan herself with elegant approval. "The columns were shipped from Rome," she continued, now apparently Lady Veitch's confidante after only days of acquaintance. But Tansy was like that, infinitely good-natured, warm, and easily impressed, and easily making a warm impression. The perfect friend for an aging widow with dim-witted, unremarkable daughters.

Full credit to Arabella and Adeline, Clemency thought gently, they were not spiteful or nasty, but nobody had ever asked a single thing of them in their lives. Their wealth and position alone made them interesting, and neither of them had aspired to be anything greater than growing into human-shaped wife material. That was perhaps for the best, Clemency decided—it was easier to swallow the barbs of matrimony if one lacked even the desire to understand why it stung so.

"Arabella and Adeline are completely taken with India these days," Tansy said, pointing out the obvious. Both girls were swaddled in bright gold-and-magenta silks, their wispy blond hair mostly concealed by orange brocade turbans. "Lady Veitch dotes on them so, she is considering redoing the whole space and calling it a Dream of Calcutta! Marvelous. Her daughters are both a vision of loveliness."

Clemency tried on another of her new, cool, agreeable smiles. "They are both perfectly tolerable in every way."

Tansy shot her a warning glance. "They are introducing me to very good society," she whispered. "It will make London quite what I have always wanted. . . ."

"I will not jeopardize your chances, Tansy," Clemency assured her, softening. "The girls are not mean-spirited, and that is high praise. They are rich enough to be whatever they want, and they have chosen to be harmless. That should be celebrated."

"I should wear a turban next time," Tansy mused, glancing over at Lady Veitch's daughters. "Perhaps I shall wear one to your wedding!"

Clemency coughed, hard, tapping at her own chest. Over Tansy's shoulder, arranged in a pleasing tableau with her daughters at the center of the room, Lady Veitch gasped in alarm.

"Stevens! Fetch Miss Fry a ginger tonic at once. At once. There is a horrid little disease making the rounds this month; I shall not have her falling prey to it, and under my roof!"

There was no avoiding the woman anymore, and so Clemency wandered arm in arm with Tansy toward the sofas. Lady Margaret Veitch fanned herself on a chair placed to the left and slightly diagonally toward her daughters, who sat like posed marionettes on a low, cushioned bench. They did not often move their hands or arms, but rather their matching ice-blue eyes flitted swiftly around the room, and in almost uncanny unison. The heavy silk turbans wrapped around their heads looked quite hot, and both girls wore a sheen of sweat that beaded on top of their perfumed face powder.

With nowhere convenient to sit, Tansy and Clemency hovered while Lady Veitch inspected Clemency from head to foot, perhaps searching for signs of the ailment she so dreaded. The old woman had once been a beauty, that was obvious, though her cosmetics and dress spoke of a bygone era of panniers and severe corsets, and she still wore a good amount of candy pink rouge in generous circles on her cheeks. She and her daughters shared a dull, porridge complexion and a rather wide neck.

"Ah! There is Stevens!" Lady Veitch sighed with contentment as a footman, also dressed like a rococo antique, hurried over, thrusting a copper cup into Clemency's hands with a bow. She took the concoction and sniffed, and nearly shed a tear from the overpowering smell.

Subtly, Tansy nudged her. She took a sip and grinned while the stuff burned its way down her throat.

"Very thoughtful, Your Ladyship," Clemency burbled.

"Not at all, not at all. I suspect you will feel much refreshed; that particular tonic is an invention of my physician and always fills me with immense vigor." Lady Veitch thumped her palm thoughtfully with her closed fan. "Stevens! More chairs. These poor ladies are looming in a most uncomfortable manner."

Stevens leapt back into action, trotting out to the gallery beyond the open drawing room doors and returning with light wicker chairs for both Clemency and Tansy.

Tansy lowered herself into the chair and smoothed out her skirts, and Clemency pretended to sip the tonic while trying not to gag just from the odor.

After she was seated, Lady Veitch gave her another close inspection. "I enjoy your company, Miss Fry, I do, and Mrs. Tansy Fry speaks very highly of you. Very highly. Though there is a sharpness about your face that I usually find unbecoming in a woman, somehow it is not off-putting on you." She squinted, and her head fell a little to the side. "Hm. The result of too much reading, I think. Yes, that is what it is, I can always detect it. Am I correct? Come now, Miss Fry, I will have your confession."

Clemency clutched the tonic close to her chest, suddenly red-faced. All afternoon, Lady Margaret Veitch had found it satisfactory to speechify on everything from her late husband's arduous struggles with gout, his love of German poetry, her daughters' endless list of accomplishments, the weather, and the horrible fashions at court, to a detailed summary of every social gathering she had engineered in the last six months. Yet now her attention turned to Clemency, and while the woman's wealth and title did not overly impress her, it was not to be missed that Lady Veitch possessed an intimidating presence.

"I do indeed have a passion for reading. Your Ladyship can hardly dispute that a woman of sense and accomplishment is expected to have an education, and to cultivate a mind for books," Clemency said, feeling as if each word were a step through a field laced with deadly traps.

Lady Veitch sniffled. "I will dispute whatever I like, Miss Fry, though it is true that the written word, in moderation, adds a certain polish to a lady's manner. A distinguished air. But under no circumstances should a lady overread. Never! For it leads to a belief in one's own cleverness, and that is never a desirable trait in a young woman of quality."

Clemency's eyes shifted slowly to Arabella and Adeline, and her only feeling toward the girls became abject pity. Well. They had traced the source of the girls' lifelessness, and it was their mother's doing. Mystery solved. She wondered what the sisters might become, how they might change, if let loose in a well-stocked library for a few months. Their only relationship with books, Clemency thought, was balancing them on their heads to refine their posture.

Sensing Tansy's growing nervousness, Clemency held her tongue, deciding that it was not the time to defend her love of Bethany Taylor, Maria Edgeworth, Samuel Richardson, Fanny Burney, and Ann Radcliffe. What good would it do? Women of Lady Veitch's age were set in their ways, and it was not worth aggravating her simply to prove a point.

A belief in one's own cleverness indeed.

"What sound advice," Clemency murmured, feeling Tansy exhale with gratitude beside her.

Lady Margaret nodded, adamant, and continued, "Knowledge is bitter, it robs the face of a round and feminine sweetness. It produces a rigid aspect to the face. I do not think you have read too much just yet, Miss Fry, for your beauty is not in question."

"Is that so?" Clemency fought to keep her voice from straining. "And what, if a woman did overstep and indulge too much in reading, could be done to restore this . . . sweetness?"

She expected Lady Margaret to entertain them all with another speech, but Turner Boyle chose that moment to join them. He strode to the space between Clemency's chair and the widow, propping the back of his left hand on one hip.

"If music be the food of love," Boyle quoted irritatingly, "perhaps it is also the restorative one might seek."

At his arrival, Lady Margaret and her daughters brightened. "There is Lord Boyle, our songbird. What a gallant voice you have. All gentlemen should sing as you do, with the clarity of heaven's own trumpets."

He gave a polite little bow and pursed his lips in a shy way. "That is too much praise for me, Your Ladyship. It was only the fineness of the room, its shape and size, that made the performance *gallant*, as you say. And some credit must go to Lord Ede. I have had the pleasure of accompanying him to hear Haydn and Mozart, and he has contributed greatly to my education on that score."

There was that name again. It was like a glass of cool wine, bringing a vibrating smile to Lady Veitch's mouth the moment he said it.

And Tansy's lovely playing, she added for him silently.

"It *is* a very fine little room," Lady Veitch preened.

"It is perfect," Lord Boyle insisted. "I should rather hear a small, intimate performance here than attend a grand production at the Théâtre des Arts."

Lady Veitch clapped her fan lightly against her palm and tossed her head, charmed. "Oh, but what do the French know about opera?" She laughed and laughed, and Lord Boyle and Tansy joined in. William wandered over, standing stiff and awkward behind Tansy. He looked frightfully out of place, a gentleman, surely, but not one made for the endless exchange of escalating compliments and deflections that made up an afternoon tea with the excessively coddled. They traded a trapped, sullen look over Tansy's shoulder.

"In fact, what do the French know about anything?" Lord Boyle asked, drawing a scream of laughter from Lady Veitch.

Clemency boiled. She could not lash out at Lord Boyle in any meaningful way, not there, and certainly not while she was meant to be playing the dutiful wife-to-be. And so she smiled primly and squinted up at him. "The Théâtre des Arts . . . Pray, when were you last in Paris?"

Was it before or after you destroyed, perhaps indefinitely, an innocent young girl's heart?

It was briefly satisfying to watch him struggle to answer. "Of course . . . Well, it was . . ." He finally shrugged and gave up searching for an accurate answer. "It hardly matters . . . Journeys abroad so tend to run together. One is always a bit blurry from the weariness and travel."

"Well stated," Lady Veitch said, unfurling her fan again and fluffing it near her chin. "I myself have never been to

Paris, but I am sure there are superior amusements to be found here in town."

"And if one is in France, then one must inevitably put up with Frenchmen, and who could possibly abide that?"

That went over even better, and a snide little chuckle chased around the room.

"Pray," Clemency began, her voice pinched, "who is Denning Ede? You both seem to think highly of the man."

"Who is . . ." Lady Veitch nearly collapsed. "He is the keeper of polite society, the arbiter of all good company, a bosom companion of King George himself!"

Clemency could only imagine what Turner could be doing with the arbiter of all good company. Boyle was suddenly quiet and steady, watching her.

"Influential in Parliament," Turner added. It seemed only for her benefit, and a threat.

"Influential *everywhere*," said Lady Veitch. "In a town rife with scandal, he is true north, how fortunate Lord Boyle is to be so frequently at his side."

The man sounded like a veritable bulldog, yet Boyle had him fooled. How, she wondered, was such a thing possible? The enemy of my enemy, she thought, realizing that Ede's spotless reputation was now masking Boyle's treachery. Audric would certainly know more, and so would she. Soon. Clemency painted on an unwavering smile and stood, Stevens dodging closer to take the cup of unfinished tonic from her. Her movement stifled the laughter, and Lady Margaret glared at her as if punishing her for ruining their fun.

"Miss Fry?" she asked.

"I am suddenly so hot," Clemency murmured. "The view

from your balcony looks exquisite, Lady Veitch, might I see it?"

"Let me escort you, here," Boyle said, solicitous, jumping to take her arm.

"Stevens? Show them," Lady Veitch commanded, gesturing them away with her fan. Before they had taken a single step, she had already returned to discussing the layout of the room with Tansy, and describing the Indian mural she wanted to place above the fireplace in that room, all of it in glass tiles, the glazing would be exorbitant but so worth it. . . .

"She is terrible," Boyle breathed when they had walked from the sofas to the other side of the room, out two tall French doors and onto a balcony decorated with a profusion of ferns in white clay pots.

Clemency closed her eyes. The breeze rolling in from the park smelled lightly of violets. Common dog-violets were probably blooming all over Mayfair, lending their delicate perfume to the neighborhood. She had always found it curious that something that smelled so charming came with such an unfortunate name.

"You seem to be enjoying her company. And anyway, she is rich," Clemency corrected him. "She is exactly how one would expect her to be."

"That's harsh. I am sure there are many people with more wealth and better sense," Boyle replied. His tone was not argumentative; it had not been, not for a single moment, since they reunited in London. Clemency glanced over at him, to maintain her façade of friendliness, and for a moment, she could forget all that he was. When he was not lying to her or berating her or snubbing her, he was effortlessly pleasant. It had been that way between them before he proposed, and she had imagined herself passing many years in his company, the two of them the rare and special love match.

"Surely not all of the very wealthy are so ridiculous," he stated with some finality.

"Like you, for example," she replied. "You are not ridiculous."

Or rich.

"There," Boyle said, beaming. "You have settled it. So clever you are, undoubtedly from all that ill-advised reading."

A joke! How sweet. Clemency nodded absently. His statement was true enough. Audric, though not of the nobility, had a fortune to rival Lady Veitch's, and he was not ridiculous. No, he was something special. *Someone* special.

Now her imagination presented her with a more tantalizing possibility—passing many years in Audric's company, the two of them giggling at the Veitches of the world, never taking themselves too seriously or letting his money rob them of compassion and humility. Perhaps they could do some real good with it, open an orphanage or a home for unfortunate mothers, something to address the unfair stipulations of society that had caused Delphine her pain. They could be the rare and special love match . . .

She blinked, hard, and felt her breath come quicker at the mere thought of Audric. Four nights was hardly an age, but she already looked forward to, and perhaps pined for, the next time their paths would cross.

"You look so beautiful just now," Lord Boyle whispered. Her skin ignited, not with passion but with revulsion. Still, she let him take her hand, lift it to his lips, and brush a kiss across her knuckles. To withstand it, to keep from striking him, she imagined Audric's lips there instead. Or where his lips had been before, tightly pressed to hers. "This light," he added, "this gown, whatever womanly secret is making your eyes sparkle like that . . ."

At that, she smiled genuinely. "Alas, a lady never tells."

He kissed her hand again. Clemency noticed the edge of a bruise near his shirt collar, the remnant of some brawl over a woman or a debt, no doubt. What would the angelic Denning Ede have to say about that? She stared at the well-formed lips that had just kissed her hand twice and imagined honeyed lies pouring out of them, fooling Delphine, and Ede, and Lady Veitch. Fooling her.

Fooling the world.

Her hand curled up in his grasp like a dead spider. Before he could notice, she jerked it away and went to place her palms on the bannister.

"A dressmaker is coming to the house tomorrow," she said, adopting a lighthearted tone. "I am to choose the fabrics and lace for the wedding gown. Honora was planning to help me sew it, but Tansy says none of the ladies in London do that. They all go to this dressmaker. It is the fashionable thing to do."

"Then, you should do it. I want you to have the best things."

Clemency smirked into the wind. She had agreed to make Boyle feel secure in his finances. "I can make do, Turner, there is no need to strain your resources."

He gave a low, rumbling chuckle and sidled up next to her, his hip brushing hers. It was an agony to stay still and let him touch her lower back, but an agony she endured for the sake of the plan. None of it would hurt as it should if he was not fully, truly in love with her. It was no small feat to make a career swindler recommit his heart, but Clemency would find a way.

"It is the least I can do," he murmured. "After the way I acted, the things I said to you . . . giving you a wedding that will be the envy of the ton is a little, little thing."

"Nothing too extravagant," Clemency murmured. "But it will be nice to meet this dressmaker."

"Of course it will be. Shame I cannot be there for an introduction," he said with a sigh. As he always did when nervous, Turner Boyle pushed his hand through his mop of red curls. "There are a number of debts I need to attend to, now, of course, before we begin our life together. I do not want another incident like the one in Round Orchard. I will never forget the embarrassment."

Clemency played the sad maiden and bit down on her lower lip. It was a mystery to her how he intended to keep the charade going. Would he really find a way to pay for her wedding gown? For a house? Just how influential was this Denning Ede person? When did he intend to make it clear that something had gone awry and their only funds would be her dowry and whatever they could beg off her father and the Bagshots?

His first night with them at the Bagshots', William had naturally brought up the help Jack Connors had given them in getting safely to London. She had watched, intrigued, as a fascinating array of emotions played across Turner's face. As her brother spoke, she could all but see Turner calculating what to say and how, though in the end he simply stated that he and Mr. Connors were no longer associated with each other, but he was pleased that they had all arrived in town without a scratch.

Clemency wondered if that was really true, if he was avoiding Mr. Connors even after the poor, strange man had gone out of his way to defend Turner. Lies on top of lies. When, she wondered, would the house of brittle kindling collapse and burn?

"Miss Fry! Miss Fry . . ." Lady Veitch's screech pierced the peaceful quiet of the balcony. "Stevens? Stevens! Bring her in at once. All that cold air will undo the tonic's effects completely! I say, Stevens, fetch them here to me at once!"

"Back into the fray?" Boyle asked, offering her his arm with a sly, exasperated smile.

Clemency was silent, and nodded, and forced her arm to obey and touch him. *This is not the fray, Lord Boyle,* she thought. *You will know when the fray truly comes, when we bring it to you. There will be no mistaking it.*

13

She had written to her sister twice already while in London, but on the fifth day of her visit she couldn't help it, she wrote Honora again.

My dearest Nora,

Words cannot express how much I miss and need you. I know I begged you to join me here in the last letter, but I will beg you again. Oh, Nora, though it seems like all is calmness and tranquility, inside me it is chaos. Today I chose the fabric and lace and ribbon for my wedding gown. A gown for a wedding that must not be! Tansy was consumed with delight, and soon I must break her heart, and Mother's heart, and tell them that it is all a great farce. What I have learned about my intended is so unspeakably terrible that I dare not write it down here. It concerns another woman and a matter of utmost privacy, and I may never be able to tell you the details of what occurred. Suffice it to say that you must imagine he has done the worst possible thing, and then think of something even graver.

In a fortnight it will all come crashing down around my ears. There is an assembly at Almack's and that will be the night when he is unmasked before the whole of society as a liar and a scoundrel. Until then, I must make him believe that I am more in love and more devoted than ever. I should hate to do it, but sometimes, Nora, I confess it gives me pleasure. It has become a little game to see how much I can grow his attachment to me before it is severed altogether. Now he wants our money, but perhaps I can coax true feeling from him.

How do you fare? And how is father? I so worry about him when I am not there. It must be miserable indeed to spend each day alone with our mother. I am sure she is all talk of London, and I am all talk of London, and now you are attacked from all sides. Selfishly, I hope it convinces you to come to me. But if it is not too terrible there, then you must stay and be happy, and keep yourself in good cheer and health. I have not yet delivered your letter because I am a lacking sister, but I promise to see it safely to its destination tomorrow. It has rained all morning, and I fear it will persist until evening.

Please be well, and do not worry about me at all. I am not suffering, and I feel quite safe and happy with Tansy and William. You will be very proud of me that Mr. Ferrand is not mentioned at all in this letter. I hardly think of him when he is not near.

Very well, I occasionally think of him. But only the right amount.

I remain your loving sister,
C

Clemency carried the sealed letter down to the front hall and found Mr. Bagshot's long-suffering valet, Langston, who greeted her with a swallowed sigh. That was fine. She could hardly begrudge him his frustrations, with her sending letters almost constantly, and to the same recipient.

"Yes," she said with a shy smile. "*Another* letter."

"Of course, Miss Fry," he said, taking the letter and the coin she had brought for the posting.

"Last one," Clemency murmured. "I promise."

"Very good, ma'am."

Langston pivoted on his foot and strode swiftly toward the front door. He was already through it when Clemency noticed that he had dropped a small sealed letter in his wake. Hurrying after him, she scooped up the message, adjusting the veil under her bonnet, for she had been readying herself to join Tansy on a walk through the neighborhood. That would have to wait, she realized, finding that fate had just intervened in her plans.

The letter had come for Turner Boyle, but it had not been opened and was marked to be returned to the original sender. It had come from Mr. Connors, and his London address was listed there too.

Voices echoed from the hall near the kitchen, and Clemency shoved the little square of parchment into the neck of her dress and pretended to rebutton her gloves just as Tansy arrived, dismissing her maid as she swept into the foyer.

"Shall we go?" asked Tansy. Lady Veitch had clearly sent over gifts of friendship, dressing Tansy like her own doll in Indian silks. The vivid magenta frock did suit her, Clemency thought with a sigh.

"Might it wait? My stomach is unsettled from breakfast."

"Nonsense!" Tansy hooked their arms together and marched toward the front door. There was no sign of Langston as the girls left, and he had apparently failed to notice the dropped letter. "A turn about the neighborhood is exactly what you need. There is the most darling park not far from here, with a willow tree and a bench; it is where William proposed to me."

Clemency shifted, trying to urge the letter deeper into her muslin gown, concerned that the shape of it wedged against her corset would be noticeable. Nodding, she used her left hand to untuck her fichu and then drape it awkwardly across her bosom, hoping for better concealment. How in heaven was she supposed to concentrate on what Tansy was saying when that thing was burning a hole through her undergarments?

"I should like to see the spot," Clemency said, finding that it was now a fine day, though a bank of clouds to the south looked to threaten rain again. "I hope I can be as happy as you and my brother, as happy as Honora was with Edwyn."

"With *Edwyn*?" Tansy almost squawked. She whipped her head around to stare at Clemency, veering left out the drive and steering them down the sidewalk toward a patch of green and trees a block north. "I only knew them together briefly, but I never had the impression she was quite content with him."

"But they were very much in love!" Clemency replied, drawing down her brow. "What could possibly make you think otherwise?"

Tansy looked into the distance, her lips twitching to the side as she mulled over the question. She fussed idly with the ribbon on her bonnet, also pink, to match her new gown, passing it over and over again across her palm. "I rather considered her resigned, not content. Truly, it shocked me to see how long she chose to wear widow's weeds. I thought perhaps she would be eager to marry again and find a better match."

"You are wrong," Clemency declared, growing a little angry with her, the letter in her gown almost forgotten. "There is no better match for her; I admire the love they had for each other."

"I suppose you must be right, dear," Tansy said with a shrug. "You have her deepest confidence, still . . . Ah well, it matters not. Honora will prove me right or wrong, eventually."

"I do not think she shall ever marry again," Clemency told her. She hadn't meant it to sound like a warning but it did. Her most protective side emerged where her older sister was concerned. "That is how deep the wound runs. And while we speak of her, I promised to deliver a letter to a friend of hers in town, might I take the carriage there after our walk?"

"Another letter! You are positively brimming with correspondence, my dear," Tansy waited until two carriages had passed and then pulled Clemency across the road. Only a few children, watched by a hawk of a governess, played in the modest wedge of nature preserved in the city. Over a low hedge and charming stone wall, Clemency saw a few well-tended clumps of daffodils and tulips, as well as the aforementioned willow, bench, and a duck pond. "You may have the carriage, but only if you tell me more of this *friend*."

"'Tis nothing like that," Clemency assured her with a

laugh. "Honora simply wanted me to deliver a message to an old friend here in town, a woman. In truth I know almost nothing about their friendship."

"Oh, how dull," Tansy muttered. She kicked at some stray pebbles on their way to the bench, following a faded, winding dirt path through a gap in the hedge and stone. "Here I had hoped to find that I was right, and your sister found a new beau."

"Time will prove me right, I fear," Clemency said with a chuckle. "Though I wish it were not so. I do hope she finds love again; it would be heartless to do otherwise. I simply worry that she is still in mourning."

They went to sit together on the bench, and Clemency silently congratulated her brother on choosing a peaceful place for his engagement. The willow bending over them provided gentle, sweet shade, and its feathery boughs dripping down felt like something out of a child's fairy tale.

Tansy patted her arm as they listened to the children laughing merrily, tumbling over one another in the grass.

"Honora still has her beauty. We shall be on the sharp lookout for any potential suitors at Almack's, yes? There will be plenty of eligible gentlemen there, and some older, and not opposed to the love of a widow." Tansy said it smiling, though it made a shallow cut. It did not feel right to discuss her sister like something used and discarded, only to be tolerated by certain gentlemen of certain ages. "What about that man that came to Round Orchard just before we left? Mr. Ferrand? Surely your mother had all sorts of schemes in that direction."

Clemency scratched nervously at her own throat. "I do not think Honora and Mr. Ferrand would be well-suited to one another."

"And why not?" Tansy shrugged. "Everyone says he is handsome, refined, of good manners, and past the draw of youthful frivolity. I shall suggest it to Lady Veitch, she must know him. Perhaps she can find some way to arrange a meeting. . . ."

"Do not do that." Clemency heard her voice raise before she could stop it.

Tansy simply stared, her lips puckered in a bemused smirk, awaiting explanation of her sister-in-law's outburst.

"Only I have met him, and he is quite stoic and strange and serious. He has . . . an intensity about him that many would find uncomfortable."

"But Nora is shy and soft-spoken; a stoic, serious man sounds perfectly agreeable for a woman of her inclinations."

"I disagree!"

"Do you dislike the man?" asked Tansy, twisting to face Clemency, her amusement dissolving into irritation. "Lord, but you are argumentative today. Oh! There is William, and in such a hurry too."

Tansy stood, watching as her husband crossed the road toward them, clutching his hat to his head as he ran. There was a fine sheen of sweat on his face when he arrived, huffing and puffing, giving them a quick bow before shoving a note into Tansy's gloved hands.

"You are to come at once, sweetheart. Lady Veitch needs you. Something is amiss with one of her daughters, that was all her valet would tell me."

"Lady Veitch! Needing me? Oh, well of course, then." She offered Clemency a frown, and Clemency stared up at her, squinting against the sunlight winking over the girl's shoulder. "Will you absolutely hate me if I run off to attend her?"

"No," Clemency replied, thinking of the letter in her dress. "You must go. I am sure it is of the utmost importance. But please, I beseech you, do not discuss with her Nora's private affairs. You know how shy my sister is, and it is not our place to meddle in her grieving."

Tansy brightened and nodded, taking William's arm as they scurried away. "You are right, Clemency. As you say, time will prove one of us wrong!"

"Sister," William said by way of apology, and then they were off.

Clemency followed them back to the house, lingering on a bench in the foyer, waiting until Tansy and William had collected themselves and gone out again before tugging the letter free of her bodice.

Clemency waited until they had almost vanished before tugging the letter free of her bodice. With eyes darting about and trembling hands, she gently unsealed the wax, trying not to damage it lest it needed to be fixed again. She unfolded the page and smoothed it across her knee through her skirts, head bowed low to read.

Turner, my love, the letter began. *I know you are in town, why will you not come to me?*

Breath catching in her throat, Clemency quickly refolded the letter and shoved it back into her dress. Mr. Ferrand had to see this, and right away. She sprang up from the bench and hurled herself out the door just in time to watch William and Tansy race down the road in the carriage she needed.

It appeared delivering dear Honora's letter would have to wait. Again.

14

"Well?" Clemency asked, insistent. "What do you make of it?"

Audric held the letter up to the window, turning it slightly translucent as he read it over again. As usual, Miss Fry had turned up at his house with no warning and turned an otherwise subdued afternoon into a dramatic frenzy. She blew into the house like a gale, startling Ralston, who brought her red-faced and out of breath to Audric's office. There they now stood, her with her hands bundled before her in distress while he considered their next move with care.

"How did you come here?" he asked, distracted suddenly by the very real possibility that her arrival had been noticed.

"My brother took the Bagshots' carriage; I had to hire a hackney," said Miss Fry, brows knit with confusion.

"Did you ask the driver to wait?"

"I did."

"Ralston!" he barked, summoning the man from his post outside the half-opened door. His valet rushed in, long hair somewhat askew.

"Sir?"

"Find Miss Fry's hackney driver and dismiss him; pay him

well for his silence. She was never here and he never drove her."

"Right away, sir."

Audric then returned to the matter of the letter, which he found a bit sad, if anything, and not the explosive shock it had apparently been for Clemency. That Turner Boyle was involved with other men, or pretended to be, hardly rated on the rogue's list of unexpected traits.

"If we use this letter against Boyle," Audric told her slowly, lowering the message and turning to regard her. The flurry of activity and the ride over had left her with a pretty glow on her cheeks; she ought to be flustered more often, it became her. "Then, we also use it against Connors. He will be implicated in the scandal. What sort of man is he?"

"Oh." Clemency chewed her lip nervously. "I had not considered that. He is not a mean sort. Blundering, I think, is the best way to describe him. A man with more money and time than sense. An enthusiastic drinker."

"So exactly like his gentry peers, I see." Audric sighed and dropped the letter on his desk, then massaged his temples with one hand.

"I thought you would be more shocked," Clemency told him.

He smiled and crossed his arms, leaning back to perch on the edge of his desk. It had become warm in his office, and he had avoided his coat, though now with her there it felt impolite and informal. "Your willingness to take part in my schemes sometimes leads me to forget your sheltered up-bringing. I suppose there was not much talk of mollies and lesbians in Round Orchard."

Clemency blanched. "I am not sheltered! But . . . no. Certainly not. That is illegal, sir."

"Not in France," Audric explained lightly.

"This is not at all the reaction I expected."

"What did you expect? For me to express disgust? For this to be some great coup for us?" Audric chuckled. "Do not take offense at this, Clemency, but there are far ghastlier things in this world than a bit of loving buggery. What Boyle has done to my sister and others, for one. His aggravating knack for eluding justice, for another."

Clemency shook her head and frowned. "Why do I feel like I am being scolded?"

"Because you are," Audric stated plainly. "But it is not with a mean spirit, I assure you. You simply are not wise to the ways of these things. It was Rousseau that said, 'I would rather be a man of paradoxes than a man of prejudices' and I wholeheartedly agree."

"Stop speaking to me as if I were a child!"

"Then stop acting like one."

She huffed and balled her fists, and for a moment he thought she might shout at him and leave. If she had, his estimation of her would have lowered gravely, but she threw no tantrums and stood still, closing her eyes tightly before saying, "You cannot fault me for my ignorance."

"No, but I can and will fault you for whatever comes next," Audric replied, watching her closely. His words had banished the lovely pink from her cheeks, and he almost regretted it. Her affronted face, however, was somewhat gratifying. "Besides, this letter only confirms that Mr. Connors maintains feelings for Boyle, not that his affection is returned. In fact, that Boyle had chosen to return it unread would only point to his innocence in the matter. This implicates Connors and no one else. Though I do not know the man from Adam nor care about his fate, he is yet another victim in Boyle's wake."

"Do you suppose he used Connors for his money?" Clemency asked softly.

"Absolutely. But your family has come into wealth again, and so Mr. Connors is no longer needed, and the risk of the relationship has outgrown the reward. I would wager that this talk of a love affair was Boyle's way of keeping Connors from retaliating." He started scratching his chin. It was odd, now that he thought more on it, that Boyle would let go of such useful blackmail. Why return the letter? It was his security against Connors accusing him of theft. "Boyle must truly dislike the man to willingly return such useful evidence."

Clemency fidgeted on the carpet, then fiddled with her bonnet ribbons before removing her hat. "Perhaps he found the implications distasteful."

"And do you?" Audric pressed. It pained him to think that she was a woman of low, mean prejudice. He thought better of her, much better, and hated to be disappointed. Many of his friends in Paris were British exiles, fleeing the pillories of London to carve out a more peaceful life in France, where men loving men and women loving women was far more accepted, or at the very least, ignored. It was nothing to anybody, and even flaunted in some circles. Audric himself felt little distinction between attraction to a man and attraction to a woman—there were physical charms to both, but his only true interest lay in a person's heart and mind. To find

a woman or man of true quality was incredibly rare, gen-
uine attraction something he experienced so seldom that
to squander it based on gender seemed wasteful. He hated
waste. And so, whoever took his heart took his heart.

"I hardly know how to answer that question," Clemency
stammered. There was that becoming flush again. Charming. "Perhaps . . . perhaps I *am* sheltered." An admission! His
brows shot up, and she readily noticed. "In some small
ways!" she hurried to add.

"Are you expected anywhere today, Clemency?" he asked.
It mattered. Her thoughts on the subject, annoyingly, now
occupied space in his thoughts. If she really was a woman of
quality, then he could be himself in front of her. His true self.
All would be revealed quickly, he surmised, after his next
suggestion.

"No." She drew out the word questioningly. "Tansy and
my brother were called away to attend to a friend. I had
planned to deliver a letter for my sister, but I thought this
matter more urgent. Why?"

"You find yourself a significant distance from Round Orchard, faced with a moral quandary for which you do not
have the vocabulary. We have a saying in France, *'Il n'y a pas
plus sourd que celui qui ne veut pas entendre.'*"

"No one is as deaf as he who refuses to listen?" Miss Fry
translated.

He nodded, pleased. "Indeed. Before you show this letter
to anyone or make any harsh judgments on Mr. Connors or
anyone of his persuasion, will you agree to listen?"

Clemency's lips quirked to the side. "What are you pro-
posing, sir?"

That was enough for him. Audric pushed away from his

desk, striding past Clemency to collect his dark blue coat from beside the door. Without further instruction, he left his office, hearing her soft little slippers padding behind him as he turned right out the door, followed the dark hall, and took the stairs down toward the foyer. Ralston waited there by the mirror to the left of the front door in hushed conversation with Audric's sister, Delphine.

"I heard we had a visitor," Delphine said mildly, a veiled smile presented to each of them. "Good day, Miss Fry."

"Hello, Miss Ferrand." Clemency waited at the bottom of the stairs, somewhat hidden, or perhaps protected, behind Audric's shoulder. The last meeting between Delphine and Clemency had been fraught, and he knew better than to say another word before the two women established how this meeting would go. He looked to Delphine, who had recently expressed her admiration for Clemency, or at least her interest in her working with Audric.

"There is a look of mischief upon you, brother," Delphine noted. "Do I dare ask?"

"Mischief indeed," he said, chuckling, then glanced to his right at Miss Fry, who worried the edge of her poor bonnet diligently. "I thought Ralston might drive us to Vere Street, to the Singing Hound."

His sister clapped her hands together and grinned. "Ralston says it is just like the old operas on Lavender Row on the rue Lamarck!"

"I only brought you there once," Audric said with a sigh. "And I regret it to this day."

Delphine craned her neck around him to see Miss Fry more clearly, her grin deepening to one of sisterly bemusement as she stage-whispered, "Dear brother no longer allows me any fun, lest I ruin my reputation further."

"*Delphine.*"

"What?" She batted her lashes and brushed by him to take Miss Fry's arm. A bold statement of allegiances, in his opinion. "It is all out in the open now, is it not? Miss Fry knows of my past; we may live in England now but I will not adopt this English habit of never speaking freely, of being polite instead of true. I am tired of being ashamed and quiet; it has not made me healthy or strong again. What do you think, Miss Fry?"

Audric could feel a hot flush roaring up the back of his neck. He spun to face them both, using his size to hover like a gargoyle. Behind him, he heard Ralston's shoes squeak as he shifted in them with unease. "Miss Fry does not carry the expert opinion on your condition, Delphine."

"Nor do you," his sister replied coolly. "Only I am the authority on me."

Audric did not know quite what had gotten into his young sister, but she stared boldly up at him with her big, consuming eyes and planted herself firmly beside Miss Fry. And in that woman she was likely to find a stalwart ally, he mused silently, for there was nothing Clemency seemed to enjoy quite so much as thwarting and infuriating him. Perhaps, by speaking aloud the horrors she had experienced at Boyle's hands, Delphine had dispelled some curse laying heavily upon herself. That said, her newfound taste for rebellion did not change what her doctors had said—that she should avoid too much rich food, exertion, and overexcitement.

"You will need my help," added Delphine. "Miss Fry cannot go without a veil and some concealment, and for that you will need my wardrobe. I offer it on the condition that I come along too."

"Devils, woman, you win. But Ralston will accompany us too and drive you home whenever I decide so." He shook his head at the reckless stupidity of it all, but this had been his idea. Typical, that these two women should wrestle it away from him. "We will avoid the Singing Hound, then, too rowdy for company such as this," Audric replied, watching his sister's grimace of determination fade into a thin if surprised smile. Yes, even he could be lenient, sometimes, and he was hopeless when it came to her demands. "Matton Hall will be better, I think."

"I will ready the carriage." Ralston snapped to the door with what Audric interpreted as giddiness. Were they that long overdue for diversion in this house?

"And I will find garments fitting for the occasion," Delphine piped up, taking Miss Fry more resolutely by the arm and leading her back up the stairs. "We shall not be long, brother. See that the carriage is prepared and brought round, and do not think for one moment that I will change my mind or be persuaded to stay indoors."

Watching the two ladies disappear up the steps, Audric could only vent a tired laugh. "Indeed, Delphine, indeed. No man is a match for the two of you in joined fortitude."

15

Matton Hall was not at all what Clemency envisioned when told she was being all but taken hostage and hied to a "molly house." In fact, it had all happened with such stupendous speed that she hardly had time to gather expectations. If she had, whatever those expectations were would have been utterly shattered by what she saw when walking through the tall, guarded, and inconspicuous doors of the assembly hall on Vere Street.

It was not at all a raucous place, and though her stomach seethed in a nervous tangle, she found herself exhaling a relieved breath as Delphine, arm tucked in hers, guided her across the clean tiled entrance toward a polished archway leading into a sort of modest ballroom filled with small tables meant for tea. The larger space was decorated with ivory bunting, wildflowers in delicate glass vases placed on each table. To the right of the archway, a number of trestle tables with refreshments were arranged, and attendants chatted amiably with those who came to peruse the sandwiches, cakes, and rolls. To the left, a well-maintained stage with a brass chandelier featured a lone fiddler, a young man in a lady's dress with no cosmetics, his short mop of honey brown hair free as he played with obvious talent and gusto.

A number of framed paintings hung on the brocade-covered walls. As they passed one, Clemency looked closer, finding that it was a bathing scene of two women in a wooded glade.

A space had been made for dancing before the stage, and two gray-haired, older ladies improvised their own steps, heedless of the rhythm or anyone watching. Most of the tables were taken, and a few curious glances were thrown their way. Clemency felt herself flinching each time, licking her lips, aware that her mother would squeeze her neck clean off her shoulders if she knew her daughter's whereabouts.

Yet none of it seemed tawdry or, as she knew, illegal. In the carriage ride over they had rattled by a number of pillories outside the establishments on that street. Was it a warning, she wondered. If so, it seemed so cold to frequent a place like Matton Hall for tea and conversation while under threat of violence.

A willowy young woman in a petal pink frock swept over to them, beaming up at Mr. Ferrand. Clemency stowed her jealous thoughts, reminding herself that she had been brought there to observe and learn, not indulge in her own meaner tendencies.

"Mr. Ferrand, what a pleasure to see you again," the woman said, then took stock of his company. Ralston had come inside with them and seemed constantly to hover protectively near Delphine's side. "And you've brought company! How fortunate."

"These ladies would prefer discretion, Miss Paisley," Audric replied, giving her a respectful bow. "But for the afternoon, they are Miss Violet," he said, gesturing to Delphine. "And Miss Rose."

For my hair, Clemency thought, and smiled behind her veil. Delphine had been kind enough to outfit her in a sumptuous jewel-blue wrap dress, just big enough for Clemency's larger frame, and a pair of sapphire hairpins to fasten a lacy black veil to her bun.

Clemency—Miss Rose—gave a polite curtsey in time with Delphine.

"And Ralston is plain Ralston?" Miss Paisley teased. "What am I saying? Ralston is as strapping as ever. All that riding in the country has done you well."

Both she and Delphine turned to see Ralston, generally unflappable and serious, turn beetroot red. Delphine tittered beneath her dark purple veil.

"Is there room for us this afternoon?" Ferrand asked.

"Of course, Mr. Ferrand. There is always room for you and your party. Please, follow me."

They did, and Clemency felt her stomach growl with hunger as they weaved through the occupied tables to one on the far side of the stage, back a ways, just close enough to enjoy the music but not so close as to be overwhelmed by it. The men held out the chairs for the ladies, and then Miss Paisley wafted away, blown to the refreshment tables like a pretty pink cloud.

Clemency studied her as she left, envious of her shiny blond hair and the intricate braids it had been styled into, each weaving into the other, then pinned in a crown across her head. Her dress too was fine but not ostentatious, in last summer's style, no doubt, but fitted so well to her figure that it maintained a timeless appeal. She had a dancer's grace and swished through the maze of tables with her hands delicately aloft, her chin high, though her manner was impeccably warm and welcoming.

"They always overfeed me here," Audric grumbled, settling into the chair beside Clemency's. He tucked his knuckles under his chin and let his eyes wander to the fiddle player. "An old Parisian acquaintance introduced me to this place when last I was in town. I had come to hunt down, well, a quarry a client wanted me to find. Miss Paisley was kind enough to help. They find the most beguiling entertainers here, voices to rival any reputable opera house in London."

"We must stay to hear them," Delphine swooned. "You know how I adore a well-sung aria."

"Out of the question," he muttered. "We will be back in Grosvenor Square before dark."

Clemency thought of the pillories out on the street and shuddered. How odd, she mused, that it should feel so cozy inside, lightly fragrant with perfumes and lacquered wood, while such an ugly threat awaited just outside the door.

Ralston and Delphine struck up an animated debate about the fiddler's style—Ralston was for, Delphine found it a bit too meandering.

In a low voice, Clemency waited until they were distracted to lean closer to Audric. "Do you think Boyle comes often to such places?"

"No, not this one. This is a fine establishment; Boyle couldn't afford it." Audric smiled as Miss Paisley returned with a tray of assorted sweets for them, as well as summer wine and a bottle of sherry. Clemency knew it was impolite, but her stomach was making demands, and she snatched a buttered tart for herself. Audric smirked at her.

"Prescient, Miss Paisley, my thanks. And quite obviously hers as well."

"Yes, thank you," Clemency replied softy. "You have a lovely establishment here."

Miss Paisley glanced at Audric with her entrancing hazel eyes and then gave an answering curtsey. "I will give your compliments to our proprietor, Miss Rose."

Again, she told herself not to be jealous as Mr. Ferrand noticeably watched Miss Paisley leave them—she even threw a look over her shoulder that was clearly just for him.

"It is hard to imagine you coming here all alone," Clemency told him. She nibbled her tart. "Or anywhere, for that matter. I can only picture you on your great hunts, pacing your office while concocting plans, spinning a dagger, and cackling at your own brilliance."

"Occasionally I cease my cackling and put down my dagger and indulge in a bit of respite," Audric replied, a little shuttered, in her opinion. "Very occasionally. And why can you not imagine me here? Among the company of women, among the company of men. Does that shock you?"

"Well, yes," she admitted. Though the veil might make deception easier, she saw no benefit to lying. He had said it himself, hours earlier—her Round Orchard sensibilities were one way, and now that needle was moving ever so slowly and ever so slightly. "Are you shocked that I'm shocked?"

"No," he said, chuckling. His green eyes flashed with interest as he too leaned in toward her. "You are taking it well, all things considered."

"It is new to me, but I see no harm in it," said Clemency quietly. "You must be patient."

"You have not run screaming out the door, nor fainted in

alarm," he observed. "So I wager there is hope for you yet. I frequent many of these places when I am hunting curs. Often, they would blow through such establishments and make a greater mess. It alarmed me at first, the things I saw, but I have found more courage, kindness, and generosity in these refuges than in all the gilded operas, assemblies, and great houses of England combined." He gestured broadly to the room. "Some of the men here might wear women's clothes, and the ladies may dress as men, but they are not masquerading, here they are their true selves. Boyle is never himself to anyone; that is more reprehensible than anything you will find here before or after dark."

"Their pastries are very good," Clemency told him, finding it was not at all easy to eat with the veil. "Thank you for bringing me here. I might read widely but there is no substitute for the education of experience."

Audric stared at her for a long moment, until she wanted to hide her face even with the protection of the veil between them. She would have paid a high price to know his thoughts just then, or for him to bestow upon her another sudden kiss.

"I fear it will not be fun and games in the coming days," he said darkly. "We must pursue Boyle's past. His connections. We must know more if we are to humiliate him."

"Denning Ede," replied Clemency.

Audric's green eyes snapped to hers with renewed vigor. Her breath caught. He leaned closer, so near that his words skittered across her chin, rippling her veil, and she sighed.

"How did you know that name?"

"At Lady Veitch's Boyle was waving his name around like a sword," she continued. "He's apparently influential, and I cannot help but wonder if Boyle is using the man's power like a parasol, shielding himself from the glare of suspicion."

Under the table, she felt Audric's hand clasp hers. She stifled a gasp, and let her fingers melt into his grip. They were plotting and planning, yet it felt as though they might be alone in a quiet garden, sharing an intimate discussion of poetry or song.

"Dear lady, you are developing a talent for the hunt."

"I merely observe," she demurred. "And listen."

"And you are correct. I have stumbled across Ede's name during my investigations too. I have been trying in vain to arrange a meeting in private, but the man is a ghost to all but the most powerful. Damnation. We must find a way to approach him, carefully, and inquire about Boyle." He squeezed her hand with finality and let go and seemed ready to stand. But Clemency reached for him, dragging him back to her.

"Music. Music! He and Boyle share a passion for music—perhaps that is how their paths crossed. Surely there are any number of musical salons we could attend, and if the right society is present, then Ede might make an appearance."

"Indeed, Miss Fry, that is sharp thinking. I will put my man Stanhope on it."

"And I will ask Tansy to inquire with Lady Veitch."

Clemency felt his hand tighten around hers again. "Now it is clear to me that I could not have done this properly without you."

His eyes looked so bright, so clear, that she feared she might be the one to break this time and kiss him. Clemency took back possession of her hand, reluctantly, and clung to her cup of wine but did not drink it. A wave of sadness passed over her as she considered what might happen after their scheme was over. She had let go of her principles once to acquiesce to Boyle, she was not certain she could happily do so again.

Yet his hand . . . His lips . . . How could she ever forget the heat of him when they were parted?

"Miss Fry?" he asked, gentle. "Are you well?"

"I have chosen a wedding gown that will never be worn," she murmured. He blinked hard and fast, and looked away from her. "But whenever I feel the revulsion rising in my gorge, I just remember what he has done to your sister, and to me, to the others I'm sure you know about but have not mentioned, and to poor Mr. Connors."

"Poor Mr. Connors, is it?" His green eyes flew back to her, and he grinned, showing a dimple that made her want to reach out and trace it with her forefinger. "Hours ago you were willing to sacrifice him on the altar of society if it meant harming Boyle."

"Perhaps I am taking after you too much," she teased. "I shall need a dagger."

"But you do not think so anymore?" He ignored her jab, leaning closer. "Do you see now why we must destroy that letter to protect his dignity?"

"I do," Clemency told him, taking an uneasy sip of wine. "We should burn the letter, and when all comes to light, tell Connors to aim higher than such a false, unfeeling man. I know I intend to. I-If," she stammered, "I ever deign to consider marriage again."

"Yes," Audric said and coughed, then fiddled with his napkin, suddenly taken with his sherry and a glazed bun. "Indeed. You deserve someone far worthier."

You, perhaps? she wanted to say. But she kept silent. Clemency's eyes drifted to the table to their right, where two well-groomed young men held hands and bounced their knees to the fiddle. To be as they were, naturally and openly in love . . . She wanted it badly but remembered how she had seen what she was desperate to see with Boyle. How she had dismantled her own misgivings about marriage to let him in, and then, he had made such a mess of things, slashing her heart and spirit to ribbons.

He would not have said that, she thought, *if he loved you. He would have suggested himself. He would have spoken up.*

"This fiddler is quite good, I think," Mr. Ferrand said to his sherry.

"He plays excellently," Clemency agreed, withering into her chair. Then she said no more, realizing she could not hear the music above the disappointed drumming of blood pounding in her ears.

"Mr. Ferrand, you appear positively morose, something that you know is expressly forbidden in Matton Hall." Miss Paisley had returned with a fresh bottle of wine for them. Ralston reached for it at once, refilling his cup and offering Delphine some too. On the stage, the fiddler plunged into a spirited rendition of "Auretti's Dutch Skipper." "Now that you have had your refreshment, a dance could prove uplifting."

He folded his napkin and wedged it next to his sherry glass. "Please, Miss Paisley. You know I have little interest and even less ability where dancing is concerned."

"Nonsense, you dance as well as any gentleman I have seen."

"Then one can only conclude that you have not seen any gentlemen dance."

At that, Delphine turned away from her conversation with Ralston and reached across Clemency to swat Audric with a fan. "He is lying, of course. He danced often and handsomely in Paris, I witnessed it myself."

Audric shifted, uncomfortable. "That was many years ago."

He seemed genuinely disinclined, and Clemency refused to join in the bullying, though he turned to face her, clearly expecting her to side with her fellow ladies.

"This tune is better danced with a group," she said softly.

"*Alors, I* fancy a dance," Delphine stated, standing. Ralston hurried to accompany her, but it was Miss Paisley who reached her first, taking Delphine nimbly by the tips of her gloved fingers and leading her away to the space before the stage.

"Del— Miss Violet," Audric grunted, standing. "Mind your condition. The doctor advised—"

"I will not overexert myself," Delphine promised with a wave.

Clemency felt strange sitting there while everyone else stood and fussed over Delphine. Staring after the two ladies, Mr. Ferrand's face had turned an alarming shade of purple, his green eyes wide and apoplectic. His concern was moving, if a bit exaggerated, and Clemency found herself reaching out to touch his sleeve. As soon as she had, Audric roused himself as if from a dream, staring dumbly at the place where her hand touched him.

Before she could regret the gesture, he had taken her hand in his, cradling it gently in his palm.

"Damnation. We have no choice but to join them."

Clemency chuckled. "No choice? Does God himself compel us, sir?"

"If she is overtaken with fatigue I should rather be near to intervene," Audric said, leading her away from the table without further questioning or consultation. "She would insist upon strength she does not possess."

Whatever her opinions of Delphine, and they were generally high, Clemency did not pretend to know the extent of her ailments. She did sometimes appear frail and sickly, but now with Miss Paisley she gave an animated performance. The two women held hands and circled, weaving between invisible couples.

"Do you know the steps?" Audric asked, releasing her hand and taking up a place across from her.

"I do," replied Clemency with a sigh. "Even in little, provincial Round Orchard we have dances, sir. You attended one."

"Of course. A silly question."

"Do try to have fun," she teased as they came together and took hands again. He grasped her with a confidence that made her feel at ease, that suggested he did, in fact, know his place on the dance floor. His face was taut with concentration, brows low, lips tightly pursed.

"This excursion was a foolish idea," he muttered.

"*Your* foolish idea," she reminded him. "We can take our leave at any time, though if we leave now, while Miss Violet is enjoying herself, you may never hear the end of it."

Audric smirked and shrugged one shoulder, back in his spot across from her, next to Miss Paisley, executing a few bars of elegant footwork before returning again to take

Clemency's hands. She tried not to glance away when they rejoined, but his gaze, boring down into her, felt at times too intimate to bravely tolerate. But she made the attempt, and let herself blush freely. The pink could be blamed on the exercise.

"And what about you, Miss Rose?" he asked, voice hushed now that they were close again, practically in each other's arms. "Are you enjoying this?"

"As much as one can with an unwilling partner."

"I am not *unwilling*," Audric corrected in a huff, but he was grinning. "Besides, you have surprising grace, Miss Rose. I'm impressed, you are a more-than-adequate partner—on the dance floor and on the hunt."

This was a concerted effort to rattle her, she could feel it, and it was nearly working. Nearly. Clemency raised her head a degree higher, skewering him with her eyes through the veil. "And you would prove a most adequate partner, but only with a less severe expression. This dance is an outpouring of joy, sir. Where is your joy?"

He had time to consider the question, and he did so across from her while the fiddle dipped and dived. A small audience gathered, clapping along and whooping, mostly praising the obvious glee with which Miss Paisley and Delphine attacked the steps. As the afternoon wore on, more folk gathered in the hall, and Clemency noted a few new faces entering from the foyer, lingering there, a gentleman in a pale blue waistcoat perusing the patrons with a fond smile.

They were nearly to the end of the tune, and Clemency wished she could tear her veil off, for it made the room very warm and the dance required a good degree of concentration and exertion, not to mention coordination and energy.

The fiddler did not spare them either, racing on, part of the fun in seeing if the dancers could meet the pace, the audience clapping along, encouraging them to spin faster and faster.

Audric, crooked grin at the ready, approached her for the final hand-in-hand trot up and down the dance floor. Miss Paisley and Delphine were ahead of them, skirts flying with the speed of the steps.

"Where is my joy?" he asked softly, only loud enough for Clemency to hear. She did not mistake the small squeeze he gave her hands, his serious expression at last banished, replaced by something softer, and kind, perhaps thoughtful. "It appears my joy is here. With Ralston and Delphine . . ." His eyes settled on hers in the most peculiar way. He squinted, as if unsure of himself, and then began to say, "And with—"

"Mr. Ferrand!"

Delphine and Miss Paisley had stopped abruptly, the taller blond woman holding Delphine's forearm as the girl breathed hard, gasping for air, both of her small, gloved hands pressed to her chest as she struggled. The fiddling died down, the audience mumbling in confusion, and then Delphine ducked to the side, reeling, before she lost her footing and swooned.

"Delphine!" Audric thundered, diving for her. He caught her before she could hit the floor, Ralston at his side an instant later, the two men supporting her as she wheezed.

Clemency watched as the girl tore at the veil on her face, revealing a shine of sweat and a horribly pale face.

"Miss Paisley!" Clemency heard herself say, finding her courage amid the panic. "Have our carriage brought around now, quickly, please."

The crowd clustered nearer, but Clemency strode forward,

warding them off while Audric gathered Delphine into his arms and helped her toward the foyer, past the man with the blue waistcoat, who looked on with his chin almost on the ground.

"Disperse, please," Clemency said, following after the men and Delphine. "It is only a fainting spell, fresh air will set her to rights."

She joined them all as Audric burst through the front doors, Delphine in his arms, Ralston sprinting ahead to meet the carriage and leap up into the driver's box.

"I'm all right," Delphine murmured as he placed her into the carriage, her eyes wide and rolling. Audric swore under his breath, collapsing onto the bench. Beside him, Delphine giggled. "Lord, what a jolly afternoon."

16

Clemency walked a slow, solemn circle around Audric's study in Grosvenor Square, finding it a curiously intimate little window into his mind. It felt like her discovery of Ede had been the key unlocking her access to the inner sanctum of his machinations.

"This is everything you could find?" Audric was asking.

His hired man Stanhope stood with his arms crossed in the center of the room, eyes fixed on Clemency as she made her own investigation. The riotous hothouse flowers on Audric's desk were no doubt from Delphine, but Clemency had foolishly and jealously glanced at them anyway, to make certain they were not from an admirer. A few glowering portraits hung on the walls, and she recognized the elder Ferrand at once. He shared Audric's severe profile and gripping eyes, though somehow even the brushstrokes looked agitated and his gaze empty. Audric's dogs dozed on the rug before his desk, crowding their master's feet, jockeying for proximity.

"We are short on time, sir," Stanhope said, impatient.

"Lady Veitch gave us nothing," Clemency added. "She hates how crowded those musical rooms become and told Tansy never to ask again."

"She sounds delightful," Audric muttered.

"You have no idea."

"I reckon these are the most promising." Stanhope leaned over the papers in Audric's hands and pointed. "Crane, Hewitt, and this one, Chilvers."

"I beg your pardon!" Clemency had found another interesting portrait, this one of Audric's entire family, but she was forced to turn away from it. "I know that name . . . How do I know that name?"

Both men froze, staring at her.

"How *do* you know that name?" Audric pressed. "It has come up repeatedly in connection to Boyle."

A memory . . . a memory . . . of black ink on faded paper, a flaking wax seal pressed with a familiar design . . .

"Mrs. Chilvers! My sister's letter!" Clemency nearly tripped over both dogs as she raced to join them at the desk. "My sister asked me to deliver a letter for her in London, and it was addressed to a Mrs. Chilvers. They sometimes correspond."

Audric blinked at her over the edge of the paper. "That can be no coincidence."

"My sister is not involved in Boyle's schemes," Clemency insisted. "It could indeed be a coincidence!"

"Not where Boyle is concerned." Audric tossed the list of salons onto his desk and shooed the hounds away. "But this is a boon. We can use her knowledge of your sister to gain an invitation. Stanhope, can you arrange it? Make it known to Mrs. Chilvers that Miss Fry and a guest would like to attend the salon."

"Sir, it's tonight—"

"I noticed. Can you arrange it quickly?"

Stanhope simply tossed up his tweedy arms, withdrew a

pipe from his pocket, and stormed to the door. After it had slammed shut in his wake, Audric gave a dry laugh.

"He will see it done," exclaimed Audric, slapping his hands together with anticipation. "And that means you and I must be ready and ready soon. Will it be difficult for you to find an excuse to be absent this evening?"

"Not at all," Clemency replied. That was hardly her primary concern. "I am not altogether comfortable using my sister's friendship with this woman to advance our scheme."

His face darkened, and he gripped the edge of the desk as he leaned back against it. "Clemency, I ask you: What is our aim?"

"To leave Boyle penniless and humiliated," she replied. "I am not wavering in that, Audric, but Honora is such an innocent soul. It pains me to think she could be at all implicated in—"

"In what? We are only leveraging her knowledge of Mrs. Chilvers to attend a musical salon, nothing more. There is every likelihood that Mrs. Chilvers has nothing at all to do with Boyle, and if we act with care and tact, we need not make a scene this evening." Audric pushed away from the desk, approaching her with open hands. She had never seen him look so . . . so . . . beseeching. "Is something else troubling you?"

Everything else was troubling her. She wanted to throttle him. Then kiss him. Then disappear. Then reappear and toss herself into his arms! Her stomach was in knots as she considered how close they were coming to the end of their arrangement. She did not want it to end.

"What if Boyle is there? We cannot be seen together," she scrambled.

"True . . . True." Audric smiled down at her, then carefully tilted her chin up so that their eyes met. His hand lingered playfully along her jaw. She told herself it would not be useful for their cause to kiss the tips of his fingers, and so she quashed the urge. Only just. Did he know what he did to her? How his presence, solid and serious and steady, made her feel like the rickety, trembling ground of her life might one day be still? That he made her feel weak in the stomach but strong at heart? *Why did you kiss me?* she longed to ask. *And why won't you do it again?*

"A pity," he murmured. "That I cannot have you there at my side."

"Audric . . ."

"Yes. My mind strays from the task." He sighed as he let go of her. That was not what she meant for him to do, but perhaps it was for the best. If he touched her again that way she might burst out of her skin. "Perhaps your brother's wife might accompany you, and we will be but polite, having shared a brief acquaintance in Round Orchard."

We shared and share far more than that, sir.

"Of course," Clemency choked out. "That will be agreeable."

It will be agony.

"Then, I will see you tonight, Clemency," Audric said, his eyes dancing and alight. "I look forward to it with the utmost anticipation."

Audric was surprised to find the Chilvers home comfortable but unexceptional, hardly the type of place to lure the most influential set of the ton, but then, he did not consider him-

self an expert on the intricacies and frivolities of the exceptionally powerful. In fact, he quite eschewed them. Yet that
evening he dressed for the part, taking Delphine's cutting
advice on all matters of fashion and grooming.

"You must look your very best for Miss Fry," his sister had
said as he left the house.

"I will give her your regards," he insisted, disappearing
into the carriage.

Wrapped in a thick shawl, she called out into the night,
"Give her your own!"

Delphine was not being at all shy about her respect for
Clemency, A long list of obstacles stood between the fantasy
Delphine imagined and the far harsher reality of their lives.
He had no idea if Clemency would ever consider marriage
again. She had been exposed to the cruelest and most pernicious aspects, the mercenary, contractual calculations that
robbed unions of all real meaning. Not all marriages were
miserable, but he had witnessed the long, slow death of his
mother's spirit at the hands of his father. Elise Ferrand sang
less day by day, smiled less day by day, crushed in the tyran-
nical fist of his father's need for control.

And there was every possibility that Clemency would
only associate him with this whole messy business. Perhaps,
if she did intend to consider marriage again, she would want
a clean start, and not to be constantly reminded of Boyle's
many crimes. It ate at Audric that he could even be associated with such filth, but it was he who had started the hunt,
and it was he who had drawn Clemency into it.

Miss Fry. *Miss Fry,* not Clemency.

A subtle, welcoming glow emanated from the windows of
the Chilvers home. Stanhope had come through with a mir-

acle, arranging invitations for him, Clemency and her guest. It was a lively, warm place, perhaps not modern but filled with obviously cherished objects—faded rugs and balustrades polished by a hundred sweaty children's fingers, greasy lamps, and rump-worn sofas, portraits of little boys in blue coats, and geraniums blossoming from the wallpaper.

The obliging maid showed him to a larger sitting room, where a dozen or so of London's finest had gathered. The musicians and their glossy string instruments waited before a red-and-gold tapestry of a medieval maiden holding a falcon aloft. He stayed to the back of the room, surveying. Hunting. He found Clemency at once, for how could he not? His gaze was drawn to her like a dancer down a line, her red-gold hair jewel bright, her gown simple, white, and flattering to her alluring shape. She must have felt his eyes upon her, for she half-turned, spying him, a flicker of a smile flaming before she remembered their ruse and she twisted away.

At once, he missed the mischievous gleam of her gray eyes.

How he would go that entire evening without taking her hand and feeling its soft strength, he didn't know.

Heaven help me.

Only their plan kept him rooted there and not flying to her side. The guests began to sit down, while the lady of the house rose to address them, the musicians dropping their bows and ceasing the hair-raising scratch from finding their note.

"Thank you so much, old friends and new, for gracing us this evening," the woman, presumably Mrs. Chilvers, said. Her straw-colored hair was piled carelessly on her head beneath a black lace cap, and she wore a gown of darkest blue, a mauve lace shawl fluttering on her shoulders like dainty

wings as she spoke. She did not project the image of a fashionable London lady, but rather of someone's kindly aunt.
"The only person who loved music more than I was my
dearly deceased husband. I know he would be so thrilled that
the works of Haydn and Mozart and Beethoven still echo
among these walls, and like a beacon they have drawn you
here."

Audric took a chair in the back row and stretched his legs
out in front of him, realizing that there was nothing to do
but wait and listen until refreshments were served later. He
heard the music, or thought he did, though accepted that if
questioned about it he could give only a recounting of which
movements made Clemency sit up straighter, or lean forward, how one particular run of notes brought her hand to
her neck, and her fingers curled into a fist, as if delicately
catching a moth. It gave her such clear pleasure that it gave
him pleasure too.

The music he did not remember, but her? He remembered
her sharply. Like a dagger he remembered her, and she was
still just there, not six rows ahead of him.

The eruption of applause at the end startled him out of a
fog, and he joined in, standing, once more on the hunt.

He noted Denning Ede drifting toward the musicians to
praise them, then standing off to the side while a maid hurried over to speak with him. Stanhope had given Audric a
detailed description—a man of six and fifty, red hair fading
to silver, tall and once a good rider but gone to fat, nearly
always wearing a chrysanthemum in his breast pocket.

There was a specific thrum in the chest that came when he
knew a hunt was almost at an end, and he felt it as he watched
Clemency deftly draw Mrs. Chilvers into conversation. He

watched her press a letter into the woman's hands and saw the joy it brought the widow. As if by perfect design, the widow drew Clemency away, down a corridor, and out of sight.

Ede, meanwhile, bent his head low toward the maid. His expression soured, nostrils flaring as he adjusted his cravat, fidgeting, then followed the maid briskly down the aisle between the rows of chairs and out toward the front hall. Audric hesitated for only a moment, trusting the strange hum in his chest, giving Ede a brief head start before swiftly embarking on the chase.

17

Clemency liked Mrs. Chilvers at once. It was no mystery why she and Honora corresponded—Clemency sensed in them the same painfully raw sensitivity, an openness to feeling and sentiment that made Mrs. Chilvers appear almost fragile to the touch. Her open, good face was lined from smiling, her eyes weary and muted with the burdens of the world.

"You have no idea how much this means," Mrs. Chilvers was saying, pouring a small measure of brandy into a glass for Clemency. They stood in a close, beloved study, filled with manuscripts and half-finished needlework. A sofa, desk, and chair crowded the one large rug. As she handed Clemency the brandy, she noticed Mrs. Chilvers's fingertips were hard and ink-stained, evidence of a woman long at her needle and pen.

"A toast to you, my dear courier," the widow added. "Honora writes so sweetly of you, and I am ever so pleased to finally compare you to the heroine of her letters!"

"She flatters me," Clemency assured her, sipping. "And exaggerates."

Mrs. Chilvers laughed and fondly placed her hand over Honora's letter, which she had set on the desk.

"My sister is the gentlest creature in the whole world, she never has a cross word for anyone. Whatever saintly description she gave you is pure generosity, nothing else."

"Oh, yes," replied Mrs. Chilvers with a wistful sigh. "And that is what makes her my favorite correspondent. With her good nature, she cannot help but brighten my days, and a widow must take her ease where she can. There are diversions, of course, music and writing, but there is no replacement for the conversation of a like-minded woman."

"My condolences, Mrs. Chilvers, until this evening I was not aware that you are also a widow."

"My great loss is what led me to knowing your sister better," Mrs. Chilvers told her. She did not look sad, perhaps, but thoughtful. "When dear Edwyn passed, I found myself penning a letter of consolation, one that, then, led to many more of ardent friendship."

"Speaking of Honora makes me long for her to be here." And it was true. But even just being in the presence of a woman her sister so admired brought Clemency a measure of comfort. One that was dashed when she remembered her purpose in coming. This widow, in her dowdy dress and handmade shawl, did not strike Clemency as the type of person to associate with Denning Ede, the golden man of London's nobility and high society.

"If we both beseech her, then she has no choice but to agree!" Mrs. Chilvers grinned and drank from her glass. Clemency found it astonishing that she should host a salon with such elevated guests while her fingers were stained almost to the knuckles with ink.

"You are so prolific," Clemency observed, gesturing to the mountain of half-finished letters and manuscripts piled on the woman's desk. "I should endeavor to write more, though my words are always clumsy on paper."

"Nonsense." Mrs. Chilvers tugged at her earlobe, spreading some of the ink from her fingers. It was fresh, then. "You must share Honora's gift for expression."

"Oh, not at all."

Mrs. Chilvers glided away from her desk, standing awkwardly beside it. Over her shoulder, Clemency noted a small doorway next to the bookcase on the west wall. She was about to thank Mrs. Chilvers for her generosity in extending an invitation when there was a sharp knock at the door. Through the window above the desk, Clemency heard raised voices.

"One moment," Mrs. Chilvers called. She swept past Clemency to the door, exchanging a few quick words with a serving girl there. "If you will excuse me, Miss Fry, I shall give you something for Honora, and I will not be but a moment."

"I am at your disposal."

As soon as Mrs. Chilvers was gone, Clemency launched herself at the desk. There had to be something of interest there. She worked quickly but discovered only abandoned drafts of letters to friends and distant family, attempts at sonnets, and a few chapters on a biography of Jane Seymour. Her penmanship was confident, bold, almost masculine.

Clemency was short of breath by the time she remembered the weird little door in the corner. There on the small blue knob was a spray of fresh ink. Minding the stain, Clemency nudged the door open, saying a silent prayer that she should not be caught poking around a kind widow's study for no good reason.

Through the door, she found a dimly lit room, hardly more than a storage cupboard. It had been converted into another study, a writing room, this one oddly orderly. The chaos of the outer study made this look straight and neat as a Buckingham soldier. Clotheslines hung between the walls, drying papers pinched there, aching to be read and investigated.

Clemency huffed, fanning her face, the guilt of this trespass climbing up her face like a spreading flame. She dodged toward the closest drying paper and read.

To the esteemed Lord Boyle—

Holy God.

You will find enclosed the birth record of one Olivier Ghrist, born March 19, 1815, to unknown parents, and subsequently adopted by James Ghrist and family. They have confirmed in private correspondence that some years after the birth they were quietly paid a sum by one A. Ferrand, the money to be used as a trust for the child's education. Mr. Ghrist has agreed to the transfer of the child, along with the money set aside for the boy's future. He asks only that he be compensated for all solicitor's fees regarding this matter.

Clemency clasped both hands over her mouth, eyes sliding to the next page down the clothesline. It was the birth record in question, and what she knew to be a completely fabricated event. Turner was attempting to claim the child

Delphine gave birth to, while wiping her name off the entire affair, and removing the boy from his new parents.

The other documents were no better. They were not for Boyle, but they were all legal in nature, and all done in Mrs. Chilvers's tidy hand.

Forgeries. The quiet, maudlin widow was producing forgeries.

Why would Turner want to raise the boy himself? Just to torment the Ferrands? Whatever the reason, Clemency knew she could not allow it. She ripped the two documents from the line and folded them sloppily, shoving them down the front of her dress and tossing herself out the door, closing it swiftly behind her.

Waiting just inside the study, Mrs. Chilvers pressed her hands together and hung her head. Clemency's heart plummeted to her slippers.

"Now you know what I am," the widow whispered. "I wonder if you will listen when I tell you how it came to this."

When Audric was just a tender lad, his father took him on his first hunt. He remembered the dry whisper of the branches across his face and the nearby churn of the river, the birdsong that crested to a panic as they were alerted to a human presence, and the ruffle of feathers as they were startled out of their trees. Away, away, to elude the hunters.

The hare twenty yards off in the brush was not so lucky. Audric crouched, unseen, his father's breath hot on his neck. The boy watched the hare's eyes, bulbous and wild, its tiny velvet nose twitching as it listened and waited but did not perceive its doom.

Audric remembered thinking the hare could see him there, downwind but surely somewhat visible among the mounded leaves. He remembered the uneasy stirring in his gut as he recognized in that animal something familiar—a will to survive despite the great bigness of the world and the smallness of himself. Powerlessness and the acceptance of that fact. His father was bearing down on him, holding him roughly by the shoulder as Audric hoisted the rifle to aim. He fired and missed the easy shot.

His father's grip turned biting and cruel.

"Always you stumble at the crucial moment. Fool boy."

He was no longer afraid of the vastness of the world, and he no longer felt powerless. He would not stumble at the crucial moment.

Concealed by the shadow of a tall, crumbling garden statue, he watched Denning Ede worry his thumb across the top of a crystal glass, pacing among the unblooming azaleas and rain-soft earth. A cold, lush smell filled the garden, the plants and bushes growing unchecked, a primitive, overrun remnant of some more refined time.

The far-off lanterns glowing along the walls at the edge of the property showed Ede to have a face older than his years. Worry lived deep in the cracks along his forehead, eyes, and mouth. Audric pressed himself against the statue as footsteps rapidly approached.

"I hope you realize you have disrupted a most pleasant evening," muttered Ede.

"Your little hobbies can wait. Until our business is concluded I own you."

That thrum in his chest had not lied—their quarry had come. Turner Boyle lurked under the high collar of a thick coat, his red hair a tangled snarl as he grabbed the cup out of Ede's hands and drank from it.

"I suppose none of this behavior should shock me," the older man said with a sigh. "You remind me so much of my younger self. It is truly humbling. And sobering."

"Inspiring, I think you mean." Boyle laughed darkly. "Ambition runs in the blood."

In the blood? Audric strained to see the two men better.

"The documents will be yours this evening. Chilvers is the very best in London. The child is made your ward, and the Boyle line is no longer extinct. Unless your godforsaken parents return from America, they will be none the wiser. It is finished, boy, do you hear me? It is finished, and you will never extort another farthing from me. I only have one final question: What makes this child so important to you?"

"He is a loose end," Boyle replied with a shrug. "This is the beginning of the rest of my very happy life, and I will not leave anything to chance."

"May God have mercy on that boy."

Boyle returned the glass, though Ede was reluctant to take it. "I am most obliged, *Father*."

"Insolent welp," Ede hissed. He took a threatening step toward Boyle. "Stupidly, I once admired your mother's soft heart, but now I see what it has produced. You should have been hided, hard and often; it might have made you a man instead of this . . . this beast."

"It takes one to know one." Boyle performed a mockery of a bow. "Thank you for your cooperation in these matters, Father."

"Never speak that word to me again!" The crystal cup flew across the garden, shattering against the statue that sheltered Audric. Glass twinkled down into the bushes, hard, glinting tears. "With this done, you are no longer my issue, you are Boyle's, and this child is a Boyle. Do not forget that this pistol is pointed both ways, boy."

"How could I?" Boyle sneered. "A bastard is never allowed the luxury of forgetfulness."

"Or gratitude. Or humility, it seems." Ede seemed to wilt, his shoulders collapsing inward. "Go and go now, before you are seen. My courier will handle what remains."

With another ridiculous bow, Boyle was gone.

18

Clemency's mind spun so fast the room tilted, a blur of bad wallpaper and Oriental rugs, an upside-down Vauxhall fireworks explosion that left her clutching the back of a chair for support. She had wandered out from Mrs. Chilvers's study in a fog, taking careful, tiny steps until she at last rejoined the other guests and lost herself briefly in their too-loud laughter.

"Clemency! Oh, you are quite pale! Are you ill?" Tansy had come, peering into her face with a worried expression.

"Some air will set me to rights," Clemency lied. She would need rather more than some air. But anywhere other than that hot, crowded room would be an improvement. "Stay," she told Tansy. "Just . . . stay. I will not be long."

The documents hidden in her bodice scratched against her skin, an unfriendly reminder of all that had just transpired. Awhirl. Her brain was awhirl. She hurried clumsily to the entrance hall and then out the door, ignoring the maid who looked stricken at the thought of her going out without a wrap.

Before she could even finish descending the stoop, a strong hand took her by the wrist and tugged. She fell easily into Audric's arms, gasping as her forehead bumped his shoulder. Away he took her, toward a bewilderingly rugged garden. Her slippers crunched over broken glass, then she felt solid stone at her back and gratefully leaned against it. Cool, galvanizing air rushed into her as she stared blearily up at Audric. His face was the flushed counterpart to her paleness.

"We have him, Clemency!" he said in an excited whisper. "His schemes are diabolical, indeed, but we have him. Oh, but the man is a scoundrel of the highest order, a cannon, and the radius from the blast . . ."

"Then, you know about the papers," Clemency replied, gradually returning to herself. She withdrew the documents hidden in her dress and offered them to Audric. It was only then that she remembered the sealed letter held tightly in her left hand.

"Boyle has been trying to patch up the scandal of his family," Audric explained, perusing what she had given him. His cheeks turned a bolder shade of red. "He should have been the Boyle heir, and a true baron, but Ede is his father. I always wondered how he could evade ton scrutiny, but Ede was cleaning up all of his messes, establishing him as the true issue of Lord Boyle, resurrecting an extinct line."

"And making poor Delphine's little boy his ward. He must be afraid of your retribution." Clemency shook her head, exhausted and disgusted. "With Denning Ede involved this all feels so sinisterly beyond my scope. It is hard even to fathom it."

Audric folded the documents and tucked them swiftly into his interior coat pocket. "You must not waver now, Clemency, not when we have Boyle in our sights. Ede too must be dealt with somehow. From his political pulpit the hypocrite preaches tradition while legitimizing his own bastard to continue another family's line. Despicable."

"Is this not all very sad?" she asked, slumping. "It will not just be Boyle ruined, but Ede and Chilvers too."

"They are complicit!"

"They are likely blackmailed!"

Audric's elation evaporated, his mouth firming up into a grim line. He took the letter from her left hand, holding it up to read the inscription.

"What are you doing?" she asked, pushing away from the statue. "That is for my sister."

"It is evidence."

"It is private correspondence!" Clemency did not ask again, snatching the letter for Honora out of his grasp. "Mrs. Chilvers was forthcoming once caught. Her husband had an unnatural end, meeting with misadventure due to his forgeries. The threats against his life and his considerable debts were passed to her, she had no choice but to survive. Honora had written of my closeness with Boyle, giving her reason to think he was an honorable man."

"She is not innocent, whatever your sympathies for her," Audric replied, crowding her against the statue. "Think, Miss Fry. Think what she would have done to my sister!"

"And now we have stopped it, and I have her word that she will stand with us against Boyle, corroborate whatever evidence we present against him." Clemency hugged the letter protectively to her chest. "And I do have sympathy for her. Once more, marriage bringing down nothing but woe and calamity."

Audric fell silent for a moment, studying her with an intensity she disliked. "This is not about marriage."

"It most certainly is. You talk of cannons and all that gets caught in the blast—that is what women are in this world. The forgotten damage. The debris left on the field. Your sister, mine, Mrs. Chilvers, me, all dependent on the changing whims of men!"

Audric took a step back, studying the tops of his boots. "This is my error. It was folly to involve you, Clemency. But you must have known that this was always our destination. Did you think destroying a man would be clean? Easy?"

Clemency shook her head, sensing his rising irritation with her. But she could not sustain his same rage. Publicly destroying Boyle might bring Audric satisfaction, but at what cost? She would not set aside her misgivings, for she knew them to be reasonable. Clemency reached for his hand, but he did not return the gesture. "I do not wish to quarrel—"

Her gloved hand hovered there, a white dove ignored. He made no move toward her, and an icy shiver speared through her. Perhaps a need for revenge occupied all the space in his heart where she might be instead.

"Then do not stand in my way."

"No one ever does, do they?" Clemency dropped her hand and wished with all her might that he would relent, and bend, and take her in his arms. There was a loving man inside there, walled off behind what pain had built.

"Except you," he said softly and glanced away.

"Yes, me." Clemency stepped around him carefully, mindful never to let their bodies or garments touch. When she sought out his gaze, he avoided her. She pleaded silently for him to fight for her, for this, for them, for what she suspected could be if he set aside his obsession and she overcame her fears. *Fight for me, love me, love me in the way of stories, of legends and fairy tales, be mine in the way I need.* Miss Bethany Taylor would shriek at such weakness, but then, it was only honest to admit that she *did* feel weak. And Clemency felt a sudden frisson of fear that they might never see each other again. It passed, but the terror lingered. Well. If he insisted on stubbornness, then so did she. "Mr. Ferrand, I will continue our partnership until the night of the assembly, and then our business and acquaintance is concluded. Good night, sir."

19

Clemency tossed another balled-up attempt at a letter into the fire, watching the parchment flare and snarl as the flames overtook it. And good riddance. She had exhausted that sheet of parchment, scratching out so many thwarted feelings and frustrations that the attempt simply couldn't be salvaged.

Mr. Ferrand, one draft read. *Perhaps my final words to you in the garden were hasty; they were said in anger.*

That felt too conciliatory. Clemency would not be apologizing. She was not infatuated with him, she insisted, she was not in love, and she was seeking only civility, not full reconciliation. Reading Miss Taylor's pamphlet again had soothed her, reminded her of her principles, and helped her realize the madness he had planted in her. In the next draft, she opened more forcefully, demanding his contrition. But that too wasn't quite right. Over and over again she tried to express herself without coming across as either too simpering or too haughty, and to no avail. *Well,* she thought, *maybe I am both simpering and haughty.* Then: *No, no, no, Honora would have a conniption if she heard me speak to myself that way. Where is the grace? Where is the kindness?*

She sighed at the little desk in the room with the pink

curtains and old quilts and let down her forehead to rest on her arms. When she was little she often argued endlessly with William, chasing him up and down the stairs, refusing to let him have the last word. When, inevitably, William finally lost his temper with her and locked her in a linen closet, her father would appear to drag her out, wipe the tears from her cheeks, and remind her gently: "You are both too stubborn! Two hard heads, impossible! Heads like stones. You can crash those stones together all day long, but eventually you will only make powder of each other."

Clemency perhaps learned the wrong lesson from this scolding. Instead of finding a way to communicate more effectively with her brother, she simply learned to avoid him. If he picked a fight, she gave him the silent treatment, a different sort of victory. Now that failure to ever really swallow her tongue and take her lumps had resulted in this cold, terrible rift with Audric. They had been going along nicely too, but days had passed with no sign of either of them putting an end to the stalemate.

If she confessed. If she admitted how deeply she felt . . .

But no.

Time seemed strange while she stayed at the Bagshots' and tried to sew and read and busy herself while her stomach tied itself in ever tighter knots. Word from the modiste came that the lace she had chosen could not be gotten in the quantity they needed in time, and so they would send over new samples for her to see. Her gown. The wedding. Time. It kept going apparently; things moved unfairly forward. She saw the family for meals, and sometimes sat with Tansy in the drawing room and listened to her recall all the latest gossip from Lady Veitch's circle, and she remained strangely

above it, floating, separated from the experiences by a fasci-
nation with how the time passed. She was waiting, she knew,
waiting either for the right words to come and then be sent,
or for Mr. Ferrand to surrender in this silent war. Neither
thing happened, and she could not help but fixate.

Now and then Turner Boyle made an appearance, all
smiles and courteous bows, just back from the club, or from
a lecture hall debate, melding seamlessly into whatever occupied William and Tansy. And Clemency would watch for
some sign of all the deception, forcing herself not to bring
up Mrs. Chilvers and Denning Ede, though she yearned to
do so. What was he doing? What was his game? In his mind,
he must be thinking that he had won. Sometimes she did
detect a crack in his smiles, just the smallest hint of something else, always as he was entering the room, the mask slipping for just a chilling instant. Whenever it happened, she
was flooded with disgust, a tremble running through her as
she remembered how he had humiliated her and made her
feel stupid and small for loving him ardently.

On the night of her humiliation, she had promised him to
be a steadier sort of woman, and so she endured and played
the part, but always took note of those gaps in his armor.
Those flashes of the man underneath frightened her, reminding her that he too was scheming and plotting, and the
stranger beneath the smile became like a player waiting to
take his mark. As Boyle entered the room, he was still not
quite onstage, and then he became someone else and the grin
spread wide and everyone who saw it was in his thrall, while
Clemency noted only the masquerade of it all. After all *she*
was playing a part too.

At last, Clemency knew she would not write Audric,

she would not call for a détente. She had let Boyle control
her life for too long, and she would not allow Audric to do
so simply because he was less odious. The revelation ought
to have ended her nausea and preoccupation, but it did
not. Still, with that settled, she considered writing Nora yet
again, but she had already sent her a truly deranged number
of letters, and it was her turn to stop and wait, impossible as
it might seem.

Her brief foray into patience paid off when, not an hour
later, while her mind wandered and she stared idly into a
cooling cup of tea, Tansy's maid arrived to deliver a letter on
a little porcelain dish.

Clemency recognized the hand at once.

At last! At last. Word from dearest Nora at last. She still
possessed the letter Mrs. Chilvers had written for her sister,
for the widow had insisted it be delivered by Clemency in
person. She devoured Honora's latest letter, of course, her
spirits and hopes lifting as she reached the treasure at the end
of the rainbow of a message: Nora was coming to London.
Clemency clung to the letter as if it were the only star left in
a darkened sky.

Nora would already be on the road to her, with perhaps
only a day or two until her arrival, the brief but agonizing
wait made easier by the knowledge that her sister would be
with them soon, and—out for the evening with Tansy, William, and Turner Boyle at Lady Veitch's salon—Clemency
kept the letter folded up in her small velvet bag, for just the
nearness of it brought her immeasurable strength. *I can get
through this; she is coming. She will be here soon. Nora will
be here soon; I can get through this.* Clemency dreaded the
conversation they might have about Mrs. Chilvers, but also

Honora knew the widow better. Perhaps she might impart some much-needed advice.

The assembly at Almack's loomed, and with no word from Audric, Clemency had to wonder if their whole plan was off and she was fawning over the dreadful *Lord* Boyle for nothing. She hesitantly kept faith and reminded herself that they had more than enough evidence to prove Boyle was a grasping, lying criminal, and Nora would soothe her, no matter what her advice. Her older sister always did.

The drizzle and rain persisted, a perfect mirror for Clemency's mood as one day oozed into the next, a gray, dismal blur. She hardly heard the others in the grand salon around her as they giggled and gossiped over cards. Lady Veitch's daughters proved surprisingly shrewd at whist and had already taken turns beating William until he was forced to retreat with Boyle to the sherry tray near a white ornamental bookcase at the back of the cavernous, soaring room.

Arabella and Adeline in their turbans and gaudy purple gowns fell to playing against each other, since nobody else in the room was their equal, not even Tansy. Well, Clemency assumed Boyle could play quite well, for what was a scheming man without a mind and eye for cards? He avoided them, however, choosing to linger hawkishly by the bookcases, idling there with a predatory energy that reminded her of Mr. Ferrand, which made her extremely cross, and so she did not look at Turner if it could be helped.

"Mrs. Fry!" Lady Veitch screamed from her customary sofa, looking regal and underplucked, with a profusion of ostrich feathers arcing up over her turban. "Entertain us at once, the quiet exacerbates the chill!"

Tansy leapt up from her place beside Clemency and went

to the pianoforte, with all the grace and dignity of a doe-eyed, scolded puppy. Her playing and singing began, and Clemency had to admit that it did somewhat improve the atmosphere.

"Now we may speak, Miss Fry, because all this evening I have detected in you what I call lover's melancholia."

She arched a thin silvery brow and leaned toward Clemency, heaving her significant bosoms in her direction, sending out a cascade of rose water and orange blossom fragrance.

Clemency winced inside, and remembered Honora's fortifying letter, reaching to place her hand over the bag containing it, clutching it like a talisman against whatever was to come. It had felt like everything was crumbling until she received that letter—now she would not be alone, left to unravel the sad mess she had made of things in London. She knew it wasn't entirely her fault; Audric had been out of line in the garden, and his demeanor frightened her. He had deserved her silence, but then, when the silence went on and on, and he did not write or call or make himself known to her at all, she realized her error.

That great and terrible silence was satisfying only until the sting of their argument wore off, and then she felt adrift, relying only on her copy of Miss Taylor's *On Marriage* for wisdom and strength.

Her existence had become a series of interwoven sighs and would remain that way until Nora arrived, and the assembly was had, and she could return to Round Orchard a solitary but ultimately *free* woman. That freedom, for some reason, didn't seem as attractive as it should. Annoying. But that would change, she assured herself, when all this business was over and it would just be her and Nora again, happily unmarried and unbothered sisters. A perfectly contented pair.

"Lover's melancholia?" Clemency forced herself to ask.

"Mother invents all manner of silly things," said Adeline with a titter.

"Your opinion was not requested, young lady, attend to your hand. From where I sit, you are losing!" Lady Veitch sniffed and fanned herself and turned her withering gaze once more on Clemency. "It comes upon us all, my dear, no need to fret. A bride before matrimony is necessarily consumed with the future, and that is never healthy for a woman. Our minds were meant for singular tasks, and to be split so is quite disorienting."

Clemency wanted to tell her that she was, at that moment, split in about sixteen different directions. Instead, she smiled mildly and said, "And did you yourself suffer from this before your wedding?"

"Naturally! Naturally. Sir John was the best of men and so very sought-after, but even so, I had my doubts. A young woman yearns for freedom until she knows the gratification of submission." She gazed around, waiting for a response, but received only Clemency's bemused smirk and her own daughters' giggles.

"Yet you yourself did not remarry, Your Ladyship," Clemency pointed out cheerfully. It was a blessing Tansy could not hear her veering dangerously into cheek. "So I wonder: How gratifying can that submission be after all?"

If nothing else, needling this rich old cream puff made her feel somewhat alive again. *Small miracles.*

Lady Veitch narrowed her eyes. "This is the result of your

unfortunate reliance on novels, which contain all forms of frippery and fantasy. It degrades one's sense of reality. Ah well, marital bliss awaits you soon, my dear, and all such nonsense is quashed beneath the yoke of a wife's duties."

"And how attractive that sounds," Clemency murmured, standing. "Bliss, indeed! I can scarce contain my excitement. Oh, look! The rain has eased, I think I shall take advantage of your lovely balcony again, madam."

Perhaps I will hurl myself off it for a real thrill and a merciful end to this conversation.

Lady Veitch sighed and adjusted her heavy skirts. "It *is* perfectly situated. As you please, my dear. Perhaps a bit of air will put roses in your cheeks again, lest that lover's melancholia take hold of you for good."

It was too late for that, Clemency thought, trying not to go too swiftly to the doors and give herself away. She couldn't stand to hear one more sanctimonious word from Lady Veitch, even if sparring with her did bring the blood up.

"Lord," she muttered, breaking out into the cold air with a relieved gasp. She inhaled deeply, fond of the crisp, wet edge to the air when rain abated.

"Do not be long, dear!" she heard Lady Veitch call after her. "I do so enjoy our lively conversations."

Clemency curtseyed and then turned back toward the road, grinning. Yes, a bit of debate *was* diverting. And in fact, it was what made her sorely miss her time with Mr. Ferrand. Joyful, one might call it. Clemency grunted and fit her hands around the railing, her fingernails scraping against the molded stone. That dreadful, stubborn, infuriating man! Everything in her heart ought to revolt at the thought of him, but the opposite was true—she thought too often of his keen green eyes and tousled black curls, of his wit, and of his overbearing tenderness for his sister.

She realized she had closed her eyes, conjuring the image of him. Why couldn't she just be smart and resolute and hate him?

"Miss Fry?"

Her fantastical conjuring would have to wait. Adeline had followed her out onto the balcony, hands poorly concealing a folded letter that she had tried to tuck into the fabric of her skirt. Lady Veitch's daughter gave one glance back toward the assembled party and then tiptoed forward, easing herself out of their sight.

"Yes?" She put on a smile for the girl, whose brow was already furrowed in consternation.

"You speak so forcefully on the subject of marriage, I wondered if you might give me counsel now." Adeline gave a weak titter, but she had gone pale. She handed Clemency the letter she had been hiding and shook her head, her turban bobbing perilously on her tight ringlets. "I have acquired an unexpected suitor. My mother and sister know nothing of it, and I find myself quite in a tangle. You see, I have never met him, but he writes so ardently of his affection for me, just the sight of me going by in Mother's carriage has moved him to almost poetic passions. . . ."

Clemency's hackles rose at once. An unknown suitor writing to a woman of great wealth and average intelligence did not fill her with hope for a wise romantic match. Still, she reached for the letter, unfolded it, and began to read. Her suspicions only doubled.

"How did this letter come to be in your possession?" she asked. "If you have never met the gentleman?"

"A strange little boy approached me along the Ladies' Mile and waited until Mother and Arabella were distracted, then prevailed upon me to take the note." Adeline frowned and pinched both of her forefingers and thumbs together. "I did not expect to find a love confession!"

"No, of course not," Clemency murmured. "I must advise caution in this matter. While the gentleman is certainly . . ." She searched for the right word, aware that this might be Adeline's first brush with romance and wary of spoiling it entirely. Even if she did not marry this odd suitor, she might still come away with a fond memory of his love-struck effusion. ". . . Persuasive, this is about general love."

"General love?" Adeline's frown deepened. "How do you mean, Miss Fry?"

Clemency returned the letter, convinced she had spied a line or two lifted completely from a Henry Fielding novel. The suitor had signed his name only as "Your Admirer." "He does not write of you but of feelings a man might have for any woman. He has no knowledge of you, of your passions, your life, your aspirations . . . This is a man desperate to be in love, not necessarily in love with you."

Adeline went still, then gradually her frown hardened into a grim line. "I am afraid you speak sense, Miss Fry." She turned to go, then paused and whirled back again. "Then I should avoid him? Truly you think so?"

Avoid love writ large, sweet girl. Maybe an errant copy of *On Marriage* could turn up in Adeline's things and steer her in the right direction.

There was no reason to prolong the disappointment. "I would say so, yes. I am sorry; it is never enjoyable to counsel against attachment, but in this case the gentleman has given me no choice. And you did want my honest opinion, did you not?"

The girl filled with resolve once more, though Clemency knew this cycle of wistful sadness and resilience might need to occur several more times. "I did. Thank you." The smallest smile graced Adeline's round face as she looked Clemency up and down, satisfied. "It is understood that unfashionable women may lack style but often make up for it with an abundance of reason, as you have just demonstrated."

In return, Clemency offered a tight-lipped smile, refusing to be offended or even surprised by a rich young woman's impertinence. "How well said."

Adeline remembered to curtsey before bustling back into the house and away from the balcony. When the girl was gone, she went again to the railing and the city spread out below, lost again in thought, wondering just what Mr. Ferrand would say to Adeline about her situation. No doubt he would have harsher words for her, having no patience for what was obviously a scheme or utter nonsense.

Clemency peered out into the darkness, pools of lantern light illuminating the rain-slicked street at intervals. Coaches went up and down, wheels sloshing through puddles, hooves clattering over cobbles, while music drifted out from every parlor window, a softly mad symphony played to the night. Standing in one such pool, across from Lady Veitch's stately townhouse, was a man in an imposing black coat, his hat under one arm, his height, stature, and silhouette achingly familiar.

"It cannot be," she whispered. But she knew it was. He had somehow found her and was standing there, watching. Her whole heart opened, and the sudden rush of relief made her dizzy.

"Escaping again? Hardly seems fair."

Damn it all. Another intrusion.

Boyle had chosen that exact moment to pounce, sherry heavy on his breath as he crowded her against the railing. With his height and vantage, he might easily see Audric idling in the lantern light across the street. Clemency stepped to the side, hoping to draw his gaze away. She wanted desperately to see if Audric was still standing there, but dared not flick her eyes in that direction.

Would Turner recognize him at this distance? Was it worth taking that risk? Did she even care? The dizziness made her reckless. But no, Audric was close now, and she must be careful and momentarily patient. Clemency felt sure her heart would tumble right out of her mouth as she pretended to laugh and primp her hair. "Oh, I am hardly escaping, I think she is hilariously entertaining."

"Then why have you fled?" The pretend baron had found a gleaming suit for the evening, the dark green a dashing counterpart to his ginger hair. He put one hand on the railing beside her, aggressively close to her own fingers.

"I am merely collecting myself for the next sortie," Clemency said. "This was a momentary rest."

"What did the old bat say that drove you out here?" His eyes searched her face, and she felt a guilty flush creep up her neck. Turner reached up and touched a single reddish-gold curl framing her face. Without meaning to, she flinched.

"Some . . . interesting talk of marriage."

"And that upset you?" He frowned and inched yet closer. His breath stank of drink. "Should I be worried?"

"Not at all," she replied, slapping on a smile. "But if I let her continue on we were at risk of Mary Wollstonecraft and Olympe de Gouges rising from their graves to throttle her, and that seemed like simply too much disruption for a Tuesday."

Turner slid his hand lower, trying to cup her jaw. Shaking her head, Clemency pushed his hand away.

"The curtains are just so," he whispered. He was drunk. Drunk on his seeming victory, no doubt, confident that Denning Ede and Mrs. Chilvers had solved all of his many, many problems. "They cannot see us. We are soon to be married, Clemency, so where is the harm in it?"

She was meant to be seducing him, drawing him in, but now it felt too burdensome. The thought of his sherry-laced kiss turned her stomach.

"You asked me to hold my feelings close," Clemency reminded him. "My passion was silly and revolting, remember? Childish and smothering. You made the words hard to forget and I am attempting to do better."

He drew up short, his expression suddenly puzzled. The trees rattled quietly, a sound like a city-wide whisper warning that the rain had returned. Boyle glanced upward and grinned crookedly. "Yes, Miss Fry, you have taken my words so to heart that it moves me. And it moves me to kiss you now. Will you not embrace your betrothed?"

Though he asked, he did not wait for her answer and

leaned close, darting his head down toward her, crashing his lips against hers while she squirmed and shrieked, his mouth swallowing the sound. This was a theft, and she heard a strange sound ripple through her head, like a crack, a fracturing. He was taking something from her, this intimacy.

No, she thought. *This isn't a kiss, it's a theft, and so it isn't real. It cannot be real.*

Clemency went rigid, then convulsed at the crack of a sudden pistol shot. It split the night, silencing all the music leaking from the surrounding windows and sending Boyle rearing back toward the railing. For a moment, she feared one of them had been shot, but no red stains appeared on his shirt. Turning toward the park, Clemency watched a puff of smoke dissipate into the rain, visible for only an instant in a pool of yellow light.

"What the devil!" Boyle huffed, searching the darkness.

"Was that a shot? It sounded like a pistol!" William appeared in the open balcony doorway, and Clemency saw her chance, rushing past both of them.

"I've had such an awful fright," Clemency stammered truthfully but in a voice she didn't recognize. She felt faint and wandered away from the sofa and the ladies, who had all leapt to their feet, cards scattered across the plush carpets. "Can one of your men take me home?"

"Of course, dear, but you must wait, surely your nerves are flustered. Sit down, now, sit and you will have a tonic and—"

"Thank you, Lady Veitch," Clemency said, pretending only to hear the first bit. She found her way out, skirt held up out of the way, heart hammering as she sped by statues and busts, down the marble stairs to the grand foyer, through the tangle of nervous servants who had also heard the shot, and out into the frigid rainy night.

She approached the nearest valet, but she saw, down the drive and out beyond the black gate, the silhouette of a tall man. He leaned against the gate, and she managed a wobbly smile.

"Shall I have the coach brought 'round, miss?" the valet was asking, rain dripping from his hat.

"No . . . No, I think I'll find my own way."

"But, miss! The weather—Lady Veitch—"

"Thank you!"

Clemency hurried down the wide stone path, half-listening to the commotion from the windows above, determined to leave before Lady Veitch could put her foot down and send the footmen after her. At some point she simply stopped hearing the pandemonium, her eyes and heart and mind focused ahead on the man who turned and began walking away as she approached. As soon as she was free of the property and rounded the gate, she felt his warm hand close around hers and pull. Clemency followed and laughed as the rain slid off her nose, and Audric's big heavy coat fell over her shoulders, guarding her from the downpour.

It smelled distinctly of spent gunpowder.

"You missed," she whispered, and he squeezed her hand.

"Ha. My carriage is not far."

"How did you know where to find me?" she asked, taking three steps to each of his.

"I will tell you all," Audric told her. No, it was a firm reassurance. A promise. She sensed that it was about far more than just how he located her. The carriage shimmered out of the mist and rain, sleek, shining, and black, the team of horses stamping, streamers of white smoke pouring from their nostrils in the cold. "I will tell you all."

"No." Clemency stopped short, skidding a little on the wet cobbles. "Wait."

Momentary patience. She had possessed it, but now it was gone. The carriage intimidated her—she could only remember what had come before when they were last alone, his anger, his stubbornness, the arguing that had driven a wedge between them for days and days.

Audric spun to face her, and drawing close, he became all she could see. The carriage, the horses, the street, London, the world, all was blotted out as both of his hands reached for her, cupping her face. She saw a strange light in his green eyes, as intense and hungry as ever, but now he looked quite starved.

Her heart stopped, the rain drove hard against them, and he gave her a trembling half-smile. "Waiting is something I can no longer do."

There in the downpour he kissed her. Clemency's whole heart was open, and then it was full, and she went up onto her toes, looping her arms around his neck, holding him there and delighting in his warm lips, the surest banishment for the cold.

This was a true kiss—not a theft but a gift, and she swelled toward him, grateful in the receiving and in the ardently returning. She had sworn off love, but how, oh God, could she swear off *this*? Surely, she would be mad to do so, even if marriage and passion and love were madness too.

His hands held her fast, and he sighed softly in the back

of his throat as they kissed. It had to go on and on, she would make it so. Stubborn, stupid, infuriating, beautiful man . . . How was she ever to forget this?

Her whole heart was open to him, and it hurt like nothing had hurt before.

20

Now that he had her alone, the words he had practiced for days did not come as easily as he expected. His refined speeches and perfect phrasings fled him, perhaps all broken and shattered by that one pistol shot, that one mad impulsive decision that led them now to shiver and exchange glances on his sitting room rug.

"First the river and now this," Clemency said, drying herself near the fire. Delphine had long ago retired to her room upstairs, and upon returning home, Mr. Ferrand had left Ralston with strict instructions that he and Miss Fry were not to be disturbed.

"I must look dreadful," she continued. "Practically drowned."

In fact, the opposite was true. With her back to him, Audric had the opportunity to gather his courage and to admire the way the silk of her dress clung just so to her figure. Her reddish-blond hair streamed behind her, having fallen free of its pins and ribbons in the carriage ride. That was his fault, he knew, for they had kissed again there, and his fingers had found their way to her hair, and whenever he touched her or held her, he was reminded again of how little she was in his grasp. His coat hung drying by the hearth too; Miss Fry had all but been disappeared by it out in the rain.

Audric smiled and ran his hand over his face, aware that he too was less than presentable.

"I apologize, Clemency, if my pistol shot gave you a fright."

She shook her head and reached back to sweep her damp waves into a simple swirl on the crown of her head. This revealed her delicate profile, and the pretty architecture of her throat and upper shoulders. He took a step toward her, a single sofa between them, one he felt sure he could tear in half with need for her. But he had let his simpler impulses rule him before, and it had resulted in a loss of temper that frightened her and left him chastened and alone, prowling his house like a forgotten leper.

Stanhope had assured him during that time that he and his minions were hard at work, but that did not soothe Audric, and so he was beset on all sides by frustration.

"Oh, no, it was no more frightening than the prospect of kissing that toad," she replied, at last turning to face him.

At that, his lip curled. "I am not proud of it, but the thought of him laying his hands on you was—is—unthinkable. No doubt he wanted to draw you into a compromising position, something untoward that he might use against you later."

Audric regretted the words at once, for they made her face fall.

She looked away from him as she removed her gloves and placed them on the mantel to dry. "Is . . . Is it so outlandish to think maybe he finds me beautiful? That a man might desire me for reasons unrelated to schemes and plots?"

Audric strode quickly around the sofa, going to Clemency and taking her hands in his. She did not resist him, and that at least was a comfort. The days of silence had stretched on and on, worsened by his obsessive need to trail Boyle. The scoundrel split his time between the club, a cheap dockside tavern, and the home of the Bagshots, though he sometimes visited the home of Mr. Jack Connors, and the two had apparently reconciled. That Boyle was on (what was for him) good behavior alarmed Audric immensely. It appeared that he was content to let the marriage with Clemency go through, to play that hand and gamble on it, now allegedly a true, titled baron, and while Audric remained confident Clemency would never really let that happen, a chance lingered . . . a small chance . . .

A devilishly small chance that made him completely insane. What if she married Boyle after all out of spite or because she felt driven to it by desperation?

His eyes softened as he stroked his thumb across the top of her hand, something he had imagined himself doing many times before. It seemed that this should have happened long ago, when he first fished her out of that river, struck by her beauty, struck more so by her quickness, her wit.

"*En effet,* are we speaking now of Boyle or of someone else?" he asked.

Clemency frowned, then quirked her lips to the side. Her eyes flitted away. "And is it so strange to ask? We are only partners after all, our roles understood and defined. Why should I not wonder if you will only pretend to want me because it humiliates your enemy?"

Audric squeezed his eyes shut and sighed, then took her by the chin and tilted it up until she relented and gazed into his eyes. "I want you everywhere, little fool."

Her lips parted in surprise, and he found them too tempting an offer to resist. When he kissed her under the hard drumming of the rain it felt like a question, and here was the answer: No amount would be enough. Many times during their acquaintance he cautioned himself that any fire lit by her presence was simply the result of her stubborn, contrary nature, that it was not passion he felt but outrage, but he had been telling himself a lie. One could struggle against the obvious truth for only so long, and the struggle proved exhausting. But with her chin in his hand, her warm little body pressed against him, her clumsy but enthusiastic kiss was undeniably, beautifully restorative. All the lies were forgotten, the truth so evident.

Clemency put her hands on his chest and opened her mouth wider, making the sweetest, most curious noise of elation as their tongues met. Her excitement encouraged him; he wanted her, but he was a man on fire standing in dry kindling, and if he was not cautious now, he might frighten her away. They need wait only until after the assembly, when her betrothal was broken and he could come to her, a free woman, as a freed man. Audric gently moved her back, holding her by the shoulders. Her lashes fluttered, and then she was peering up at him with hot, searching eyes.

"This time without you has been a torment," he said, hoarse. "And I brought it upon us both. My father was a cold, unmovable man, never ruled by passion or gentility. He crushed my mother's spirit to ash, and I promised myself many times that I would never become him, but I crept too close to his shadow when I refused to hear your concerns. You were right to waver in the garden. What we do here is challenging, and terrible, and the consequences will be serious; to ignore such things is only stubbornness, only pride."

Clemency sighed and shook her head. "I behaved stubbornly too. I tried to write, Lord but I tried to write."

Audric couldn't help but laugh. "God. So did I."

"You should know that I have taken the counsel of books and thinkers wiser than I and sworn off love."

"Indefinitely?" He grinned.

"Do not smile. Do not laugh at me!" But he did, only gently. It was not a mocking gesture, for how could he mock such a decision after all Boyle had done? He himself had done the same. Many times. "I have sworn it off."

"Could you be persuaded to reconsider?" Audric asked, schooling his expression to one of seriousness, which she noticed.

"I . . . maybe. How did you find me?" she asked.

The fire beside them was growing cumbersomely hot, and Audric's chest was already simmering with another sort of heat. He guided her away from the hearth, back to the sofas, fetching them both a measure of fortifying sherry before sitting beside her and watching the flames over her shoulder turn her reddish-blond hair to fiery gold.

"It's all around the club that your brother and his wife have become Lady Veitch's favored companions. It occurred to me that you might be dragged along to her salons too." Audric was intent on schooling himself back to a state of reason, but he couldn't help but reach out and touch one of the dangling locks framing her face. It was gratifying to see her blush.

"Mm. Just how long were you waiting there in the rain?"

Audric stuffed his nose down into his glass. "Your charms are many and not to be underestimated, Clemency, but you will never know the answer to that question."

"Then I will draw my own conclusions." She smirked. "And I have concluded that you were there for hours and hours, gripped with melancholy devotion."

Oh, if she only knew what he really desired in that moment, to meet her impertinence not with a sneer or a kiss, but with a lover's forceful ardor, taking her to the floor beside the hearth and shredding her damp gown. *You would retract those cutting words, miss, if I had you at my mercy.*

Audric growled into his cup.

"Believe whatever pleases you best, Clemency."

"I quite will." She smiled, very happy with herself indeed. After a sip, she pressed her lips together tightly and he wondered if they shared the same thought—that their kiss and the liquor made for an intoxicating combination. Given the sudden flush creeping up her neck, he trusted it was so.

"Tansy and William will worry," she said softly, and with clear regret. "If they arrive home before me there will be questions."

"It would be terribly impolite of me to keep you," replied Audric, almost relieved. If she stayed any longer, he might tell her what was in his mind, what he imagined for them, and then, knowing her, she would insist on staying. Or perhaps she would be scandalized. Either way, it was time for her to be respectfully returned to her family. The assembly was near, he assured himself, and then those lusts could be sated. "However much I wish to keep you."

Placing her empty glass on the table before them, Clemency stood and smoothed her rumpled skirts down her thighs.

Her hands trembled. Did she suffer as he did, ready to snap and laugh at caution and propriety and all the rigid expectations keeping their clothes on and their bodies apart?

Of course she did. She must. He had recognized the hunger in her eyes. He still couldn't say if he had kissed her first or if she was the instigator.

"And however much I want to stay," she murmured.

"How much is that?" he asked, watching with eager eyes as she slid her hand around the arm he offered. Her touch put a torch to that kindling at his feet. It was hopeless.

Clemency giggled softly, and the blaze threatening to consume him spread. "Well, your charms are many and not to be underestimated, Audric, but you will never know the answer to that question. After all I have promised myself not to love and not to marry."

He crowded her against the wall just to the left of the door, a portrait of an ancestor above her head, gazing down at him in dry amusement. Kissing her, he swallowed the light gasp that escaped her throat. Again she rested her hands on his chest and again he wondered how long his restraint would last. Paper-thin, that restraint. Flimsy, and ready to tear.

As he stepped away, Audric managed to school his expression into one of stern consternation. Predictably, the unflappable Clemency simply smirked.

"Was that a warning, sir?" she breathed.

"Not a warning, no," Audric replied, leading her to the door. "But a promise. You will love again, that much I know."

They encountered Ralston half-asleep in a chair in the foyer, slumped back with his head against the wall. He gathered himself quickly and pulled on his coat, then hurried to look awake near the front doors.

"See that the driver takes Miss Fry home with all haste," Audric instructed him.

Ralston snapped to action, plunging out into the continuous rain and whistling, the clip-clop of hooves on the cobbles coming a moment later.

Now that they were no longer alone, Audric observed all expected courtesies, bowing at the waist while Miss Fry gave her curtsey, their eyes lingering over each other before she gave him the scantest, strangest smile and then left. Ralston went after her into the rain, the dark and the mist swallowing them faster than Audric liked.

The step behind him creaked, and he blew out a tired breath through his nose.

"'Tis awfully late for company," his sister, Delphine, mused from the stairs.

He turned and shrank somewhat from the power of her sisterly superior look, as though he were a young man caught with his faced stuffed in the larder.

"Which is why you should be abed," Audric reminded her, going to the foot of the stairs and leaning against the bannister.

"You are blushing, brother. A momentous occasion!"

"If you want me to be embarrassed, then I refuse."

Delphine pulled her heavy black shawl closer about her shoulders and laughed, then turned to retreat upstairs. She had only come to briefly tease him, and make sure he knew that she knew what he was up to. The dogs had followed her down, now whining for either bed or a late-night refreshment. "Embarrassed, no? Only I hope you are happy, brother. I truly do."

Audric rubbed fretfully at his temples. "Surprisingly, I *am* happy, Delphine."

"Ha! There's nothing surprising about it. I knew you would love her from the beginning; it was always in your eyes, and a sister knows. A sister can tell."

21

"My God, the air in London suits you, sister. You're practically aglow."

Clemency shied at her sister's praise, for while she was bursting to tell Honora the truth, she knew it was wiser to keep the secret until after the assembly. All that mattered in that moment was that Honora had come, and she could embrace her sister, and take her hand, and walk with her and talk with her. After, of course, Tansy and William had done their fawning too. It was chaos in the foyer of the Bagshots' house, while Honora held Clemency at arm's length, inspecting her, and Tansy fluttered and fussed, directing the valet, Langston, who had already departed upstairs with Honora's modest luggage.

Chaos, but Clemency was glad of it. Tansy's father greeted them, a round-faced bull of a man, stooped and strong, but with a kind face and an open invitation of a smile. The cook had done a beautiful roast and all manner of vegetables and pig bits suspended in elaborate jellies, and Mr. Bagshot brought out the finest bottles in his cellar. They all sat down to dine at the long table with three small candelabras throwing merry golden light down the linens, the candles flickering in a way that made smiles shimmer, like they

were all feeling a little mischievous. And there sat Clemency
beside her sister, teeming, teeming, teeming, brimming with
secrets.

Secrets but not love. No, never love. I have sworn off it.
Maybe.

"But where is Lord Boyle?" Honora had asked as they
were all at last settled down at the table and surrounded by
the clinking music of knives and forks at work.

That was the last subject on Clemency's mind, yet she
drummed up a cool smile. She did not have to pretend to be
unbothered at his conspicuous absence. "He has some business out of town to settle," Clemency replied.

"Any respectable man settles his accounts and readies
himself before marrying," Mr. Bagshot pointed out from his
place at the head of the long table. She didn't mind his unwitting assist.

"Oh, but it is so soon!" Tansy squealed, scrunching up
her nose. She and William sat across from each other, just to
Honora's right. "We shall all gossip our way back to Round
Orchard after the assembly, and then our Clemency will be a
married woman."

"Hard to imagine," William said with a chuckle.

"Why speak of me when Honora is here now?" Clemency
redirected. It was uncomfortable to be the subject of their
teasing and joy when so soon the cause for it would be dismantled. Indeed, Honora's coming could not be better
timed—she could attend the assembly in two days and be
there in person for Boyle's unmasking. She only hoped Mrs.
Chilvers would not be too implicated.

"What is there to ask?" Tansy replied lightly. "We have
already asked her thrice about the road conditions."

"Clemency has been kind enough to keep me abreast of all your many adventures in London," Honora said in her effortlessly polite way. Below the table, Clemency patted her knee in thanks for changing the subject away from Boyle. "Lady Veitch is frequently mentioned. . . ."

And that was all it took. Tansy launched into her usual glowing recounts of their evenings with Lady Veitch and her daughters, and then veered suddenly to tell Honora of the most alarming pistol shot they heard just three nights before.

Clemency, more taken with what had come after the shot, had almost forgotten all about that part and flinched when Tansy pounded her fist on the table, mimicking the boom. Afterward, she could feel Nora's eyes burning into her cheek. A sister's intuition . . .

How unfair that she had to wait to tell Honora all. She yearned to write to Audric but knew they must be careful now that the assembly was nearly upon them. It was a risk, what she had done—kissing him in the rain, speeding off into the night in his carriage, kissing him some more. Thankfully, she had arrived home before Tansy and William, and dried herself down and tossed herself into bed before any of them could start up interrogations. The next morning, talk only revolved around the subject of the mysterious shot, and that was just fine with Clemency, who stared into her porridge, lost in thought. She must have looked dreadful, for she had slept not a wink that night, revisiting in her mind every moment she had spent in Mr. Ferrand's company, every detail of his face and the exact warmth and pressure of his lips upon hers . . .

Lord, but she wanted to write to him. There was so much to say! So much to ask! She wanted to study him like a long-forgotten book, a tad dusty but attractive and serious and leather-bound, wanted to search through every word and all the marginalia for information. What was he like as a boy? Had he been in love before? What operas did he yet desire to attend? Did he possess a favorite dish? A favorite wine? Where might he want to holiday, and so on.

Clemency pushed her roast around on her plate and sighed. And none of it could be told to Honora. How was she to hold her tongue for three whole days? And after Honora had noticed there was something different about her too?

She was becoming a tangle of contradictions. A woman who eschewed love yet found herself tumbling helplessly toward it. A grand, romantic love. Miss Taylor would groan. How many times must Clemency forget and relearn this lesson?

When the dinner ended, they adjourned to the sitting room; general witticisms were exchanged, the pianoforte was by turns adequately and exceptionally played, motes danced in the butter-yellow candlelight. Then yawns were stifled and excuses made, beds more enticing than cards, and Clemency at last found herself alone with her sister, who would be occupying the room across the hall. Of course, after washing up and changing into her dressing gown, Honora came to her and the two of them sat on Clemency's bed with their knees touching, just as they had done as girls in Round Orchard.

"Is it true?" Honora asked, running her fingers idly across the edge of her knit shawl. "Has it been Lady Veitch's luxurious salons and nothing else all this time? How have you not gone mad?"

"Of course not," replied Clemency, rolling her eyes. "We

must convince Tansy that she will not inherit Lady Veitch's great fortune, no matter how many lectures she endures!"

Nora grinned. "And you have delivered my letter to Mrs. Chilvers?"

The name somewhat diminished Clemency's joy. "Yes, I have. Only . . . I hesitate to tell you this, but she is part of this business with Boyle. It will all come as a shock, Honora, and you must prepare yourself." She fetched the letter from Mrs. Chilvers, which she had kept under her pillow all those days.

At that, her sister frowned. "I cannot see how she is involved. She does not speak of him, though I have mentioned him in passing, and only in relation to you."

"Yes, she said as much. In fact, we spoke at length, Honora, about some misfortunes that have befallen her. Life has shown her so much unkindness, and to survive she has taken regrettable actions." Clemency took a deep breath and pressed the backs of her hands to her eyes. "You should hear it all from Mrs. Chilvers herself, Nora, but I cannot promise that Boyle's downfall will not include her."

"It is hard to imagine," Honora breathed. She held the letter gently between her palms, her cheeks suddenly pink. "I thought Mrs. Chilvers had given me her true confidence, for we have shared so much of our lives through our correspondence. . . . I never for one moment thought she might be an unsavory character."

"She is not unsavory," Clemency insisted. Mrs. Chilvers was not a Denning Ede or a Turner Boyle; she refused to believe it was so. The widow had been so contrite, so sincere. . . . "She is complicated, and she has promised to give testimony against Boyle when the time comes."

"So many secrets," said Honora, eyes downcast. "If she is aiding Boyle, then Mr. Ferrand must despise her."

"Do not worry about him. Mrs. Chilvers will not move against us."

"*Us* is it, now?" Honora asked, perking up. A slow smile spread across her face. "Your letters mentioned Mr. Ferrand frequently. For a man you profess to dislike you certainly do speak of him often. Is there more to tell? Come, I am your sister, Clemency. You know I can be trusted."

Naturally she could be, but Clemency felt protective of her scheme with Mr. Ferrand. Their interactions, experiences, even their friendship, must be kept hidden, and the plot itself, while also a secret, felt truly theirs. A unique bond, if an untoward one. She leapt from the bed and crossed to the window, fretting with the edges of the lace curtains that billowed gently from the humid night breeze.

"Clemency . . ."

"Oh, do not use that warning tone! I am powerless against it."

"I know." Nora laughed softly but made no attempt to follow her. "What have you left out of your letters? I know something has changed, sister. You look different. You seem changed. There is . . . a shift in your demeanor that I dare not try to explain. A private smile that I recognize, as I have worn it myself."

She knew. A sister would. Clemency squeezed her eyes shut and let the curtains drop from her grasp. "You . . . You are imagining that."

Honora had the grace to wait for a moment or two before murmuring, "Dearest, are you in love with him?"

"Oh God! No!" Not love. Never love. Clemency wilted. "No! Yes. I must be! Dreadful! Dreadful, dreadful," Clemency wailed, crushing the heels of her hands into her eyes and spinning. She found her way back to the bed and collapsed upon it, and at once Nora stroked her hair and back. "You mustn't tell anyone."

She could hardly admit it to herself.

Honora laughed again, supremely gentle. "You know I would never. Besides, he is a single man with a fortune, why should you not love him and marry him? How is that at all dreadful?"

Clemency only tiptoed up to the idea of marrying Audric, for thinking about it in detail gave her prickles up and down her arms. Would they even be happy? Would they drive each other mad? "There is no understanding between us, Nora, not like that."

"Could there be? You need not go through with your marriage to Boyle. And yet what would your cherished Miss Bethany Taylor have to say about this?" she asked, wryly.

"That I am a fool," she wailed again. "I should not be falling in love. I should be avoiding men altogether!"

"We are all fools in love, surely even Miss Taylor could not begrudge you a happy heart?"

Clemency rolled gracelessly onto her back and pouted. "There is so much to untangle! I had no interest in ever marrying, but then Boyle changed my mind, and then he changed it yet again. And for weeks I had thought myself decided on spinsterhood, and yet Mr. Ferrand . . . the thought of a life with him, a forever life, does not *seem* dreadful. Rather, it moves me. It moves me to dream. But dreaming is so dangerous, and dreams are terribly fragile."

Nora patted her hair again, then giggled and swooped down to plant a kiss on her forehead. "Then dream away, Clemency. You are quite allowed to change your mind. Your smile tells the story, and if that smile tells true, then it will be a happily ever after."

22

Clemency realized she ought to appreciate the glamour of the assembly hall more, but it was all a bit fuzzy behind the knowledge of what must be done that evening. Her skin felt alight, as strange and hot as when Audric touched her or embraced her, or even glanced at her with his intense emerald eyes. The assembly had seemed a distant thing for so long, but now it had come, and she must play her part, and Audric must play his—Turner Boyle must be disgraced, confronted with his scheme to legitimize his title before the whole of the ton, so that he might not squirm out of the scrutiny and accusations again.

And then Clemency would be free of all the games and nonsense, free to finally profess her heart to Audric.

That sent another jolt of fear through her. She stood under the dazzle of candles made crystalline by the many chandeliers and handled her cup of punch rather roughly, spinning it ever in her silk-gloved fingers. Beside her, dressed in a ravishing green gown, Honora tapped her fan lightly on her wrist to the beat of the music, her ringlets bouncing as she pursed her cherub lips and searched the sea of unfamiliar faces.

A green dress. Searching. That at least broke through the

fog of nerves gripping Clemency. She leaned into her sister, both of them squashed against the wall near the dancing while a steady river of attendees ran by, a constant stream of beaded silk and fluffy cravats.

"But where is your Mr. Ferrand?" Honora suddenly asked.

Clemency swallowed hard and shrugged. It was best not to think of him yet. She knew he would appear at the right time, when all was to be revealed. First, Boyle must show himself, must ask Clemency to dance, and then he would be shown the papers they had taken from Mrs. Chilvers, the forgery plot revealed. They hoped to keep Ede's name out of it, as he was powerful enough to enact his own reprisals, and thus she would reveal Boyle's true parentage only if he forced her hand. Then, at last Audric's presence would be required, as he would swoop in to gallantly take her hand, wrenching her from Boyle and toward the dance floor for a triumphant turn.

She began to sweat.

"Let us not speak of him," she told her sister. "For it has come to my attention that you have shed your widow's weeds. This shade of emerald nearly does you justice, sister. But who is it for?"

Honora paled and fussed with one of her curls. "What a foolish question. No, your love life is far more interesting of late."

"Tonight is not about love, Honora, but about revenge. Besides, if Mr. Ferrand is here we will quickly find him; he is not difficult to spy in a crowd." No, thought Clemency, it was hard to look at anything but him when he was present. "Tell me more of this gown, Nora. I insist!"

Clemency finished her punch and felt Honora's delicate

hand take her by the wrist firmly, then tug her into the flow of folk leaving the dance hall. They snaked their way through the overpacked, perfume-soaked room to the west corridor running alongside, with large French doors placed at intervals where one might peek in and observe the festivities. They found a quietish corner near an imposing bust of someone or other, Honora's forehead nearly touching the bust's pointed beard as she sagged against it.

"Nora, are you well?" Clemency frowned and leaned closer.

"I . . . am. I think. Oh, I do not know! The gown . . . You are right, Clemency. Something has changed in me, just as something has changed in you. And just as you are made different by blossoming love so am I."

Clemency's eyes grew wide. She couldn't help but be enveloped by a smile, for nothing could bring her greater joy than knowing her sister could open her heart again. "Nora! How could you? Who is he? I must know, tell me at once and let us find him here so I might apply my most vigorous judgment. Is he handsome? Is he kind? Say he is kind—"

"Dearest . . ."

She still looked pale, the roses in her cheeks faded away. It occurred to Clemency, then, that they must be twins with their pallor and perspiration. But what made her sister so anxious?

"Something is the matter," Clemency murmured, brow furrowed. "He is married or . . . or destitute. Out with it, Nora, you know I threaten to judge only in jest. It matters only that you are happy."

"No, no." Nora sighed and pushed away from the statue,

throwing up her hands and nearly dropping her fan. "You have it all wrong. But how could you not? Oh, but I am stupid. Stupid, stupid . . ." She shook her dark ringlets, then turned back toward Clemency and gasped, pointing with the tip of her fan. "Look! Boyle has come. He approaches with a most determined stride."

And so he did. Clemency steeled herself, pretending to laugh ardently at something Nora had said, fluttering a hand over her heart. She knew the rosy pink stripes of the gown flattered her, that it was a perfect complement to her red-gold hair, and that the low scooping neck showed her advantageously; better yet, the dreamy concoction had all been made with the scandalous gift of fabric and ribbons from Mr. Ferrand, lending it a secret power known only to a few. . . . But still, knowing all that did not lessen her dread. She wanted to appear perfect, so that the loss of her would hurt Boyle all the more. She felt she knew him somewhat now and thought the theft of a desirable jewel would sting and sting deep.

He would not just lose the right to his title tonight, but his right to her.

His blue eyes lit at the sight of her, and he swept a courtly bow over her offered hand, whispering a kiss against her knuckles.

"The radiance of the evening is made shabby by your beauty," he purred, giving them both a catlike smile. His timing could not have been worse. Clemency kept hold of his hand, itching to toss it away, but twisted back around to her sister, giving Honora a helpless sigh.

"Go," Nora said. She grinned and seemed almost relieved for the interruption. "Nights like this were made for young couples. Go, enjoy yourselves." Then, knowing of course that Clemency's heart remained with someone else, she said more softly, "Know, sister, that I am not far."

Clemency nodded, her hands perspiring hard, and let herself be led back to the sweltering crush of the dance. Her sister would follow, she knew, in case she was needed. Also, she suspected, to watch for the mysterious Mr. Ferrand.

Boyle led her through the assembly with the unearned confidence of a man who stood, he thought, on top of the world, having gotten there through deceit and cruelty. He did not know, however, that the world he stood upon was cracked and ready to crumble, the weight of his hubris enough to bring the whole thing crashing down. Even Clemency could admit there was an elegance to his profile as he held his head high and escorted her, and when they had found the beating heart of the dance, and he brought her forward to take their places in the Allemande Cotillion. They were steps she knew well, but Turner's hand holding hers firmly felt all wrong, and her hand had become slimy beneath the glove.

"Miss Fry," he said softly, his voice just above the music as he bowed to her. Clemency gave her curtsey and smiled, one eye on him, the other fixed over his head, searching urgently for Audric. In the wall of faces behind Turner Boyle, she spotted Tansy and William, and her sister. Lady Veitch and her daughters would be elsewhere, with the more fashionable set, if they had deigned to come at all. She spied Denning Ede arriving, and her corset felt twice as tight. He must be left out of Boyle's humiliation if at all possible.

Where are you? Clemency thought desperately. How long would he make her wait?

They began to move in a circle while the violins soared,

Turner oddly close for the demands of the dance. His lips lowered to her ear, and she braced for more of his lies.

"I must admit, you played a cunning hand."

Clemency jerked her head away, smile still firmly and uncomfortably in place. "What are you talking about?"

"You and Ferrand. You really almost had me, might have humiliated me entirely and given the game away. But you must keep your eyes on your cards at all times, my dear. Your focus drifted, and now the advantage goes to me." His hand gripped hers so hard she gasped, and Clemency broke protocol to swivel her head and glare at him.

"I have no idea what—"

Turner's blue eyes became ice, the ease and grace of his movements directly contradicting the cool edge to his voice. "I know what you're about, and what you think you can prove. You can dig into my affairs and follow me, Clemency, but I can give chase too. Imagine my surprise when I discovered you making a fool of yourself all over town with Mr. Ferrand. But then, foolish recklessness runs in the family."

The frost in his gaze penetrated her, and her blood ran cold. Clemency tried to force her hand out of his grasp, but he only gathered her closer, his other hand clamping down on her hip, keeping her anchored to his side. Some of the other dancers had begun to stare, and while a chill ran through her, her face flamed, burning with sudden fear and shame.

"You have discovered some of Mrs. Chilvers's secrets, but I'm afraid not all. Your sister and that Chilvers widow are engaged in a most scandalous arrangement, which you must have known or at least assumed," he sneered. "What would the *ton* say if they knew? If I made their letters public? Your

sister would be disgraced, and you the cause of all her unhappiness."

Nora and the widow? Clemency almost buckled, not out
of shock that her sister might love a woman, but that Nora
would keep such a thing from her. It did make sense to her
then—the urgency with which Nora had wanted her to deliver the letter, and both of the women widows . . . They
must have found such comfort in each other, in their shared
experiences and similar status in the world. And now Turner
could use that love against Nora, and the thought of it made
Clemency ill. If Mrs. Chilvers's criminal activity came to
light, it would only reflect even more poorly on her sister.

She gripped him back, but only because she had become
dizzy. The circle of the dance felt impossible to endure, the
room suddenly rocking from side to side.

"Chilvers provided useful documents to claim my son as
a ward, but I can do it with or without her. You've accom-
plished nothing, really; that boy is mine by rights. A man
always has a right to his son. Ferrand will be entirely without
recourse when I have the boy under my control."

"No." Clemency finally found her voice, gasping.
"Delphine . . . You will not wound her that way. You will not
hurt her, and you will not hurt Honora—"

"Me?" He had the audacity to laugh, crinkling up his eyes
as he threw his head back. "I would not dream of hurting
them, not, of course, if you keep your promises, Clemency,
and marry me. I will even give up on claiming the boy as my
ward. You see? I promised you a baron, and now in the eyes
of the Crown I am one. You might try to prove otherwise,
but Ede is too powerful, too connected, and too close to all
of this nasty business. The man so hates a scandal—one

whiff of your intentions and he will crush you and Ferrand like the scrabbling rodents that you are."

"He would turn on you first," she hissed. "You are the source of all his woes."

"Perhaps. Care to take that gamble?"

Somehow, through the flames searing against her cheeks and the dizziness overcoming her, she saw Audric, tall and brilliant, slicing his way through the crowd. People parted for him, aware, as she was, of his solemn, powerful presence. The cello and violins raced toward the climax of the dance, the circle spinning faster, Clemency carried along by it, and by the man clutching her with painful force. If only the floor could swallow her up, disappear her from this nightmare . . .

Why had he chosen that moment, of all moments, to appear?

And yet he could not save her, and his radiance, and his clear emerald eyes, and the sweet, knowing curve to his lips, none of it could intervene.

I must save myself.

"I cannot let you do this," Clemency told him through clenched teeth. It was her turn to clutch him, letting her fingers bite into his sleeve, into his arm. "I will fight you, Boyle, for I am not the naïve young woman you persuaded with your pretty words and empty promises."

"You will not fight me," he grunted, giving her the small satisfaction of showing pain for the force of her grip. "You have not a soldier on the field, Clemency. The war is over, and I have won."

"No—"

Before she could speak another word, Turner Boyle had

turned to the short young couple dancing to their left. The woman of the pair, obviously a little deep into her punch already, beamed up at him with a sweat-sheened pink face.

"Good evening!" Boyle called to her over the music. "Tell me, have you heard the latest gossip of out Round Orchard?"

"Oh?" The young lady frowned but then shook her head and giggled. "Is it terribly wicked?"

"It concerns a widow by the name of Hono—"

"Lord Boyle!" Clemency stomped, hard, on his foot, and mercifully he shut up, tearing his attention away from the other couple. "Stop! Stop this instant."

"Then relent." His smile held the cold white gleam of a string of cheap pearls. Clemency shivered and bowed her head and felt a surge of pain at the base of her skull. "Or shall I say more?"

"Why?" she wheezed, breathless with confusion. The dance would end soon, and they would be expected to part and smile, and bow, but she felt too weak to do any of those things. "Why would you want to marry me when you have nothing but contempt for me and my family? When we so clearly revolt each other?"

"There are other rich women," Boyle said with a shrug, loosening his grasp on her at last. She sagged. "But I would not have the power over them that I have over you. Step one toe out of line in our marriage, my sweet, attempt to outmaneuver me or contact Mr. Ferrand and Delphine Ferrand's child will be mine. Your sister's life? Ruined. Mrs. Chilvers? Ruined. How freeing, don't you think? To be the husband I want to be, and not the husband you or anyone else expects me to be. I suspect it will be rather liberating." His smile turned brilliant, and it even reached his dead, cold eyes. "Yes,

I suspect I will infinitely enjoy being a married man. The delicious icing on top is that I have taken you from Ferrand; he will likely flee back to France and never show his face in London again."

Clemency could not risk exposing her sister's secret, and she could not risk gentle Delphine's awful dealings with Turner Boyle becoming public knowledge. She was stuck, trapped, and as the dance ended and they made their curtsey and bow, she and Turner came back together, and his hand closing over hers was like the sealing of a tomb.

Her mind raced while her body went completely still. Across the floor, Clemency found Audric, felt his eyes drill into her. His happiness, his anticipation, was palpable in the high, tight line of his shoulders. There he was, ready to swoop in and be at her side, to humiliate the man that would humiliate them both, and Clemency could do nothing but let her face fall.

A wave of regret washed over her, but there was nothing to be done. She simply closed her eyes hard, once, then opened them, hoping Audric could detect the sadness in her gaze. Then she shook her head, and looked down at the floor, and let Lord Boyle lead her away.

23

Clemency was drowning, and the last thing she remembered seeing was the flicker of shock and recognition in Mr. Ferrand's eyes. Her legs went numb, and she felt Nora and Tansy at her sides, their sure, soft hands keeping her upright as she dipped toward the ground.

"Air!" she heard someone, most likely William, say. "By God, move, the lady requires fresh air!"

The faces in the ballroom became nothing but a nauseating blur as she was rushed away from the dancers. Boyle was somewhere, she knew, gloating over his victory. She couldn't stand to think of him, of the life she must now forfeit to him in order to protect Honora and Delphine. And she was not even allowed the honorable step of explaining to Mr. Ferrand why, with no warning or good reason, she had chosen the horrid Boyle over him. How could he forgive her for spurning him in such a callous way? Had he done the same to her, her heart would have shattered.

Well, shattered into an even finer dust than the pulverized mess her heart had become.

"Nora," she whispered, leaning against her sister. "I am not well."

"Of course, dearest, we'll leave at once."

The colder air outside proved a blessing, but it offered only temporary relief. Clemency opened her eyes wide enough to realize they were lifting her into Tansy's family carriage, and Nora was stepping in behind her. When the door closed, the muted warmth and silence became instantly unbearable. She cried. Great, shivery, and sucking sobs that sounded more like someone dying from the cold than someone suffering their heart-death.

"What is the matter? Oh, Clemency, you are so pale!" Honora clung to her, held her. "What has happened?"

"I—I—cannot—say. . . ." She could hardly get the words out between sobs.

"But you must tell me. You have me so horribly worried."

Then Honora would have to remain worried. Her concern could not be addressed, for Clemency knew her sister well and felt sure that Honora would throw herself on the deadly sword of London gossip if it meant freeing her sister from Boyle's clutches. But she refused to hurt Nora that way, to tear her away from Mrs. Chilvers, and give Delphine's child to Boyle.

The future joy and contentment of two women had to take precedence over her immediate unhappiness.

She sobbed harder.

"Has something transpired between you and Mr. Ferrand?" Nora pressed. Clemency felt numb all over, and though the carriage rocked fiercely, she barely noticed. "I hardly caught sight of him before you collapsed. Oh, tell me what is the matter! You must!"

Inadvertently Nora had given her the words she needed. Putting them in the right order and speaking them coherently required every sinew of concentration. Her voice shook, but she managed to whisper, "Yes. Something transpired. What-ever understanding was between us is . . ." *Say it and have done. It's gone. Say the word, say the hardest word in the English language.* "Gone."

Honora fell abruptly silent, her hands stilling on Clem-ency's shoulder and side. For a moment, there was nothing but the strike of hooves over cobbles, the creaking of the car-riage door, and the call of the driver as they raced back to the Bagshots' home.

Softly, as if any sound at all might undo Clemency com-pletely, Honora murmured, "And . . . And Boyle? What is to become of you two? Dare I ask, sweet sister?"

Clemency curled in on herself and indulged in one more rattling cry. Her face felt fit to burn, covered in a sluice of hot tears. How could it be said at all? And if spoken aloud now, in confidence with someone she loved and trusted, how much truer and more final did it make this lifelong sentence?

Tell her the truth. Do not suffer alone.

But what was braver? Taking this bullet to the heart spared two others. The mathematics were obvious. When it was finalized, Clemency told herself, she must never consider herself a martyr. This was her mistake, her doing; she could blame nobody for the curse of Turner Boyle but herself. She had been the one to believe his lies, to listen to his promises over the wise, sober words of Olympe de Gouges, of Mary Wollstonecraft. Of Bethany Taylor.

It is vain to expect virtue from women till they are in some degree independent of men, wrote Wollstonecraft. And oh how Clemency felt that acutely now. None of this pain or torment would have come had she held fast to her beliefs and simply avoided both Boyle and Audric.

She would not forget again.

"It appears . . ." Clemency whispered, becoming strange and vacant. The pain was unbelievable, and she wondered if the absence of that pain would somehow sting too. A remembrance of a remembrance of what might have been for her and Mr. Ferrand.

Audric, forgive me.

"It appears that where Turner Boyle is concerned I remain . . . entangled. Mrs. Chilvers will not have her secret exposed after all."

She wondered if Honora understood every way in which Clemency meant that. The carriage was quiet again. Clemency imagined a house, vibrant, full of life. A family lived there, but one by one they left and took their belongings. Then men came and put all their possessions into crates, and covered the sofas and tables with silky white sheets. The house gradually became empty and dark, no candles burning in the windows, and no laughter heard in the halls. Love left it as the dust settled, until all the tears cried and kisses exchanged and hands held were not just a distant memory but ghostly and distorted.

Love a haunt, and her the hollow, darkening house.

When Audric's fourth letter went unanswered and unacknowledged, he knew it was time to believe a once impossible notion: that Clemency Fry had chosen another, and she had chosen his sworn enemy.

He watched the priceless vase sail across the room and smash into the far wall with a vague, detached pleasure. The sound ought to have resonated deep in his chest and released the hot knot of agony coiled there. Yet he craved to throw more. He found an empty brandy bottle in reach and hurled that too. A powder of glass shimmered like ice under the sitting room window, the accrued detritus of his confusion and his rage.

The bottle shattering against the wall covered the sound of the door opening behind him. His man Ralston cleared his throat and kept his voice to a respectful murmur.

"Sir, your sister is becoming rather concerned."

Delphine. God. How would he ever make sense of this for himself, let alone poor Delphine? They might have been a little family, strange in their way but content.

Robbed. Robbed of his moment of vengeance, robbed of love, robbed of . . .

Her. Happiness.

Audric squeezed his eyes shut. He had never been a graceful loser, and now, in this moment of greatest humiliation, when his temper ought to flare beyond reason or fathoming, he could only muster concern for Clemency and Delphine.

Something must have happened. The phrase—no, the truth—repeated in his head, a maddening refrain.

Something must have happened. She loved me. She loved me. Something must have happened.

But what? But *what*? He knew, in his bones he knew, that Turner Boyle was somehow to blame, that he had outmaneuvered them in the last, most important moment. Not just because he had been there, holding on to a ghastly pale Clemency with a gloating sneer. He had made some kind of threat, or perhaps concocted an elaborate lie about Audric and his sister that convinced Clemency to quit their acquaintance.

Yet she was a smart woman and wise to Boyle's ways. They had all the evidence, so why abandon their plans? It was risky, naturally, but they had worked so hard. And what could make her withdraw her affection so abruptly? He would not sleep nor know peace until he had answers, and he had learned through the observations of Lee Stanhope that William and Tansy Bagshot, accompanied by Honora and Clemency Fry, had unexpectedly quit their London house and returned to Round Orchard.

Turner Boyle had gone with them, departing in the same carriage as Clemency.

"Ralston? Prepare the house. We will be leaving for the country at once." He ran a trembling hand over his face from forehead to chin. "I find suddenly that I despise London."

"Sir, if your intention is to nurse the sting of Miss Fry's—"

"Leaving," Audric declared. "At once. *Par Dieu,* I will pick at this scab to my heart's content, Ralston. No man or god may stop me. I will have answers, and after that? Satisfaction."

24

One day bled into another while Clemency found that the lonely house of her heart did not wish to remain so. Visitors tried to come and go, and each attempted entry proved harder and harder to withstand. She had to keep herself locked tight, but even a gentle knock on the door hurt and hurt deeply.

Five days after the doomed assembly, she stood at the garden door of her family's home, watching spring jut its way through the soft earth, daffodils unfolding tentatively despite the lingering spring chill. Those innocent shoots poked above the gleaming mud hoping for the tenderness of sun and finding more mercy than Clemency. She had wanted to find solace and reprieve in that old house and in the changing season, but it served to remind her of what she could not have—early morning walks with Audric across the sprawl of his grounds, long rides through the country, a spontaneous trip to Dover to wander the cliffs in warming weather. Now none of it would happen, and she could not feel the spring, only that stubborn winter chill.

A few slants of sunlight climbed their way across the stone path, over the well spigot, gaining ground toward the house, and toward her slippers, positioned just against the threshold.

She clung with both hands to the frame, nervous that even a slight breeze might tip her one way or the other. That day would be her wedding day, and while the house woke up around her and began to descend into matrimonial preparation and chaos, Clemency stood empty-stomached and empty-hearted, faced toward the house Audric still possessed but did not inhabit, her eyes becoming fixed on the narrow stream that she had tumbled into and that he had pulled her from. If she closed her eyes, she could still feel the sure strength of his hands as he gathered her up and out of the muddy water.

Before she could command her body to behave, she had taken six steps out the door, striding across the garden and toward the border of their properties. There it was, that peaceful river, now an unmistakable Rubicon. There had been a flurry of activity at his house in recent days, but Clemency knew it could signal only one thing—he was preparing to abandon that estate, the last tie between them slashed away. But she went anyway, suddenly possessed, eyes filling with tears as she picked up speed along the stone path.

Go to him, go to him, go to him. It is not too late. . . .

"Dearest? Where are you going? Mother is frantic; it's time to depart for the church."

Clemency froze. A moment later Honora's hand landed lightly on her elbow. "Clemency? Are you well?"

Too late.

"Certainly."

Her sister sighed, turning her carefully back toward the

house. "There have never been any secrets between us. It hurts so that you should choose to keep some from me now."

Clemency shook her head, her slipper crunching one of the bold-faced dandelions, its yellow head smeared across the stones. "I am keeping no secrets, sister. You know everything there is to know."

And that was true. For Honora knew of Delphine's tragedy and of her own relationship with Mrs. Chilvers, the two knife points upon which Boyle kept Clemency balanced.

"But you seem so unhappy," Nora said, stroking her hair. "You should be all joy and lightness on your wedding day, dearest."

"Whoever is? When marriage is the man's game."

"Surely it is not so bad," Honora murmured. Her sister stepped ahead of her and into the house.

"It's worse," whispered Clemency. If Honora heard her, she made no indication of it. She had always assumed that if she married, it would bring her and Honora closer together. It would be a shared experience, one that, though Honora's ended in tragedy, would bond them, and Clemency might go to her for advice and comfort, but now what could she say of her marriage? Keeping secrets, even for a noble reason, might only tear them apart. Honora's wisdom lay in her heart, in her intuition, and for one as sensitive as her sister, there would be no mistaking the pain radiating from the open wound of Clemency's spirit.

"I was nervous too," Honora said softly, coaxing Clemency into the house, through the kitchen, and through the salon toward the winding staircase. Holding Clemency's hand, she patted her like a fretting child. "Who would I be? I wondered. Would I feel not myself? Like I had given my whole being away? In the end, it was just a few words spoken in a church. Even if I felt the presence of God there, or if my happiness increased, afterward I was the same person."

Clemency huffed out a dry laugh. "I promise you, Nora, I will not be the same person after I speak those words in the church."

"Yes, you have always had your qualms with marriage. . . ."

Her instinct was to argue, but Clemency found she had grown very tired. Every step toward the bedchamber where she would dress felt like a chore. At the open door, her mother waited in her frilliest and finest, the ostrich plumes of a tall bonnet brushing the ceiling as she gave a soft squeal of excitement. The maids were there. Everything was prepared.

She took Clemency's other hand and squeezed it hard enough to bruise.

"Oh, smile," her mother said with a sigh. Her own bedchamber had never felt colder or more foreboding. "You are going to your wedding soon," her mother reminded her, "not your funeral."

Audric felt much like a gargoyle as he stood at the bannister on the wide balcony overlooking the west lawn of the Beswick estate. From that height, the grounds gently sloped through sparse forest, down to the stream that wound like a fine blue ribbon across the green velvet of the grounds.

A perfect day. A horrid day.

A gargoyle he remained, stony, silent, hunched, waiting for the bells to toll at the church and signal proof of his torment.

Yet the French doors behind him swung open loudly, no doubt Ralston's attempt to warn him in case he was up to any humiliating weeping. Audric's face remained dry as he glanced over one shoulder toward the doors, finding Ralston there, straight and serious as ever, and beside him a stout, well-muscled gentleman with a square face and reddish nose.

"Mr. Jack Connors to see you, sir."

Ralston knew that Audric was accepting no visitors, particularly not that accursed morning. He was about to remind his man of just that when he noticed the intruder, Jack Connors, gulping desperately. His eyes never seemed to stay in one spot, jumping from Audric's face to his hands to his feet, and back again. This had every indication of a confession.

"I beg your pardon, sir—" Connors began, stumbling forward on clumsy feet. He had the bearings of a man who boxed for pleasure and boxed enthusiastically but not well.

"No, I beg yours. I am not receiving company today. Good day, sir."

Audric had hoped the finality in his tone was impolite enough to shock the man and make him leave, but Connors held his ground. In fact, he strode forward, impertinently joining Mr. Ferrand at the bannister. Audric pulled his hands away from the stone with a grimace and inhaled sharply through his nose.

"I know what you will say," Connors blurted. He shook his head vigorously. The deep, dark smears under his eyes spoke of many sleepless nights. "But today is not yours alone to mourn. I suspect many of us are in great pain today. . . ."

Ralston disappeared before Audric could call on him to dismiss their unwanted visitor. No matter, Audric would see to it himself. He held out his hand toward the French doors and cleared his throat.

"You are invited most forcefully to leave, Mr. Connors. You do not know me and you certainly do not know my state of—"

"Lee Stanhope."

Audric arched one brow. "What of him?"

"Turner—Lord Boyle—knew about him. He's no man of honor, only a man of greed. He doubled your payment and had Stanhope report all of your dealings in London to him. Miss Fry's too."

"Preposterous," Audric thundered. "Stanhope is a friend. And you say Boyle doubled my fee? How? With what money?"

His temper, which had been quelled by the shattering of many a vase in London, flared again and more dangerously. He crowded Connors against the railing, his vision blurring at the edges as if the man's accusations had driven him to the verge of madness.

"With mine," Connors murmured, shrinking. "Might be a baron, but never had a farthing to his name. He had you both followed. Every step you took in London, he had you followed, and he did it with my money."

A misplaced urge to strike the man rose sharply in Audric, but he stowed it, taking a pronounced step back and away from Connors. All of his questions, all of his swirling, spiraling thoughts, might be answered by what this man had to say. But to be betrayed by both Clemency and Lee . . .

In how many places and configurations could a man's heart break?

"Why come to me with this now?" Audric barked.

"The drink had me and . . ." Connors shuddered and
tugged at his chin. "And so did Boyle. God help me, I loved
him. Love made me a fool, but no more. My eyes are open,
and I have no doubt he'll expose my secrets to the whole
world. Let him. I don't give a damn; a man has his pride and
his code or he has nothing at all." He paced away from the
bannister, grabbing his head with both hands as he hurried
on. "I found at last the receipts that had bankrupted me.
Boyle spent a fortune having you followed and buying off
Stanhope's loyalty. I tried to confront him but he already had
what he wanted. Listen now, Clemency was always kind to
me, and even knew of my proclivities but told no one—"

Audric raised his hands, trying to convince the man to
slow down.

"What exactly does Boyle intend to do?" Audric asked
carefully.

Connors threw up his hands but ceased his pacing, turning to him with a splotchy, pale face. "He has already done
it. Miss Fry had no choice but to marry him, to protect her
sister, to protect you and your family." Connors pinched his
mouth shut as well as his eyes. "To protect me. Oh, he is a
fat, contented spider abiding in his web, a ruinous scandal
his prized clutch of eggs."

Audric heard only *to protect you and your family*.

Delphine. Perhaps they had found the forged documents
too late. Perhaps Boyle was already in possession of the
child. If not, then only Clemency's decision to marry might
have kept him from procuring the boy.

"In the late and lonely hours so many unkind thoughts
have come to me," he whispered, not caring if Connors heard

him or not. "I allowed myself to imagine Clemency as the worst sort of person, unfeeling and callous, deceitful, cruel . . ."

Connors grunted. "Boyle holds the axe above all our heads, sir. Clemency is keeping it aloft with this marriage."

"And I can do nothing."

"But, sir—"

"My sister's past, her secrets, are not mine to share, nor her pain a plaything to be toyed with carelessly."

Connors riffled for something under his jacket, then produced a pistol, boldly aiming toward the wood below the balcony. "Now that I have come to my senses I just need one shot. One chance . . ."

But Audric gently lowered the man's pistol. The hunt was over, no blood would be spilled. "We both know Boyle is cleverer than that. He will have put contingencies in place. There are others in possession of his secrets, powerful, rich others."

Hell and damnation. Boyle was going to win after all. Audric could forget his pride, but not the knowledge that Clemency was sacrificing her happiness to save them from Boyle's wrath, to protect Delphine's innocent child from him.

"Then there is nothing we can do," Connors murmured, holding the gun in his hands and staring down at it.

"Nothing *you* can do, perhaps."

Audric set his jaw, slowly swiveling to regard his sister in the open doorway, her black gown and shawl ruffled lightly by the morning breeze.

"How long have you been listening?" Audric asked, glaring beyond Connors's shoulder.

"Long enough," his sister replied with a shrug. "I have

made up my mind, Audric. This has gone on long enough. I refuse to let Boyle control all of our lives like this. Word will be sent to London. All the scandal sheets may know of my past, of what Boyle did to me, of the child it created, and the loss I endured. If he wants a fight, then so be it, I will contest his right to take that child."

Audric pushed past Connors and met Delphine at the doors, taking her by the forearm. At once, she eased out of his grasp.

"I forbid it, Delphine. You will be ruined, any future prospects—"

"What future prospects?" She laughed. Her big eyes shimmered with tears, but strangely, she smiled and pulled the shawl closer around her arms. "There is no man I love better than Ralston. I have no intention of aiming higher, for I know he can protect and love me as no one else could. A man is not his fortune or his breeding, he is his word and his actions. He has shown me all the love, protection, and loyalty a woman could ever desire."

Audric glanced around for Ralston, but the man was nowhere to be found. Perhaps he had foolishly missed what was right in front of his eyes. It would not be the first time. And that conversation could wait, Delphine's heart was not in question, but her safety was.

"Delphine, you will not do this—"

"'Tis already done."

"What?" Audric recoiled. "How—"

"The messenger has been dispatched," Delphine told him calmly. "My past is one less card in Boyle's sleeve." She breezed by her brother to join Mr. Connors at the railing. Primly, she set her hands on the bannister and drew in a deep breath. Her eyelashes fluttered shut briefly before she opened her eyes to survey the grounds as Audric had done.

"Let the whole world say what they will about me. I will be here, where I am safe and loved, and you . . ." Here she turned to face her brother, though she gave Connors a look in turn too. "You will mount your horse and go to that church, and you will not let Clemency marry the architect of all our misery. Because you love her, because she deserves better."

Audric did not know if the lump in his chest was from pride or fear. He did know, in that moment, that his sister had never looked so lovely or so strong.

"Because I love her," he repeated, his right hand curling into a fist.

"Go," Delphine whispered. "Now go to her."

Audric did not hear her, he was already gone.

25

Someone had brought her wedding gown and laid it among a table of flowers in her room. Someone, presumably her mother and sister, had seen to it all—the gown, the invitations, the breakfast that would follow, the flowers spilling out of the church and lining the pathway that would take her and Boyle to the open-air carriage and, afterward, their marriage.

Someone had taken care of it all as Clemency drifted through what felt like another person's life. The gown was sewn to her size and the flowers were what she preferred, all of it evidence that this was indeed her wedding day, despite what her heart insisted. Round Orchard was a very small, very close place, and it was not uncommon for most of the town to attend a wedding, and if not to sit in the church during the ceremony, then to celebrate afterward as a general sentiment of joy and future bliss swelled through the village, into the tavern, down the roads, like a sweet colorful mist perfumed with wildflowers and promise.

And every moment, Clemency expected another woman to walk through her own bedroom door and take her place. She trod to the table with her dress, past the vanity where she brushed her hair, and touched the delicate lace of the skirt.

This was hers and it was not, and when her skin brushed the fabric it felt hot to the touch. Never mind it had been sitting under the sunshiny window, Clemency was sure it would burn her up, incinerate her until there was nothing left but ash, the ash of a dream once had and now impossible.

It might have been a gown meant for a different day, for a wedding to a different man, for the joy of real love deeply felt.

"I cannot do this," Clemency whispered. She imagined, all at once, Boyle's touch as his fingers skimmed her face, the sickness she would feel sitting beside him at every church service or walking out with him at a dance, the horror of expectation, of the children that it would be her duty and burden to bear him. The fake heirs she would bear for a fake baron. Clemency could only resolve to be the best mother possible, and believe that somehow she could mother and nurture away any of Boyle's vile influence.

And each time she glanced at the boy, she would remember Delphine's pain.

"No," she said, closing her eyes. "No, no, no . . ."

Clemency backed quickly away from the gown and turned, fleeing out the door and into the back garden of Claridge. Down the lane in the church townsfolk and extended members of the family waited, and terrifyingly, Turner Boyle.

She walked to the big tree with a dilapidated swing, where she would spend hours and hours reading as a girl. When she sat down on the crooked wood, it threatened to buckle. Facing the valley and the river and Beswick, she tried to conjure Miss Taylor and wondered what her favorite writer would have to say.

"You were right," Clemency whispered. "All along, you were right. The scholar, the poet, and the philosopher can all agree that love is an ungovernable mystery," she recited. "And yet we seek to govern it."

"Govern, Miss Fry, or preserve?"

It was the last voice in the whole of England she expected to hear. As far as she knew, Lady Veitch was not even aware of her specific wedding day. Clemency shifted, swiveling to look back at Lady Veitch as she stood in the shade of a poplar and a scalloped-edge pink parasol. The frothy concoction of her gown sparkled, glowing from the sunlight shining behind her.

"Lady Veitch . . ." Clemency whispered, dumbstruck. "Forgive me for asking, but what are you doing in my garden?"

She noticed an elaborately enameled barouche waiting on the graveled drive to the left of the house. The old woman tilted her head to the side, imperiling the silk and feather bonnet pinned to her gray curls. "You may think me a very old, very traditional woman, and I am that, something of a relic from a bygone era that you now sneer at, but I also cannot abide injustice when I see it unfold before me." Lady Veitch closed her parasol and stabbed the pointed end into the dirt with a flourish. Behind her, Clemency saw both Arabella and Adeline peering out at her from the waiting barouche. "*Mr.* Boyle is a snake and a liar, a rude pretender who is not a baron's heir, and indeed hardly a man. The insult cannot be supported."

Clemency gradually stood, clinging to one rope of the swing for support. She opened her mouth to speak but Lady Veitch would not allow it.

"I find myself in the difficult position of thinking you hopelessly misguided, Miss Fry, but loathing Mr. Boyle, and as life is a series of lesser evils chosen, I have decided to intervene on your behalf. Tansy is a darling girl, and dear to me, and she assures me that you are worth the effort, though indeed I remain dubious."

"Lady Veitch, I am already quite at my wits' end and—"

The old woman chuckled and stabbed the ground with her parasol again. "By and by your wits may be spared, young lady. Mr. Boyle will not be arriving to marry you today, and unless I have gravely misunderstood the situation, I should think you will be very happy indeed to hear that."

It was shock and not relief that almost brought Clemency back to her knees. "N-No, whatever you have done you must undo it. You do not understand how dangerous Mr. Boyle can be!"

"Oh, I am quite aware." Lady Veitch snaked through the rosebushes toward her. She pursed her lips and then glanced through squinting eyes at Clemency. "Miss Fry, it was brought to my attention that a suitor of dubious means had become . . . unduly attached to my daughter. As I became aware of this, I also became aware of your role in steering her away from this unsavory character. Through my own means I discovered that the rogue in question was none other than our mutual acquaintance Mr. Turner Boyle."

Clemency covered her face with both hands. "That is hardly surprising, yet he is in possession of such damaging secrets, such ruinous information, that I cannot risk angering him. Please, Lady Veitch, I beg you—"

"There is no need for begging, Miss Fry. He is already apprehended and, I should think by now, on his way to Fleet

Prison. Worry not about his pernicious ways, I have already put about to every corner of London society that his lies are not to be believed. And do not worry about Denning Ede." She reached down and picked a bit of leaf off Clemency's sleeve and flicked it away. With a sniff, she turned her face toward the church. At Clemency's gasp of surprise, she said, "Oh, yes, I am aware of his involvement now. If it is his wish to remain free of scandal and advance his promising career, then he will not debate me. I hardly think King George would look fondly on his dear friend elevating an upstart bastard to be the heir of a disgraced, extinct family. The Boyle line is well and truly dead; they have no legitimate son. Lord and Lady Boyle fled London when Ede discovered the boy's true parentage, but America is not far enough. They will hear of this."

Clemency opened and closed her mouth, speechless. That Lady Veitch would intervene on her behalf in such a spectacular way, she could not fathom. She wondered if it could all be attributed to her conversation with Adeline over that suitor's letter, or if indeed Lady Veitch's pride did not allow her to be befuddled by someone like Boyle. Perhaps knowing she might have lost her daughter to such a man had inspired her to this extreme action.

"We must not let such men win," Lady Veitch said in closing, offering Clemency a broad smile topped with twinkling eyes. "Even your Miss Taylor would agree with me there, I think."

"Most ardently," Clemency whispered, astonished. "Most ardently. But I can never repay this kindness, Lady Veitch, and certainly the cost of besting Boyle was great indeed."

"'Twas money well spent," the old woman replied lightly.

She unfurled her parasol again and made a long arc to return to the gravel path and her daughters. "And the most adventure I have experienced in an age. I suspect, Miss Fry, there is another man somewhere more deserving of your affection?"

Lady Veitch grinned as she continued her grand, deliberate parade through the garden. Distantly, from the direction of the church, bells rang out.

"There is, y-yes," Clemency stammered.

"There now." Lady Veitch chuckled and waved off a spray of dust and grass as Clemency raced by. "All is not well, but all is well enough."

26

Most vividly she would remember the flashing halo of light around his silhouette as he came riding toward her, up the lane leading to Claridge. She knew him from his shape, his height, the slant of his shoulders, and the tilt of his hat. She knew him as a moth recognizes flame, as a tree knows sunlight and bends innately toward it, seeking and seeking, and then rewarded with indelible warmth.

She had hardly made it ten paces out of the garden when she saw the dust rising from the hell-bent rider. Then came a spray of gravel as he pulled up the reins short and his horse veered and stamped, prancing in a circle before coming to a halt. With the light in her eyes, Clemency could only see the outline of his suit as he leapt down to the ground, and his hat as he swept it off and tossed it aside.

Somehow her feet carried her forward, and she kept going, and at last they met and she felt his arms lift her, hold her, encircle her . . .

"The bells," he murmured into her quickly unspooling hair. Audric kissed her cheek, her temple, the corner of her lips. "I heard the bells. Tell me, Clemency, tell me you are not married to him."

He set her back on the ground, and Clemency slid partly

away with a ragged laugh. "He is not here, Audric. He's gone. Gone. Imprisoned. All of his secrets go with him, and I am blessedly free."

Audric stared at her, then steadied her by the shoulders, staring down into her eyes with his particular ferocity. "But how? I have heard nothing of this. . . ."

"Lady Veitch," she said simply. "Boyle tried to toy with her daughter and paid for it with his freedom. She has met with Ede and spent dearly to silence him, and I can never repay her for it." Clemency hooked her arms around his neck and pulled him close. "Oh, you must know I never wanted to marry him! I could not say a thing without risking Delphine's secret, and my own sister's love for Mrs. Chilvers. He would have ruined them both, even if I so much as wrote you! I would never—but of course—you must believe me. You must."

"With all my heart I believe you," Audric replied, smoothing her hair back and leaning down to kiss her once more, and on the lips. "I suspected you might be acting out of affection for my family, but I had no inkling of your sister's predicament. That you would hold my sister's happiness above your own . . . but of course you do not know! She has taken matters into her own hands on that score. Against my advice she has admitted to the entire business with Boyle. What happens next I cannot say."

"She is brave," Clemency murmured. "So unspeakably brave. But that she should be forced into this position! And by the man who caused all of her pain!"

"She made the choice. I think she has found her peace and now she does not fear him or the whispers, and I can do nothing but try to protect her from the worst of it." Audric sighed. He shook his head and then pressed his face to hers, a pained gasp escaping his throat. "But what of your family? Do they know about Boyle?"

Clemency gestured to the house behind her, where an explosion of flowers still waited to celebrate someone's nuptials.

"They are all waiting. Waiting for a groom that will not come and a bride who loves another."

Audric dragged his fingers through her red-gold hair, his chest rising and falling rapidly as he chewed his lip and then nodded his head once. "Then shall we send up to the house for Delphine and Ralston? There could still be a wedding in the church today."

"But all of your plans! All of your anger and your vengeance, what becomes of it?" Clemency asked, holding desperately to the lapel of his jacket.

"It is all forgotten. The hunt is over, and we have played our part."

"Yet—"

"Listen to me, Clemency—we lived well and loved each other, and lost track of time and revenge. Perhaps this is the unexpected reward." Audric drew back, clasping both of his large hands over her small, warm, shaking ones. "Delphine has found her peace and let me find mine. He cannot harm us any longer, that I was not responsible for his end is meaningless beside the . . . the joy, the unbelievable relief and joy I feel in this moment. Damn it all, so that I can try to be better for you. To know I have you."

It didn't seem possible, that in one moment she could be so full of dread and fear, and in the next overcome with perfect happiness. "Joy, yes! Joy. But do we deserve it? Haven't we been wicked? Planning and plotting as we were?"

Audric kissed her again gently, and then not gently, and Clemency forgot all about words like *deserve*.

"Perhaps." Audric smiled, his lips still pressed to hers. "And if so, then let us be wicked together."

She did not have to remember the warmth of his embrace or the comforting strength of his arms—those sensations had never left her, though she had walled herself off from the memory. There was a remembrance sunk deep inside her of every dark hair on his fingers, every scar, every rough callus. There was a remembrance of his frank green eyes and the black waves of his hair, the dimples carved through his cheeks, the serious lips that now seemed so suddenly prone to smiling.

Her face fell for a moment. "But marriage . . . I had resolved never to consider it again."

Audric sighed, his smile collapsing. "Ah. That."

Clemency chewed her lower lip fiercely, worried that the desperation of the moment was leading her into a hasty decision. Yes, the church was decorated for a wedding, but she could still be the master of her fate. A few wasted buntings were nothing when compared to her lasting happiness. Marriage or solitude? When she glanced at Audric's face, the thought of being without him opened a hopeless pit in her stomach.

"Marriage is a compromise," she said slowly. "But we are clever enough to bend it to our needs. Delphine and Honora, they may need our protection to have the lives they deserve, and if we vow to embrace them as family and support them no matter what challenges they might face, then marriage is a compromise I am willing to make."

His eyes lightened, his smile returning. "That is an easy vow to make, almost as easy as the one I hope to make to you when—if—we are married."

Clemency had thought him a hard, impenetrable man, but something in him had softened, a sweet blurring around the edges of the gruff stranger who had approached her those weeks ago at the Pickfords' assembly. The man before her, enveloping her hands, hardly seemed like the same person, or maybe the light had shifted and she was no longer looking at him in the dark.

"The suspense, Clemency, is terrible." Audric laughed and scrunched up his eyes. "Have pity."

She looked again at the house and the flowers, then turned toward him with a crooked grin. "Then I have a proposition for *you,* sir, if you will hear it."

"Despite all your insisting, I knew this day would come."

Clemency wanted to roll her eyes at her sister but could not. After all Honora knew her best.

"What gave me away?" she asked, staying very still while her sister waited beside her outside the church door. Soon they would go in. She heard the restless shuffling and whispering of those inside the tall, dusty stone structure. There was no doubt quite a bit of story-swapping and confusion, given the last-minute change of grooms.

"You always had your nose in a book, and books are full of dreams," Honora replied. Smiling gently, she reached up and fixed a flower that had come loose in Clemency's hair.

"Love is a dream, fleeting and precious, best in the moment, and mourned when it is gone."

"And your dream of love?" Clemency turned, her own impending happiness momentarily forgotten. Clutching Honora's hand, she waited until her dear older sister looked into her eyes. "Mrs. Chilvers . . ."

Honora tried to tug her hand away.

"It is all right, Nora. I know how it is between you. How it truly is."

"What must you think of me?" Honora whispered.

"Only the best, as I always have and always will. Whatever money must be spent to free her of her husband's debts it will be yours."

"And Mr. Ferrand would help us this way?"

"I know he will understand," Clemency assured her.

A far-off smile spread across her sister's face. "Then she can give up those regrettable pursuits and find a better use for her talents. I want to trust her. I want to forgive her. Do you?"

Clemency nodded. "Time will show her true character. And she will have money now, so if indeed she is your true love's desire, then we are both becoming rich women."

Honora scrunched up her nose, pressing two fingers hard to her forehead. "That is not funny, dearest."

"It is a little funny."

"Only because all has ended this way," Honora reminded her. "I still feel the edges of a shadow about us."

"That will pass," Clemency promised. "All has not ended. Your life, whether it be with Mrs. Chilvers or another woman—"

"Sister—"

"Or another woman, will be a safe and happy one. I will not rest until you have all that you deserve, for you were always the sweetest of us. William is a fool, I am a tyrant, but you are all softness and light."

Honora embraced her, and she felt warm tears against her cheek. Both of their tears.

"Softness and light," Nora repeated, sighing. She stood back and held Clemency at arm's length, admiring her in her wedding finery. "That is what I wish for you. This love you have with Mr. Ferrand, it began in darkness. But here . . ." She glanced up and closed her eyes, a rainbow of light cascading down from a stained-glass window bathing her in a divine richness of colors. "Here you are, coming together in the sunshine."

"Then let us go in."

The doors opened and her mother was already weeping, of course. Audric waited for her at the end of a flower-strewn path. She had never seen him look so shy, his hand tucked in front of his waist, his posture confident yet his eyes boyishly darting.

I am sure enough for the both of us.

Honora departed, scurrying up the aisle to be with their family. Tansy clapped her hands like a child under the bemused gaze of Lady Veitch and her constantly flurrying fan. Even Mr. Fry shed a dignified tear into his handkerchief.

Clemency let Audric's green eyes be her guide. She walked herself toward them, not to give herself away, but to accept all he was willing to give.

27

It had never occurred to Clemency that a wedding could be such a breathless thing. Indeed, from the moment she slid into her crisp, new gown and tucked flowers into the ribbons woven through her hair until they trotted away from the church in the carriage hastily brought down by Ralston, she could scarcely remember taking a single full breath. It was with that same reedy, light-headed, and gauzy brain that she climbed the steps of Beswick, entered the great house, and found herself alone again with Audric Ferrand. Her husband.

Her husband.

Though they had stood together unchaperoned many times, Clemency now plunged headlong into terra incognita, aware all of a sudden, in a way she had never been before, of Audric's body. She stood in the cavernous and generously frescoed bedroom, awaiting a maid she did not have, at a moment when she did not want one. Yet she had no earthly idea what to do with her hands. The dogs, Talos and Argus, slumbered by the foot of the bed. The house creaked and settled. The fire crackled.

I should have read tawdrier novels.

Audric, for his part, did not seem nearly as out of sorts

with the idea of them being alone in a context far different than any they had experienced before. He went purposefully to the hearth, where a fire had been lit. The room itself was far too large for ten people, let alone two, yet it housed a single opulent bed, ornate in a way that made Clemency think he had nothing to do with choosing the furnishings for Beswick. A pair of naked, playful cherubs pointed fingers at each other on the carved and lustrous bedframe.

She felt acutely aware of the bed too.

Tugging his cravat free, Audric leaned near the fire and picked up his monologue where it had trailed off while they had climbed their way to this room and this, for Clemency, meaningful aloneness.

"My sister and Ralston. I can hardly believe it, but then, I'm certain you noticed. I am always the last to know these things."

"They do seem to share quite the profusion of glances," Clemency replied, finding something to do with her hands by skipping them along the edge of the bedframe. Her forefinger landed on a rotund cherub bottom and she quickly pulled it away.

This was patently ridiculous. Wasn't she a full-grown woman and he a full-grown man? She was a full-grown *married* woman. And had she not imagined them alone more than once, in all manner of wicked configurations that were not encouraged or described by the books she read? Yet her heart raced—his body and her own had never seemed so vital or so alive; she could practically hear the blood thrumming in her veins. She watched his pulse jump in his throat, coated gold by the fire, and realized with fading shame that she wanted to kiss—no, lick—that spot in particular.

Audric shed more clothes, and she discovered that she sincerely liked the way the fire sculpted his body, exaggerating hollows and angles she had never glimpsed before. With her gown still very much on, he came to her, and she reached out with fluttering hands to trace the broad plain of his chest, covered in coarse black and gray hair. A thread of fire tied itself to where her thumb brushed across his warm skin, a thread that ignited a path through her chest and belly, and startled her when it came to rest between her thighs.

"I think I am afraid," she whispered.

"There is nothing to fear," Audric told her. He took her hand and their fingers knitted together. "You may trust me as you trust a friend. Are we not friends?"

"We are," she said and smiled. "You are my dearest friend."

"Friendship is a serious affection; the most sublime of all affections," Audric quoted, half-solemn and half-grinning, "because it is founded on principle, and cemented by time."

"Mary Wollstonecraft, impressive," Clemency murmured, chuckling. "Sir, I am seduced. Or maybe convinced."

His smile remained, but in it she detected something wolfish and hungry. If there was more laughter to be had, it was swallowed and silenced by his lips descending, capturing hers, unexpectedly obliterating her fear. She felt the broad, intimidating strength of him just there beneath her hands, inviting now, and tempting.

Bethany Taylor had failed to mention the benefits of marriage in this regard, and Clemency, perhaps sheepishly, felt possessive of the heat and blood and bone that now felt *hers*. Hers forever, hers to explore and cherish and know. Truly know. Miss Taylor warned that marriage diminished a woman, and maybe that was so, maybe that ugly surprise was yet to come, but so far Clemency only felt like more of herself, expansive and growing, a plant tended and watered with affection. If this was imprisonment, Audric made her feel strangely free.

Free.

Her gown was in his hands, flying over her head in one instant and cast onto the floor in the next. Neither of them had time to make sense of the tangle of her corset laces, not while locked in a frenzy of kisses, not while navigating around the end of the bed to the middle, and then the soft, giving mattress.

She had not anticipated wanting to cry out, and to cry, and to gasp so much—was that normal? There did not seem to be time to stop and ask. Each new foray of his hands up her bare legs or across her shoulders taught her a new hunger—to devour, to sate, to taste, to remember the new richness on the air, a scent she hadn't known before, of their mingled perspiration and the wet trails of saliva left by seeking, wanting mouths. There was a certain music to this new activity that she had not expected but now relished—the sighs of open lips startled that way by pleasure, of smacking, of rustling fabric and nails scratching down heated skin.

At last Clemency found herself trapped beneath him, feeling the full weight of his body as it came to rest between her legs. The hearth fire blazed in Audric's eyes, and he pulled her red-gold hair free of its ribbons, letting it spill fully over her shoulders. He craned forward and raked his fingers through her hair, the bite of his fingernails against her scalp a near undoing.

"You ignite me as no other woman could," he told her, his

teeth scraping across her neck, his hands searching and pulling, releasing the confines of her corset and exposing her
breasts to the warm cupping of his palms.

She arched and keened, robbed of words. No, she had not
read of this, or even come close in her occasional delves to
this corner of her imagination. Nothing compared to the
rich heat of his mouth around her nipple, or the flutter of
her belly when his hand reached lower, a single nervous gasp
managed before his fingers traced the slick heat of her sex,
and nervousness turned to wonder.

The want devastated any desire she had to solve the mystery of lovemaking slowly. There would be other nights—all
the nights in the world—to meander. She remembered mar-
veling at the strength in his shoulders, poised and tense, and
she remembered the expression of almost pain as he found
her gaze and entered her for the first time. There was pain for
her too, pressure like a pinch, but it was one wilted flower in
a field of lilies.

Far more she knew she would remember Audric's thumb
worrying gently along her brow, and his whispered concern
for her, then the brief flash of a smile when he was consoled
by her whimpers of pleasure. She would remember his brow
furrowing in concentration and the slap of their bodies meeting. There was a moment when the pain was gone, and
Clemency felt herself open to him, and it felt like truth
dawning—she had him, and they were married, and she
could give herself over to the idea completely. She could let
herself chase the itch that felt like it stayed in the back of her
throat—to scratch it she needed more of him, and faster, and
to be empty and full, and empty and full.

It was a word on the tip of her tongue, and then, finally,

she remembered it. He clutched her hips hard, and went suddenly tense, then finished. Clemency remembered the word and gasped as he spilled inside her.

Complete.

Breathless again. Just like the whole of the wedding. Clemency laid on her back and Audric sprawled across her, both of them a sweaty tangle. The noises. The scents. The inescapable moistness of it all. No, none of her novels had communicated it well. She rubbed a small circle over her belly and let herself indulge in the odd feeling spreading through her and the almost pleasant soreness between her legs.

"Was there anything to fear?" Audric asked, crawling off her and turning onto his own back with a huff.

"No," she said, giggling. "But much to learn."

"In this discipline may we both become scholars."

Clemency smirked and flicked him on the shoulder. "I'm too warm."

Sliding out of the bed, Clemency used her own discarded shift to sop up the wetness they had made and then found a dressing gown sized for Audric hanging by the hearth. She shrugged it on, the hem dragging behind her as she left the fire and stepped out into the coolness of the balcony on the other side of the bed. The night washed over her heated skin, a much-needed balm, and she tipped her head down, looking over the rolling greenery between her new home and her old one.

Audric joined her, forgoing any dressing gown of his own, the heat of his naked chest a comfort as he enfolded her in his arms and kissed the top of her head.

"Nora is playing," Clemency said softly, pointing across

the estate grounds to her old family home. A few candles burned in the windows, a very, very soft piano song carried across the fields on the wind. The house was still full of life, and perhaps they were celebrating.

"Home," she said. "And home." Shaking her head slowly, she reached up and gathered her hair over one shoulder, peering up at Audric as he detached from her and leaned against the railing, facing the house. "I thought you were a lunatic when you first came to me with your schemes and allegations."

"Ha! And now? Do you regret agreeing to my proposition?" he asked, outlining her jaw with the edge of his hand.

"I only regret I did not listen to you at the Pickfords' ball," Clemency murmured. "We might have avoided so much unnecessary pain. I feel as if my indecision is to blame; I should have known Boyle for a villain at once."

Audric pulled her dressing gown closer about her shoulders and stood tall again, then leaned down to brush a kiss against her cheek. "Your good counsel to Lady Veitch's ridiculous daughter saved us all from a regrettable fate. Without her influence, without Denning Ede to support her story, we might never have rid ourselves of Boyle so cleanly."

Clemency nodded and tried to believe him. "And now I am married."

"You are," Audric said, chuckling. "An end none of us could have foreseen, with all your loathing of it. Tell me, were your heroines right? Is it all horror and gloom?"

She smiled and fit herself into his chest, turning them both toward her family's home, where the lights blinked out one by one. A darkening house, but one still full of life and love.

"Bethany Taylor said that the scholar, the poet, and the philosopher can all agree that love is an ungovernable mystery and yet we seek to govern it." Clemency breathed out, warm and held and safe. "I'm not sure I agree with her. In our bumbling way we seek to control it, to control each other. But I think our marriage might be different. We can do some good with it, not just good for us, but for others too."

"Oh?" Audric grinned. "And how will our marriage be?"

"Not love governed," Clemency said. "But a love story, and like all stories, we simply write it and hope, hope against hope, hope passionately that it endures."

ACKNOWLEDGMENTS

In the spring of 2020, I began writing this novel as a distraction for my mother while she recovered from a serious illness, and while I too struggled with my own debilitating sickness. With the pandemic raging, I couldn't fly to be with her, and so I fell back on the thing we bonded over and shared when I was a child: Jane Austen. As I sent her each chapter, I tried to give us both a Regency adventure that would make those dark days feel a little easier and brighter. I want to acknowledge and thank her for introducing me to the world of Austen, which led to my obsession with Regency romances of all kinds. This book wouldn't be here without her influence.

As always, I would also like to thank my wonderful agent, Kate McKean. Thanks is also due to the amazing team at Penguin Random House—Shauna Summers was instrumental in developing and polishing this work.

Lastly, I want to acknowledge my partner, family, friends, and early readers. This one took a village, and I'm grateful for your support.

About the Author

MADELEINE ROUX is the *New York Times* and *USA Today* bestselling author of the Asylum series, which has sold over a million copies worldwide. She is also the author of the House of Furies series, and several titles for adults, including *Salvaged* and *Reclaimed*. She has made contributions to *Star Wars,* World of Warcraft, and Dungeons & Dragons. She lives in Seattle, Washington, with her partner and beloved pups.

madeleine-roux.com
Twitter: @Authoroux
Instagram: @authoroux

About the Type

This book was set in Sabon, a typeface designed by the well-known German typographer Jan Tschichold (1902–74). Sabon's design is based upon the original letter forms of sixteenth-century French type designer Claude Garamond and was created specifically to be used for three sources: foundry type for hand composition, Linotype, and Monotype. Tschichold named his typeface for the famous Frankfurt typefounder Jacques Sabon (c. 1520–80).